CAITLYN

Arthur Butt

Solstice Publishing - www.solsticepublishing.com

Caitlyn
A Novel by
Arthur Butt

Dedication

As always, to my wife Susie

Chapter One

The moving van sped away from the house, empty, hurrying to the next stop. Within the home, sofas, chairs, tables, and endless boxes were tucked into corners, awaiting unpacking and rearranging by the new owners.

In her room, Caitlyn sat, tired. Tired of the move into the new house, and tired of the suburbs, although she'd resided in her new home for less than one day. Unseen apprehension and anxiety flooded her, radiating from her shoulders and neck, spreading wave-like into her arms.

She stared around the strange space. Brown packing cartons with her name scrawled across the sides in black magic marker stacked precariously, each threating to tumble onto the floor at a moment's notice and create more havoc than she already felt. Her old dressers from their apartment in the city stood empty against the blank walls, waiting for her to fill each drawer. She'd rearranged her furniture twice, trying to decide where each piece fitted best and then given up in weariness. The room could stay a shambles. What her own little space looked like didn't matter. No friends would stop by to hang out and she wouldn't be in this town long enough to become comfortable with the furnishings no matter where she stuck each.

From along the wood floor hallway connecting the bedrooms to the rest of the house, the faint noise of a radio mixed with the clatter of tableware banging against each other. Caitlyn's mother unpacking dishes and plates in the kitchen. Mrs. Brennen sang off-key, but upbeat, as if trying to convince the cups and saucers the strange cupboards were a wonderful place to take up their new residence, and they would be as happy as she was.

Why does Mom have to pretend to be so cheerful?

Sighing, Caitlyn summoned the energy to push herself off the bed and wandered over to a stack of boxes, staring at the topmost blankly. *Might as well start. The cartons won't unpack themselves.* She ripped off the tape and hauled out clothes, shoving piles into the dresser haphazardly without really caring which drawer shirts and pants arrived in or in what condition.

At the bottom of the first box, she ran across her old cheerleading spankies and skirt, including the gold chain and medal she'd won at cheerleading camp. Caitlyn held the medallion up and flipped the disk over. Engraved was her name and date. She looped the chain over her neck and tucked the medal under her shirt. She paused, trying to decide if she should keep her uniform or dump the whole mess in the garbage, discarded along with the rest of her past life and dreams for an exciting last year in high school.

Welcome to the 'burbs where hopes go to die.

She was supposed to be head cheerleader this year. Now? Different school, senior year, no friends. Four years dieting and exercising down the drain demonstrating to her peers what an athlete and leader she'd grown into. Was the time worth the trouble trying out for a new squad? Probably never make the team; these things were all politics, and there were girls who'd been cheering at the new school for years. They wouldn't boot one to make room for her, no matter how good she was.

Caitlyn sighed and left her uniform in the box, wondering why she packed the outfit in the first place. Another piece of garbage she'd dump when taking the trash to the curb.

Scratch the band, too. She'd been first seat playing the clarinet for two years, battling off contenders for her position by practicing night and day, and a lock for this fall, also. No one dared challenge her. Marching band, gone, and she'd enjoyed doing the games. Everyone came to see her. She knew the fans did with their claps and shouts. Her father use to call her the Mighty Mite, running off the field, only to reappear a few seconds later in her cheerleading uniform. He'd whistle and stomp his feet along with the rest as she proudly stood on top of the pyramid, arms raised in triumph. He would have understood why she wanted to stay in the city for her senior year.

Too bad he died of a heart attack and her world fell apart around her.

Caitlyn understood her mother was upset and missed him. She did too. Late at night, when her mother thought no one else listened, Caitlyn hear her mother talking to her father, crying she missed him so bad. The funeral was hardly over, though, when her mother bought this house, gave all her father's clothes away to Goodwill. She refused to sleep in her bed. Instead, she'd stretch out every night on the couch in the living room with a blanket thrown over her.

She coulda bought a new bed and mattress. We coulda stayed in the city for one more year.

"Well, look at you. Finally moving that butt of yours." Mrs. Brennen stood in the doorway of Caitlyn's bedroom, hands on hips, and surveyed her daughter in mock sorrow. "Hurry up and finish unpacking. Lynn is almost done, and so am I. As soon as we're ready, I want to visit the pizza parlor we saw yesterday downtown in the village and see what's on the menu. We're exploring to locate a place selling good Italian food."

Caitlyn shoved the empty box containing her uniform onto the floor and ripped the tape off the next carton, taking out a fistful of socks and dropping the clothes on top of the already full pile in the drawer. "Mom, I know I asked before, but maybe could I spend the last school year at Carla's? She asked her dad and he said staying at their place was fine by him." She stared at her mother without much hope.

"Now, Sweetie, we've been all through this before." Mrs. Brennen stepped into the room and laid her hand on Caitlyn's back, rubbing along her spine gently. "It was always your father's dream to have a nice home in the suburbs for you and Lynn. I won't have his family broken up so quickly after his death. Soon enough you'll be off to college and Lynn right after." Her voice broke and she dabbed at her eyes. With a shake of her head, she squeezed Cailyn's shoulder. "I'll hear no more about you living at Carla's and her parent's apartment, or with anyone else for that matter. Now, hurry up, okay?" She scrutinized her daughter for the first time and felt her shoulder again, patting along her side. "My, I never realized how skinny you've grown." Her fingers moved up and down Caitlyn's back and ribs. "You're nothing but bone. I know the last year's been hectic for all of us, but—have you been eating right?"

Caitlyn edged away from her mother and pulled out more clothes from the carton. "Sure, Mom, but I've been dieting and exercising. I'm top of the pyramid, remember? Have to keep my weight down. The rest of the girls don't want a lard-ass standing on top of their heads." She flashed her mother a smile. "I'm fine. Besides, looks like I won't be doing cheerleading this year. I'll have plenty of time to add on weight."

Mrs. Brennen nodded in understanding. "From now on I'm keeping an eye on you, young lady. I can't have you withering away to nothing before you go off to college, now, can I?" She swung around and strolled to the door, trying to sound as chipper as when she first walked in. She called over her shoulder, "Hurry up. I want to go and return before it's too dark to see. I think we all deserve a nice relaxing evening in our new home. We've had a busy day."

Caitlyn waited for her mother to disappear and dropped onto the bed again. *Put on your big girl panties and act your age, girl. I guess I'll have to tough out this year. Won't be so bad, I guess. Boys to meet, girls too, and mom's right, next year I'm off to college anyway. New friends. Keep practicing and working out, try for college band and cheer squad. No scholarships, but I can ask for recommendations from my old teachers in the city.*

Throwing off the depression hanging over her, Caitlyn returned to unpacking and emptied out a second carton. With a grunt of determination, she started on a third as her sister ran in, her ponytail bouncing behind her. She halted at the doorway. "I found Mr. Piggy," Lynn exclaimed, holding up a raggedly stuffed pig. Her mouth puckered into a serious expression and she wagged a forefinger at the doll. "This is Caitlyn's room." Her sister swung the pig in a wide circle so the toy could survey the whole interior. "You must never, ever, sneak in here without being invited first. You know how strict she is about her privacy. Understand?" Lynn beamed at Caitlyn. "See, you saw me tell him, right? Now he knows. No excuses."

"Yeah, great, squirt. Now if we could teach you the same thing, we'd be all set, right," Caitlyn said, sarcastically. "Stick around now you're here. I'll put you to work helping me unpack my junk."

Lynn took a step into her sister's room, unsure if Caitlyn was joking or not. "Well, if you really want me to…"

A wave of tiredness swept over Caitlyn and she dropped abruptly onto the bed with a moan.

"Are you okay?" Lynn sat beside her and peered into Caitlyn's face. "You look kinda pale and stuff."

"Must be catching something, a cold—flu." Caitlyn rubbed her arm trying to ease the soreness. "I'm achy all over." She nudged her sister away. "Don't sit too close to me. I wouldn't want you to catch whatever bug I have. One of us being sick is bad enough." She tried to grin. "Being nauseous and queasy will ruin the beginnings of your sophomore year in this wonderful new school were attending, in the beautiful 'burbs, right? We both don't need to be red-nosed messes to impress the hicks."

"I'll tell Mom and maybe—"

"Don't bother," Caitlyn breathed, "she's busy pretending everything is hunky-dory in the sticks." She pushed the hair out of her face. "I'll dig out the nasty cold and flu stuff she always makes us drink." The pain subsided. Breathing a sigh, she glared at the unpacked boxes waiting and rose to her feet. "If you're not going to help, scoot out of here and leave me alone. I have to pretend to accomplish something today or Mom will never let me hear the end of how lazy I am."

Lynn stood, cradling Mr. Piggy in her arms. "Me too. I still have to make my bed and put books on the bookshelf. If you're not finished by the time I am, I'll stop back and help you polish off whatever you haven't done, okay?"

Caitlyn waved her away. "Don't bother, I'll manage." As her sister turned to leave, Caitlyn said quickly, "Hey, wait a minute. I do have a mission for you."

Lynn halted. "What?"

"Do you know where these stupid wires go on my computer?" She gestured to her desk where tower and monitor rested. "I should have labeled each connection when I took the dumb machine apart. Now I can't figure out where to plug the jacks."

"Sure." Lynn stepped over to the desk and began plugging wires in. A few minutes later she said, "All set and ready to go." She pushed buttons and the machine whirred to life. "Anything else?"

"No. Your good deed for the day is done." Caitlyn waved in dismissal. "Thanks."

After she'd completed unpacking half the boxes, Caitlyn surveyed the room with grim satisfaction. The place wasn't perfect, certainly not like her old room in the apartment. Needed a few posters on the walls. She'd bought three new ones of her favorite singers, if only she could remember in which box she'd packed the pictures in. She had to admit, though, the place was more spacious than she ever imagined a room could be.

As Caitlyn wondered if she should start on the remainder of the boxes, or her mother would be satisfied once she saw the progress already made, the muted roar of a lawnmower flowed to her from outside the house. She strolled to the window, curious to see who was making the racket and pulled up the venetian blinds, while absently noting she'd have to go shopping with her mother to pick out curtains matching the color of the room.

The view from her upstairs window let out into the garden separating her yard from the home directly behind hers. A young man in faded blue jeans and white t-shirt industriously pushed a hand-mower back and forth across the length of the yard, stopping occasionally to empty the grass bag. Even at this distance, she detected the beginnings of dark stains forming under his armpits in the late morning heat.

Kinda cute, sandy-brown hair, my age or older. Caitlyn observed with growing interest as the young man halted, bent over, and shoved grass trimmings into an oversized green trash bag. *Nice butt. Maybe living in the 'burbs has some benefits after all.*

The boy straightened and casually surveyed the rest of the lawn still waiting for him to cut. His vision lifted and swept over the garden and into Caitlyn's yard, and finally centered on her window. His eyes locked on Caitlyn's as she stared out the window.

He waved.

Caitlyn hastily retreated from the casement and fumbled at the blinds, dropping the shade and stumbled over her feet in her panic to disappear from view. "Oh, gosh. He must think I'm a pervert, or peeping Tom stalking him or something," she giggled to herself and held one hand over her mouth to keep from bursting out laughing.

Her face burned hot as she crept back to the window. Standing to one side, she cracked open the blinds wide enough for her to peek through the slates without being seen. The boy was staring at her window, head cocked to on side in puzzlement. Shrugging, he continued to mow the grass.

"Caitlyn, are you ready?" her mother called from the living room. "I want to leave now before we hit the afternoon lunch crowd and find ourselves stuck in a line for an hour."

Caitlyn looked toward her door, and then at the window, a bemused expression on her face, thinking. "I'm going to stay here, if you don't mind, Mom," she called back. "I don't feel so hot, and I still have unpacking to do. Maybe I'll take a walk around the block afterwards, see what's happening. Bring me back a couple of slices, will yah?"

Her mother appeared at the door. "Alright, but don't go far, or lose track of time," she cautioned, "and I'll bring you more than a couple of slices of pizza. A salad, too, I'd say. We have to grow some meat on those bones of yours, and keep you healthy for the new school year."

"Fine, Mom," Caitlyn said. She smiled weakly.

Her mother surveyed the cartons still unpacked. "I expect to see all your clothes put away also. Just because I'm not here to stand over you...."

"Yeah, Mom. Of course. Jumping on the rest of my junk right now."

After Lynn and her mother left, Caitlyn hurried to the window again and peered out the blinds. The young man was still in the backyard, finishing his mowing. *Well, let's go exploring. Time to meet and greet the neighbors. The unpacking can wait until later.*

She debated whether to take her pocketbook or not, which lay on her bed and decided she didn't need the extra articles inside. *Only going next door, not on a safari.* As she left her room, the sharp pain returned, harder this time, hitting her in the back, radiating along her arm. She grimaced. *Stupid pain. Probably pulled a muscle shoving furniture around all morning.*

She ignored the throbbing, pushing the hurt to the back of her mind, walked outside, and wandered along the garden path until she reached the gate. A tingle of excitement raced through her body as the young man came into plain view. Hanging over the fence, she watched the boy working until he glanced up and saw her standing there.

Caitlyn waved. "Hi, I'm your new neighbor."

***

John pushed the lawnmower up and down his parent's back lawn, the late summer sun causing him to sweat and itch from the dust that was tossed up. He paused and arched his back, brushing at his shirt, and reflected this was the last time he'd cut the grass for a long while. *Tomorrow morning I'll be in the army. Better enjoy this while I can.* He'd heard basic training was rough, a lot of marching and P.T., worse than football camp. He hoped he wouldn't be one of those guys crying in his bunk at night to go home, or on the phone with their parents desperately begging Mom and Dad to find some way of busting him out of the military.

Issuing a grunt, he surveyed the rest of the yard, concentrating on the jobs left to do. He regretted his decision to volunteer weeding the garden. Maybe four, or five hours more work, he decided, but what the heck. No one else was around, his parents weren't home. Sunday was church and lunch afterwards. Most of his friends were on vacation with their folks, or taking advantage of the last days before school started to enjoy themselves. He had nothing else to do. There was no rush.

To his left was Mr. Rue's home. He like the old man, a retired postal worker. Mr. Rue asked John to watch his house. He'd driven to Maine, a small weekend trip, and left Friday morning to visit his son. John had gone over every day to rattle the doors and check the windows. Mr. Rue said he'd return late tonight or Monday afternoon.

On the other side was a person he didn't know, other than the guy's name was Steve. An electrician, he thought. John met him once when the man first moved in and walked over to borrow a ladder. He received the impression the person was divorced. John never saw a woman there, except once when Steve barbequed in his back yard. The man was never home, mostly working and returning to his house late at night, spending weekends on the golf course. In fact, John noticed him leave early this morning, loading his golf bag into his trunk before driving off.

John noted new people moved into the home behind his, and wondered who they were, or had any kids his own age. His parents were good friends with the Cowins who'd owned the house, playing cards with the couple every Saturday night. His mom and Mrs. Cowin talked over the fence for hours about the garden, neighborhood, or swapping recipes. When his dad enclosed the yard with a chain link fence, his parents stuck a gate in so the Cowins and they could walk back and forth and visit. Their daughter, April, even babysat John when he was small. Too bad they retired and moved to Florida. He hoped the new neighbors would be as friendly. John remembered grumpy old man Smyth who'd lived next-door before the electrician moved in. Always complaining about the noise the kids made or peoples' dogs barking at night. Having bad neighbors was never any fun.

A car drove by the house. John glanced through the breezeway toward the driveway, expecting to see his parents arrive.

He remembered another chore. "Darn, I forgot I promised Dad, I'd go into the crawlspace under the house and shut off the main waterline for him." It was hard enough for John to wiggle his way through the window opening between the house and garage and to low crawl to the valve. For his dad, with a beer belly, the operation was impossible. John decided the plumbing could wait. This wasn't a task he enjoyed doing anyway. The space under the house was dark and he was always nervous spiders or snakes lived in there. His father wouldn't start changing the faucets on the bathroom shower until after he returned home.

Well, let's get back to work, daydreaming isn't accomplishing anything, and I still have plenty to do. Exhaling a good-natured sigh, he emptied the bag on the lawnmower, and checked the garden one more time, planning the next task, and trying to decide which areas needed the most attention. When his eyes rose, he saw the blinds on the upstairs window on the Cowin house drawn up. A girl watched him, a pretty girl with blond hair.

A smile crossed his face and he waved. *Well, nice neighbor. Too bad I won't be around longer to know her better. Wonder what grade she's in?*

The face in the window disappeared and the blinds hastily dropped. John released a chuckle while staring at the house. *Bashful, are we? I kinda like shy girls. Maybe sixteen or seventeen? Didn't have time for a good look. She disappeared too quickly. Maybe if I have leave after basic, I'll meet her.* He shrugged. Didn't really matter anyway, he decided. Tomorrow he'd be history. Tomorrow he'd be miles away in the army, and who knew if he'd receive any leave.

He finished cutting the grass, two big lawn bags full of leaves, twigs and clipping ready to haul out to the curb. Pieces of debris clung to his pants and shirt. He looked down at himself, grimaced, and brushed at his clothes.

"Hi, I'm your new neighbor."

John jumped and glanced around. His eyes resting on the back fence and the girl he'd seen watching him from the window. She hung over the gate, a lop-sided grin on her lips, blond hair framing her face in a pageboy cut. The sunlight filtering through the leaves of the trees overhead made her hair shimmer as if brushed with gold. The first impression John received was a china doll he'd seen in a magazine at one of his friend's homes. He doubted if she weighted ninety pounds soaking wet, and her shoulders barely cleared the top of the four-foot chain link fence.

What is she, ten? John's vision left her face, roved over the rest of her body. He decided she *definitely was* not ten. Thirteen? Fourteen? Guessing age was hard with girls when they applied makeup—even a dab changed their age wildly. Some actresses he'd seen on TV played teenagers into their thirties. He grinned back and strolled over to the gate. "Hi yourself, new neighbor. Welcome to the neighborhood. My name's John." He stuck his hand over the fence for her to shake.

Her small fingers crept into his with a firm clasp. "Caitlyn," she announced brightly. "Out of the big city and now," she glanced over her shoulder at her house, "residing in the 'burbs. I figured you could supply me the four-one-one on what's happening around here. You know, the school, stores, places to hang out, if you follow what I mean." She focused on the lawn mower and leaf bags, and realized she was talking too much, too fast. "If you have time, that is. I see you're busy."

Nervous. "Nah, all finished here." He fanned his arm across the plants surrounding the fence and marching to the lawn. "I should rip out weeds but—" he pursed his lips and shrugged "—they're not going anywhere. Anything else can wait until later, anyhow." He rattled the ornamental scrolling on top of the gate. "Come on over. It's time I took a break, anyway." As an additional invitation, he reached for the latch, opening the gate, and swung the entrance wide for her to pass into his yard.

She giggled and gave a quick curtsy. "Thank you, sir. You're a gentleman," she said as she strolled through the opening, gazing around as if this side of the fence provided her with a new view of the shrubs and flowers.

They stood awkwardly for a moment, not quite knowing what to say to continue their conversation. John pivoted and walked toward the back stoop of the house, Caitlyn taking two steps to his one as she hurried beside him. To break the silence, he asked, "How old are you anyway? What grade are you going into? I don't mean to be rude, but you look like you're about twelve."

This invoked a smirk and quick chuckle. "I wish. Seventeen," Caitlyn replied. "I'll be a senior this year, but I'll admit, I'm short for my age. You should see my sister, Lynn. She's fifteen and already half a head taller than I am. "You?"

"Eighteen. I graduated last June."

"Oh." Caitlyn's attention slid from him to the ground.

The two reached the house and John sat on the stoop. Caitlyn dropped beside him and wrapped her arms across her chest. John glanced surreptitiously at her out of the corner of his eye.

Disappointment was etched across her face. Having talked with her, even for so short a time, the feeling was mutual. Her looks and personality enchanted him. The girl was someone he'd enjoy knowing better. He tried to place a good spin on the situation and added, "I know lots of juniors who'll be seniors this year. Maybe tonight after supper I can call some of my buddies and their girlfriends and we can hang out together. I'll introduce you around, okay? How does the idea strike you? At least you'll know people at the beginning of the year."

Caitlyn brightened. "I guess so. Sure, why not. Sounds like meeting your friends would be fun."

On impulse, John waved to the house and said, "Why don't you come in, I'll find us something to drink." He shoved a finger toward her home. "Parents won't mind if you stay over here for a while? They're not waiting for you, or anything?"

Caitlyn shook her head. "No, everyone's gone for lunch, pizza, and it's Mom and my little sister. My dad died a couple of months ago. That's the reason we moved out here in the first place."

John paused as he opened the back door. "Oh, I'm sorry. You musta had a rough time, losing your dad, moving to a new town and all."

Caitlyn entered the house. "Yes, it has been."

Chapter Two

Caitlyn took a seat on the sofa in the TV room, a small area a few steps down from the main floor, and connected by the dining room and kitchen. John called over the divider between the kitchen and television room, "Soda, beer, water?" He rummaged through the refrigerator, took out a can of beer for himself and popped the top open while he waited for Caitlyn's reply.

"Uh, I really shouldn't, but I guess one beer won't hurt," she replied nervously gazing around the room at the pictures on the wall, the kitchen, and dining room beyond. "Looks like a nice place," Caitlyn commented. On the way in, she'd caught a glimpse of the living room covered in dark paneling, bricked fireplace, and mantle above cluttered with glass knick-knacks. She wished her house had a fireplace.

"The house is," John agreed as he walked down the steps and set a can of beer on the edge of the end table next to Caitlyn within easy reach. He took a seat beside her on the sofa. He pointed out the rooms. "My dad kept adding additions to the place: the dining room, rear bedroom, and dormer upstairs," he explained eagerly, "even a half basement dug when the back rooms were added. We don't use the downstairs, mostly storage for junk. All the original house had was a crawlspace."

"The place musta been tiny when your parents first moved in," Caitlyn remarked as she estimated the size of the front room and kitchen.

"Sure was," John said. "I can barely remember our house the way the place was originally in the beginning." He waved a hand to the television room. "This used to be an enclosed patio. My dad broke out the exterior wall between it and the kitchen and dining room, redid the place and opened all three rooms up as you see the interior now."

"Wow, all the work must have been expensive." Caitlyn took a sip of her beer and studied the room once again with new interest.

"Not really," John replied. "My dad added the additions over a couple of years. Did most of the inside work himself, the sheetrock and painting. He's pretty handy using tools—did construction when he was younger. My parents never told me how much converting the patio was, but Pop would have gone ballistic if the contractor asked too much."

Caitlyn swept the room one more time and changed the subject, trying to keep the conversation going. "So, are you off to college this fall? Join a fraternity, be a frat boy?" She chuckled at her half-joke.

John smirked along with her. "Nope. Joining the army," he said proudly. "Gonna be a soldier boy. I leave tomorrow morning, in fact, to in-process and start basic training. I gotta be at the recruiting station by six o'clock in the morning. Next time you see me, I'll probably be a general."

"Oh, I hope I see you again before you're promoted to an officer, or someone shoots you," Caitlyn quipped, trying to act serious. She laid a hand on his shoulder. "Aren't you afraid, all the fighting in the Middle East and terrorists attacking everyone?" She took another sip of beer and scowled at the can. "I would be. So much hate and violence over there."

John shrugged. Deep down inside he was nervous, never could tell what would happen, but he wasn't about to admit his fear to anyone. Especially to Caitlyn or his friends, and after twelve years in school, college held no appeal for him, not yet anyway. He needed to be out doing something on his own, learning a trade and experiencing the real world. More classwork would happen later in his life.

"Lots of people are sent overseas, chances are I'll survive," he replied, nonchalantly, in an act of bravado. "Who knows, I might wind up in Alaska and be sent to Europe afterwards. All I have to worry about then is being eaten by a polar bear, or how much beer and wine I can drink."

Caitlyn winced.

"Say, are you okay? I didn't mean to frighten you." He peered closely into her face. You're all pale." She couldn't be that scared of someone shooting at him. She'd just met him, and he hoped she realized being eaten by a bear was a joke. Perhaps she didn't enjoy the taste of the beer. Caitlyn was squirming, touching her left shoulder and arm while making a face.

"Not frightened," she replied. She grimaced and rolled her shoulders and head trying to work kinks out of her upper body. "Pain in my back, arms, my whole chest and muscles feel sore. Musta pulled a ligament during the move here or packing, pushing furniture around and carrying boxes. Been hurting all day. The pain will pass," she said as if to reassure herself, "I'm tough."

"Done the same thing myself during the first few days of football practice," John said. "I ached all over like someone hit me on my body using a baseball bat. Take care of yourself. A nice hot bath tonight and soak in the tub. I wouldn't want to lose you now. I just met you," he joked.

"You can be sure I will. As soon as I go home, I'll pop some vitamin C and cold medicine, jump into bed early and have a good night's rest. All the drugs will fix me right up."

"Anyway, I should be back from basic for a couple of days before I start advanced training," John continue. "I'll be checking on you to make sure you're still alive. We can hang out, take in a movie, go bowling if you want to, and get to know each other better." *I wonder if she has a boyfriend. Too attractive not to be seeing someone, at least part-time. One way to learn. Let's climb the tree and ask.* "You're not dating anyone, are you? I mean back at your old school, seriously. I wouldn't want to cause problems between you and your steady boyfriend."

Caitlyn closed her eyes for a minute, gathering her thoughts. "There was a guy. He lived down the hall from us and we attended the same school. I was sorta seeing him," she admitted, "but, you know, with moving here to the suburbs and all, going to different schools, long distance relationships, we figure it would be better to break off our relationship and be friends—call on the phone and stuff and see what happens. He doesn't drive and I don't have a car yet."

The alcohol was making John feel light-headed. He hadn't eaten breakfast, missed lunch, and felt reckless. He said, "You know, in this case maybe you could give me a picture of yourself. I hear all the soldiers carry photos of friends and family. I can tape your pic to the inside of my locker and tell everyone you're my girlfriend. This way the rest of the guys won't think I'm a total loser."

Caitlyn's eyes widen, startled. She drew back from John slightly, her lips fluttering in amusement as she studied him critically. "Sure, why not," she said at last, "but don't go making up stories about what we do when we're alone, okay?" she cautioned. "I want people to think I'm a hottie, but not that hot." She batted her eyelashes. She said archly, "I start finding my name and phone number on bathroom walls, or tanks and jeeps stop in front of my house, and you're in trouble, stud. You hear me?"

You're a hottie, alright, and you know you are. If I had my choice, I'd keep you all to myself. John stuck out his hand. "It's a deal."

***

Caitlyn felt an unnamed emotion swell up inside her when John asked for her picture. Something akin to fear, but excitement also, and icy tension ran across her chest. *This one moves fast considering we've only met each other for a half-an-hour. No messing around. He's either desperate for a girlfriend or he wants me for one.* So she wasn't surprised when he suggested he'd tell everyone they were dating. She'd save him for a reserve. A boyfriend was always a useful excuse to keep the geeks away, and who knew? He said he'd be back after basic, probably be in and out of his parent's house for the next couple of years while on leave. He was kinda cute, too. Maybe in the future…?

I'll give him a thrill. Let him have a taste of what he might see if he behaves. Show him my sexy cheerleading look. Caitlyn displayed her best pose, pushing her chest out, hands on hips, flashing a dazzling smile. "Maybe a pic like this? Make the U.S. Army drool?"

"I don't know about the rest of the military, but if I have a photo like you showed me, I sure would want to take a bite out of you," John agreed wholeheartedly.

One thing bothered her, though. She'd known some boys who were lying stinking weasels, who'd say anything for a chance to get into her pants and move on to the next conquest. Was he dating another girl? Or two? "I take it *you* don't have a girlfriend?" She watched his eyes. His lips might lie, but the eyes never did. She'd be sure he wasn't telling the truth if he didn't look her squarely in the face.

John kept his vision center on Caitlyn. "Yeah, well, it's sorta the same situation as you, I guess. When she learned I'd enlisted in the army, we decided to go our separate ways," he explained. "Doubt if I'll ever see her again. You know how life is. She's leaving for the West Coast in a few days for college, anyway. I bet in a couple of months, she won't even remember my name. If I'm lucky, I'll receive a letter telling me how much fun she's having."

"Oh, true," Caitlyn agreed. *Of course, he had a girlfriend, I wouldn't expect otherwise. He acts as if he's telling the truth, too.* "Different time zones in California, I would imagine, and schedules. You don't have Christmas and Spring Breaks in the army I suppose, do you?" She mentally face-palmed herself. Of course, soldiers didn't have Spring Breaks. She pictured tanks and airplanes dropping men off at a volleyball game on the beach, bikini-clad girls running around in the sand, bombs exploding, and cringed. She must sound like an airhead to him. She hurried to correct herself. "I mean, you'll be returning home for leave sometimes, whenever you have the chance, but who knows when that'll be, and if you're overseas, flying all the way to the States might not even be worth the time, or an option."

"I wouldn't think so. The military doesn't call the war off for weather, either. And as far as my ex was concerned, well, we weren't really boyfriend and girlfriend in the strict sense of the word, anyway, if you can understand what I mean," John admitted. "I was in a lot of sports, and she was a cheerleader. Everyone sorta expected we'd hang out together." John stood and walked into the kitchen, throwing his empty can into a recycling bin. He called out over the divider, "I mean, we liked each other, had a bunch of laughs, always someone to go out with on a Friday or Saturday night, but we were never serious." He walked back and sat beside Caitlyn again.

"She's a cheerleader? So am I," Caitlyn exclaimed, "or at least I was until the move out here. I mean at my old school. I was supposed to be head cheerleader this year, in fact."

"Yeah? Gonna try out for the team this fall?"

Caitlyn kept her voice even, but the bitterness shone through in her tone. "What's the use? Senior year,

I'll never make the squad," she retorted. The injustice of the past months pushed on her. She took a deep breath and released the air slowly through her nostrils. "This year has been terrible already. I don't need any more disappointments."

John dismissed her statement by a wave. "You can at least try. You'll met some of the girls tonight, I'll make sure a couple are there. I know the new captain of the squad. I'll call her and introduce you. Who knows, right? Worst case scenario, they put you on as an alternate if someone hurts themselves. Even if you don't cheer at least you can make practices and keep in shape. Have your name in the yearbook."

A glimmer of hope flashed inside Caitlyn. *He'd do all of this for me? Maybe....* Her pulse quickened. She didn't wish anyone bad luck, of course not, but accidents did happen.

John's voice took on a tender note and he said quietly, "I know you said your father died." He edged closer until their legs brushed. "Want to talk about what happened? Tell me how you feel. Up to you."

An invisible hand squeezed Caitlyn's throat remembering her father. She replied in a low monotone, "Heart attack. Dad was only fifty. He was a dentist, Mom's a bookkeeper and kept the accounts for the office. He wanted a home for her and us out here in the suburbs, figured he'd save half the house as his office, the rest we'd live in. Always use to talk about his dream home." She stopped speaking as she remembered her father's rants. "Hated paying rent to landlords. Disliked what the neighborhood was turning into, with all the violence and crime he heard about on the television."

She took a deep breath. "One day his assistant walked into the office and..." Caitlyn recalled vividly the early morning telephone call her mother received. "She found him slumped over in a chair, dead."

The weight of despair bore down on Caitlyn. John watched her sympathetically, nodding his head, and waited for her to continue the story. She took a long sip of beer and went on. "Right after the funeral, Mom sold the business, took the insurance money, and ran straight out and bought this place." She waved vaguely with her thumb toward her home. "Said the house was Dad's last wish." Caitlyn felt her eyes moisten. "She acts as if he's still around. He'll walk through the door any moment wearing this big, cheery smile on his face like he always did when he came in at night." Caitlyn choked, sniffing back tears, trying hard to take a breath. "I guess this is her way of coping, but dragging us out here sure messed me up." Her voice threatened to break. She stopped, hopeless, unable to alter the situation. Whatever happened in the past wouldn't change. "I guess you think I'm a big crybaby now, right?"

John wrapped his arm around her shoulder in a light hug. "Of course not. Anyone in your position would feel the same way, and I'm sorry," he said quietly. "I wish I knew what to say. I know words won't makes things any better, but I'll mail you my address when I know where I am, and you can send me a note. I'll write to you, too, okay? We can tell each other our problems. Maybe relieve some of the frustrations we have, if nothing else." He gazed into her face and flashed her a warm grin. "You're my girlfriend, right? The rest of the guys would think I'm lying if I didn't receive letters from you."

He's really nice. He understands. "Thanks—I think—I think I will," she replied, trying to return his smile. "Having someone to write to would be nice. Like jotting my thoughts down on paper. Something like a diary, but one replying back to me."

"I never thought of exchanging letters that way." John paused, considering, "and you know, if you ever grow tired of writing, you can always 'Dear John', me." He threw her a lop-sided smirk. "It is my name, you know."

Caitlyn laid a hand on his chest and giggled. "Oh, I could never do something so crass. Much too formal if I'm writing to myself." She said mischievously, "I'll make the heading 'Dear Johnny'." She broke out in laughter, her eyes beaming in delight at her quip as she gazed up at him.

At that moment, John thought she was the most adorable girl in the world, the way her mouth lifted and her eyes looked into his face. He bent over and whispered in her ear, "Maybe we should seal our bargain with a kiss?"

Kiss? Sure, why not. Maybe the way he acted, as if he were on her side, ready to exchange secret thoughts, feelings, perhaps the alcohol helped. She leaned in close to him, giving faint disregard for the flu, or whatever sickness she felt. *What the heck, it's not as if I have AIDS or anything.*

Eyes half-closed, mouth open, she wrapped her arms around his neck. "Okay," she murmured, heart pounding in anticipation.

Their lips met. John's tongue probed lightly into her mouth, caressing the sides and roof. She gently sucked back, feeling his arms enfold her in an embrace, tugging her body tightly against his. Caitlyn savored the tangy taste of the beer in her mouth, staring into John's eyes as he gazed into hers.

The pain plaguing her all day in her back and arm returned, creeping into her chest like a smothering blanket. John's hand dropped to her knee and rubbed slowly upward along her inner thigh.

Caitlyn's eyes widened. *Slow down, mister. Let's not become this friendly yet.* Her heart beat faster, the pain increasing.

She dropped her fingers onto his wrist to stop the advance. A spasm of heartburn shot through her chest, centering between her shoulder blades, a hot flaming knife hammering away at her insides ripping her body apart.

"Ohhh," Caitlyn moaned. The pain clutched her chest, a gigantic fist squeezing. She struggled to push herself away from John and hold herself at the same time. He didn't release her.

"Hey, I didn't mean anything. I thought...."

Caitlyn barely heard him. The agony grew worse, so intense she could barely breathe. She gasped, "Help."

John was shaking her. Why was he shaking her? She needed a doctor, someone to stop the agony racing through her body. She broke free of his grasp and tried to stand. The pain refused to allow her. She moaned, "Oh, God, help me."

John's voice was loud in her ear. "I didn't do anything. Why are you screaming? Cut the shouting out, you'll have the whole neighborhood over here." He held her arms, rocking her violently back and forth in his grip.

Caitlyn's head dropped forward against her chest. She stopped yelling.

John stopped shaking.

***

"Hey, you okay? What was the screaming about?" John stared into Caitlyn's face. Her eyes were closed shut, head bent at a strange angle as if she were a broken doll, the stuffing missing from the neck. "Caitlyn, you alright?" he taped her lightly on the cheek using two fingers, sure she was putting him on for some reason. He expected her to bust out giggling, yelling "Gotcha!"and tell him what a dog he was for running his hand up her leg.

Caitlyn did not respond.

"Quit the act now, will you? This isn't funny anymore. You're freaking me out."

John stared at the girl pretending to act unconscious and frowned. *Is she afraid I'm going to rape her? She put her hand on mine. I stopped.* "C'mon, Caitlyn, answer me." This time he nudged her cheek harder and shook her lightly, trying to elicit a response. Her head bobbed sideways against his chest, hair covering her face, body limp and heavy against his.

John stood. Caitlyn slumped onto the arm of the couch. She didn't stir.

Crazy girl, she fainted on me. Why did she faint? John hastily ran to the kitchen. He returned carrying a glass of cold water. Dipping his fingers into the cup, he flicked the liquid onto her face, an uneasy tightness gripping his throat. "Snap out of it, will ya?" he said loudly, as if the harshness of his tone would make her wake up.

John waited and looked closer at Caitlyn. The uneasiness changed to panic. He couldn't see her chest moving. Pushing down the feeling he was somehow molesting her, he placed his fingertips on her chest, trying to locate a heartbeat. Caitlyn didn't awaken, nor did he feel any movement.

A static buzzing rang in John's head. He froze, gazing blankly at the girl and snatched his hand away. Apprehensive, he seized her wrist, remembering at the last second to feel for her pulse using his fingers instead of his thumb as he'd learned in first aid class. All the while, he repeated to himself, "I didn't do anything. What did I do? Was the shaking responsible—did I break her neck?" He felt no pulse.

John dropped her wrist, wiping his fingers on his pants as if they'd touched something dirty. His sight narrowed, centering on the pale arm and face of Caitlyn, filling his vision, nothing else existing in the world.

I DIDN'T DO ANYTHING.

John stood in horror. Full-blown terror was coursing through his body.

Caitlyn was dead.

Chapter Three

Call the police? He'd be thrown in jail for murder. The cops would say he'd killed her, broken her neck in a fit of rage, maybe attempted to rape the girl and she resisted. John kept staring at the body, frozen, trying to think and unable to do so. A strange sense of lightness entered his body. The sole thought circulating in his mind was that the rest of his life had ended. From this day forward, the police would search for him as a wanted criminal and lock him away forever.

John spun from the corpse and paced up and down the length of the TV room, refusing to look at the body. Tell his mother and father? No way. They'd call the police, his parents must. What choice did they have but to hand him over? His parents weren't criminals. No one could help him out of this. Caitlyn's death was his fault. They should be home soon any minute. What was he going to say? How could he explain?

I didn't mean to. I didn't do anything wrong.

Wetness streamed down his cheeks. The urge to hide under the covers of his bed was the first idea crossing his confused mind. He dismissed the idea as stupid. How would hiding help, or running away? Eventually the cops would locate him, place signs in every post office in the nation. He must do something to make this right, cause the murder to vanish, disappear like he'd never met the girl.

John glanced out the back window to Caitlyn's house. He saw no movement. She'd said her mom and sister went out to eat. Then he raced to the front picture window in the living room and ripped the curtains aside, peering along the street. No cars, no people. All was quiet.

Mr. Rue wasn't expected until late tonight. The electrician in the next house was still at the golf course. At least until his parents returned from lunch, his own little square of the block was free of eyewitnesses, his to move about in as he wished.

Whatever he did, he must act fast. Snorting as hard as he did when running a hundred-yard dash, John pushed his confusion aside and made a decision. He only saw one course of action in the matter as far as he perceived, and he could pull the plan off if his luck held. John decided to hide the body.

The backyard was out of the question. Someone was bound to notice he'd dug a hole in the earth and buried something. His parents would ask what he did and why. The police might even bring search dogs into the area, in fact the authorities were bound too once the hunt started for the missing girl. The cops would investigate every backyard on the block and comb every square inch of the town. Anyone walking along the street might see him digging and remember, say they saw John Baker carving out a hole in the earth and think he acted odd. Once Caitlyn didn't return home the police would ask questions, canvass the neighborhood showing a description of her. The same was true if he took the body and dumped the corpse in the woods no matter how far away he drove. Every TV show he'd seen, or newspaper article he'd read, always mentioned a witness, some evidence left for investigators to discover.

He kept glancing at the clock on the wall, surprised to see only a quarter of an hour passed, but time was working against him. He must start moving, not stand around like an idiot wondering what to do. His parents would reappear any minute and Caitlyn's mom was sure to begin searching when the day grew too late and she didn't return. He paced, a rat caught in a maze, not knowing where to run. *Get a hold of yourself, boy. Slow down. Work the problem out. If I'm going accomplish this, the body must be hidden perfectly.* John took deep, calming breaths, trying to concentrate and clear his mind.

His striding through the house brought him to the back window again. As if his brain were detached from his body, he remembered he still must finish weeding the garden and shut the water off for his dad. His parents would wonder what he'd been doing all day if he didn't finish the chores he'd promised to do. John pictured the dark crawlspace under the house, the single copper pipe jutting out of the earth. The shut-off valve attached in the middle. Cobwebs clung to the cinderblocks, more in grey profusion dangling in dark corners and covering the floorboards above the dry, brown dirt.

Of course, the crawlspace. No one goes under there. They have no reason too, unless the water needs switching off for the whole house, and that only happens every few years at most. Even if someone did go in, the person would concentrate on the valve, not on searching for hidden bodies concealed in the ground. I could hide her there. Scoop out a grave in the earth and bury her deep. No one would see. No one would know where she is.

Could he stuff the corpse into one of the lawn bags he used for the grass trimmings? She was five foot nothing and hardly weighed a thing. The sacks were big enough, but strong enough? He was afraid the plastic would burst apart.

He was glad he'd paid attention in school, listening to the side remarks from the teachers. His history class discussed disposing bodies one day. He'd have to wrap Caitlyn in something, sprinkle lye or lime on the corpse to make the body rot faster and eliminate the odor. John recalled from class the teacher saying the body of William the Conquer swelled and exploded from the gas built up inside, while on exhibition after he died. The stench was horrible.

Burlap and lime. His father kept both in the garage along with fertilizer. The burlap to wrap the bushes in before winter so the snow didn't weigh down the branches and break the wood, and lime for the lawn every few years to cut the acid buildup. Did he have enough for what he needed to do? He thought so and his dad would never notice the items missing. John was in charge of yard chores, only mentioning the supplies and asking for money to buy more when he ran out. The plan would succeed, but he must hurry. Every second he delayed brought him one step closer to discovery and he had a lot of work to do.

John strode to the couch, cringing inside, and blanked from his mind what he was about to place into motion.

Caitlyn was heavy. John was surprised. He'd expected her to weigh no more than a bag of dry leaves, as small as she was. Instead, her limp body caused his arms to tremble. The sensation of holding a sack of warm Jello flooded his mind as if water filled the body, and she sloshed every time he moved. Before he left the house, he scanned the exterior yard, surrounding homes, and street carefully to assure himself no one saw him. With difficulty, he carried her outside through the back door to the side entrance of the garage. John hauled the corpse inside, while repeating to himself, "I have to do this. Covering the evidence is the only way."

Two large bundles of burlap stood in one corner. John laid the body on the concrete floor, grabbed a roll, and uncoiled a length of the coarse material, pushing the corpse on top.

Tears leaked from the corners of his eyes. John wiped his face and closed his mind. Without thinking, he tore off his high school ring with his initials etched inside and slipped the band onto her finger. She'd remember him, he hoped, and knew he didn't mean any of this to happen—

a mistake, a dumb mistake. Struggling to contain himself, he took a deep breath and started to conceal his crime.

He kept rolling the remains while unwrapping the burlap until Caitlyn resembled a brown soft mummy and the fabric was gone. He debated whether to use the second roll and decided not to. He'd bought the additional bundle out of his own money when he saw the material on sale months ago and forgotten to tell his father about the purchase. Now he was glad he hadn't. No one would ever miss the burlap.

The side door of the garage stood directly opposite the small window leading into the crawlspace under his home. A breezeway connected the two buildings. John peeked out the door, checking the front and rear of the house for signs of passersby, assuring himself no one would see him as he moved about carrying the body and his materials. In three quick steps, he opened the window, and returned to the garage, carrying the corpse across the cement walk. Stooping, he pushed the body underneath the house with a grunt, shoving Caitlyn's remains as far in as possible and hurried to the garage to collect the rest of his supplies.

On the shelf in the rear of the building, five bags of lime were stacked one on top of each other alongside of extra bags of lawn fertilizer he hadn't used in the spring. One by one, he dragged three of the bags to the window, pushing the sacks inside next to the wrapped corpse.

John kept his emotions tightly constrained during this operation. As he wiggled in beside the body, he lost control of his feelings and they broke through his shield. A pang of sorrow stabbed him in the heart. The horror of what he was about to do washed over him, a wave crashing on the beach crushing anything standing in the way.

A dog. I'm burying her as if she were a pet animal, loved and then forgotten, shoved in the dirt or flushed down the toilet. "I'm sorry, Caitlyn," he whispered.

Shaking his head to clear the thoughts, John scanned the small, enclosed space under the house. *I can't use a shovel, the ceiling's too low. I should have brought a pot or trowel. Not enough time to find one now. I want this over and finished before my parents arrive home or someone stops by.*

He'd have to claw out the grave by hand. Sweating profusely, he slithered to the farthest point away from the water main, a dark corner never explored even during the few trips he'd made under the house over the years.

The earth was soft and dry, undisturbed since construction of the building twenty years ago, the body small. John kept scooping dirt, breaking his fingernails as he hit rocks, and praying he didn't run out of time. He kept casting fast glances toward the window, straining his ears for the sound of anyone's approach, or his name called aloud by his friends or parents. Even in the coolness of the semi-darkness, perspiration continued to run down his forehead, stinging his eyes, and mingling with the dust he raised to create a muddy mask on his face.

His arms ached, the muscles in his shoulders and back screamed in pain from his frantic digging. After he'd excavated a shallow grave he dragged the bundle over and pushed it into the hole. Dirt from the edges of the pit fell alongside the corpse as the earth eagerly claimed the body. *Not very deep, but the pit will have to do. I can't waste any more time. My parents are sure to be home soon.*

In the gloom, he stared at the remains. *I'm sorry. Whatever I did, I didn't mean to do.*

Moisture flooded his eyes again, making rivulets where the sweat and dirt coated his cheeks with grime. The bags of lime came next. John ripped each one open, sprinkling the powder evenly as possible on the burlap, coating the fabric in a thick, white pile. When he finished, he shoved the remaining dirt on top, until the grave appeared to be a large mound of earth in the darkest shadows of the crawlspace.

Finished. This never happened.

Without looking back, he shimmied his way out into the fresh air and bright sunshine. John scurried to the backyard, carrying the empty lime sacks while crumbling each into small balls. He stuffed the evidence in the lawn bags containing the grass clippings, mixing the paper in until the bags disappeared into the middle of the trimmings, and hauled the last proof of the crime to the curb. The garbage men would collect the trash tomorrow morning and whatever remained of the murder would vanish. Drawing a huge lungful of air, he frantically ran to the garden and started ripping out weeds, not caring where they landed or daring to look around to see if anyone watched him work. He waited tensely for a tap on the shoulder from a police officer. Positive he'd been seen and arrest was minutes away.

"My, you certainly are a mess."

A jolt of fear shot into John's heart. A shadow passed over the patch of weeds he scratched at wildly. He jerked his head up. His mother stood behind him, clutching a shopping bag to her chest, a frown creasing her face.

How long has she been here, watching? Did she see me wiggle out of the crawlspace? His mind spun rapidly, he felt sick. "Oh, you scared the wits out of me. I didn't hear you drive up. Just get home?" He tried acting normal, willing his heartbeat to slow, his breathing to appear regular, sure the guilt of the murder shone all over his face in big letters. On hands and knees, he stared up at his parent and pasted a sickly grin on his face. "How was lunch? I expected you home hours before this. I was about to send the dogs out searching for you and dad."

His mother waved a hand glancing at the bag she held. "Oh, we stopped off at the mall, and then the hardware store. Your father wanted to pick up another handle for the shower as long as he was changing everything else. You know how he acts when he walks into those stores." She said the last with a sigh, discarding the fact she'd spend an hour at the mall buying a skirt. "Strolls up and down the isles looking at everything else when what he needs should take him five minutes to buy and pay for."

"Hardware stores are interesting," John said in defense of his father, glad she made no mention of seeing him emerge from under the house.

"Oh, you men. Tools, paints and glue," his mother replied. "Of course, then he has to rush to finish whatever project he was starting on in the first place. In fact..." she glanced toward the house, "I think he wants to get going now on the shower before the time grows too late. Did you shut off the water as you promised?"

"Uh, no." Damn, he should have turned off the valve when he was under the house. Crawling in and out once was a dirty job he hated, now he'd have to repeat the operation, with the *thing* still fresh in his mind, waiting.

"What have you been doing all morning?" his mother said, studying the garden area and lawn. "Doesn't appear as if you've completed very much."

"Umm, well..." John tried thinking of an excuse. "I did take a break for an hour or so." *Please, don't question me anymore.* He ripped out a dandelion. "These weeds are rough, especially in this dry dirt, and uh...."

"What's the matter, you look scared," his mother said. "If you don't want to help your dad do the plumbing, I suppose your father could —"

"NO—no. I'll do it. I—um..." he glanced down at himself, trying to appear as if he were silly for appearing frightened, "Wiggling around under the house isn't the most enjoyable job I like to do. It's creepy under there, dark, and I didn't want to make my clothes all dirty, but I suppose I'm filthy enough already, huh?" He stood and brushed ineffectually at the dirt and leaves clinging to his pants and shirt. "I'll crawl in now and shut the valve off. Let Dad know, okay? The quicker he's finished, the sooner I can have a shower and change my clothes."

The space was darker than an hour ago. John shimmied his way over the dirt keeping his eyes averted from the mound in the corner. He made it to the wall, grabbed the valve and twisted. Despite himself, he turned and looked where Caitlyn lay.

John swore he saw the earth shift, clods of dirt falling off the top of the pile as if fingers tried to claw their way skyward. A chilling splash of terror crawled up John's neck. His sweaty hand slipped around the valve, the tap firmly shut, in a fruitless attempt to tighten the spigot further. Releasing a shuddering wheeze of air, his overwrought brain imagined an arm reaching to grasp him. John crawled out hastily and stood in the breezeway, shivering.

The movement was his mind, playing tricks on him. The earth settling. Caitlyn was gone, never to return to life—dead and buried.

John strode to the back door and called in, "Water's off, Pop. Let me know when you want me to shimmy back under." A muffled reply echoed from the downstairs bathroom. John returned to pulling weeds.

The daylight failed. In the twilight, John hoped his father would hurry. He kept glancing up from the garden to Caitlyn's house watching for some indication of life. A light switched on in the kitchen, a head passed the window, and then the bedroom lights sprang into existence. Caitlyn's people were home. His body tensed, wondering what was happening inside, when the search would begin.

His mother strolled out of the door and called, "Your father says to switch the water back on. He's finished." She thrust a flashlight into his grasp, glancing at the sky. "Here, take this. It must be pitch black underneath the house by now."

This time he refused to look around, keeping his attention on the pipe ahead, the glow of the flashlight creating a pale white circle, illuminating the cinderblock wall behind the valve. A faint scurrying noise sounded from the corner, a whispering, halting suddenly. The hackles on the back of his neck rose in fear. Senses taut to the breaking point, he spun the cutoff open and pivoted to leave.

"Your father says to wait a minute." His mother's feet and ankles framed the window opening. "He wants to make sure everything is working properly and there's no leaks before you crawl out."

John's head snapped up, hitting the wood from the floorboards, making a resounding thud. "Ow."

"Did you say something, honey?"

"Tell him to hurry up. This place is creepy." John rubbed his scalp.

"I'll tell him, dear." His mother's feet disappeared.

The rustling started again, this time along the wall. Automatically, John shone the light in the direction the noise issued from, making a slow circuit where cinderblocks met dirt, a hissing breath leaked between his clenched teeth.

A small, brown shape silhouetted in the brilliance, froze, and issuing a high-pitched squeak, disappeared into a hole underneath one of the blocks.

A mouse. I'm ready to pee in my pants because of a lousy mouse. Gotta get control of myself, there's nothing under here planning to hurt me.

John's heart hammered in his chest. He crawled to the window, praying for his mother to return.

"All set," his mother called.

After he'd wiggled out the window, John pretended to stared at his filthy pants and shirt while he waited for the thumping of his chest to still. "I'm gonna take a shower," he finally mumbled as he rubbed his forehead and ground dirt even deeper into his skin.

"Are you alright?" his mother asked. "You're as white as a sheet."

"Nervous about leaving tomorrow," he lied, not daring to look her in the eye. "I'll be fine once I wash off all this muck and relax. I've had a long day."

In his room, John ripped off his clothes, the very feel of the fabric against his body making his skin crawl. The tiles were cold on his bare feet as he entered his bathroom. He fumbled at the tap of hot water until the shower ran full blast and the sting burnt his flesh. When he could take the biting pain no longer, he switched the flow to a cooler temperature, hoping the lukewarm liquid would relax his body, wash away his sin. Breathing deeply, inhaling the steam, he kept repeating, "God, don't let anybody find her. The murder never happened."

When he stepped out of the shower he felt no better.

John dried himself, dressed in clean clothes, and stood by his rear bedroom window, staring at the house behind his. Caitlyn's home. The place was ablaze in lights. Even the outside ones illuminating the yard shone a brilliance on the dark green lawn. He tried to imagine what was happening inside. Did her mother and sister think Caitlyn was late, lost, kidnaped? Would her people wait before calling the police hoping she'd return, or the police been notified all ready and on their way to investigate?

John spun from the window, ashamed and guilty about the pain he caused Caitlyn's family, and walked downstairs to eat dinner.

"I see what took you so long doing the yardwork this morning," his mother said, glaring at the kitchen garbage can. "You know what I think about you drinking."

The empty beer container he'd thrown away sat atop a pile of coffee grounds.

Oh, geez. I left Caitlyn's sitting on the end table. "Huh, I only drank one." He hurried to the television room, grabbed the can and held it up, walking quickly to the kitchen sink. "See, one. I didn't have a second 'cause I knew you'd be mad." John poured the contents of the half-full container down the drain. He crushed the can and dropped the evidence on top of the other empty, hoping his mother was satisfied and forget all about the beer.

Did he leave anything else of Caitlyn's laying around? John couldn't remember, the morning clouded into a blur in his mind. Was she carrying a purse maybe? He casually walked into the TV room and glanced around, lounged on the sofa, and ran his fingers surreptitiously inside the cushions. Nothing.

"I guess one won't hurt you," his mother said, still frowning, "but I don't want you to make a habit out of drinking alcohol. You're too young."

"Huh? Oh, yeah, Mom. I'll remember." *Anything outside, in the garage maybe, fallen from Caitlyn's body before he'd wrapped her in burlap?* He didn't think so. He was safe.

John ate supper quickly, expecting a rap on the door, a police officer waiting, ready to take him into custody. When he finished eating, he announced, "Heading up to bed. Gotta be up early and at the recruiter's office by six a.m. I'll leave my car there." He said to his dad, "You can pick the old bomb up for me if you don't mind whenever you have the chance. I won't need a ride for a long time."

"Don't bother, son," his father replied. "I'll drop you off on my way to work. I drive right by the recruiting office."

Before he went to bed, John stood at his rear window one more time to check the house behind his. Caitlyn's home was still glowing with lights. In the distance, he heard the wail of a siren and wondered if the police were on their way. He shuddered and lay down.

Sleep wouldn't come. John tossed and turned, the scenes of what he'd done flashing through his head. He kept running over in his mind, what went wrong. How could he hurt Caitlyn so badly she died? He shook her, yes, but so rough he broke her neck? During football games, he often tackled people harder, so rough he'd knocked the wind out of the kids and they were taken off the field. The players never died. She wouldn't stop yelling. Why? Why? WHY?

The questions kept spinning around and blurred into a mixture of images. Her face. The girl screaming. The body in the grave. When his alarm rang in the morning, he felt as if he'd never slept during the night. He swung his legs out of bed, still half asleep, at first thinking the day before was part of a bad dream, a nightmare brought on by the thought of entering the army. He was John Baker, athlete, student, and soon-to-be soldier, not a ghoul burying corpses in the basement.

As he dressed, however, and his mind cleared, he realized yesterday was not a dream. He stared at his hands. His school ring was missing. He remembered slipping the band onto Caitlyn's finger before he disposed of the body. For all the scrubbing, faint traces of soil still lined the inside of his nails as if he'd been permanently stained by a stigma of his deed.

His father left him outside the recruiter's office in the morning. "Good luck. See you in a couple of months." His dad grinned and added, "Remember, this is basic training. Try not to kill anyone unless you're in combat, and the people you're shooting at are the enemy."

John returned a frail smile. "Never have. Don't plan to unless I'm forced into defending my life or a buddy's."

As his father drove away, relief, fear, and regret, all mingled into a flood inside John.

He walked into the recruiting office. The sergeant behind the desk rose. "Right on time," he exclaimed clasping John on the back. "Hope you tied up any last minute details. No business you have to take care of, right? You'll be busy for the next few months."

"All set, sergeant. As far as I know, I'm free to leave."

Nothing so far. No police, no questions. It's over. What happened was a different part of my life. I was right, yesterday was a bad dream. Keep truckin'. The death never happened.

Oh, Caitlyn. I'm so sorry.

Chapter Four

"Caitlyn, we're home," Mrs. Brennen shouted as she and Lynn entered their home. She pulled off her sweater and tossed the garment on the couch before strolling into the kitchen and slipping a pizza into the oven. She switched the stove to warm and dropped a brown paper bag on the table. "Lynn," she called over her shoulder, "go find your sister and tell her supper's here. She's probably in her room, still pouting. I hope Caitlyn finished unpacking her clothes, at least. She's taken all afternoon."

"Yes, Mom," Lynn yelled back from the living room. She hurried along the hallway to her bedroom, tossed her jacket onto a desk, and then crossed the hall to Caitlyn's. She rapped on the closed door and shouted at the same time, "Hey, Cat, we're back. You in there?" When she received no answer, she opened the door cautiously in case her sister was asleep and stuck her head into the room. The lights were off, the bedroom unoccupied. She switched on the overhead light. Some of the boxes were still unpacked and sitting where they were left when she and her mother drove to the pizza place.

Typical. Took off and probably leaving the rest of her junk on the floor until I help. Lynn called back to her mother, "She's not here, Mom. Didn't I hear her say she was going for a walk around the block? Maybe she's still outside somewhere." She stepped over to the window and checked the backyard. No Cat in sight there either.

Lynn hear the clicking of her mother's shoes as she walked along the hallway and entered Caitlyn's room, inspecting the chamber for herself. "Yes, but we left hours ago, and she didn't finish putting away her clothes either."

She frowned, annoyed. "She's growing worse every year. Never listens to a word I say." She regarded Lynn for a long moment. "Would you mind very much taking a quick walk around the block and see if you can spot her? She knows better than to wander off and not leave a note." She glanced out the window, estimating how much daylight remained. "Not too long, though. The sun's going down and it's growing dark. I don't want to go searching for you too in a strange community."

Lynn beamed back at her mother. "Sure, no problem. I'll only be gone a couple of minutes." She ran, scooped up her jacket and hurried out the front door. *Stupid sister, now I have to go tracking her down when all I want to do is kick back and relax. She'd better not ask me to help unpack her things.*

Lynn circled the block at a fast walk, attempting to peer in windows and backyards, but fell short of stalking people's properties, afraid someone would accuse her of trespassing while she searched for her sister. The last thing she needed was to have the new neighbors think she was nosy or a thief. When she finished her circuit of the homes and returned to her house, she decided to check the opposite block. She set off at a dogtrot and a few minutes later finished checking the homes in either direction without success.

She stood in front of her mailbox, hands on waist, glancing up and down the street while worrying her lower lip with her teeth. *If I was a stupid jerk sister, and wanted to aggravate my mother and sister, where would I be?*

Lynn swung in a wide circle, as if she were a search dog sniffing for the scent of her lost sibling. Lynn stopped, her nose pointing over a row of houses toward a lighted spot in the sky. Of course. Next block over and up the hill. An elementary school. Her, her mom and Cat drove up there last week while exploring the area to see what the place looked like. Lynn noticed groups of kids, some their own age, hanging out and playing basketball. Cat mentioned she thought the school grounds would be a cool place to investigate, and said she'd check out the woods, ball fields, and a church picnic yard beyond as soon as she could. Cat was probably up there now with a bunch of guys she met, BSing and being her cute self. Lynn took off jogging, swinging her arms in a rhythmic beat, while muttering words under her breath about people who could not tell time and wasted hers.

The schoolyard stood deserted except for two children on the swings, parents in tow receiving a few last pushes before it was time to leave. Lynn glanced around, drew a deep breath, and bellowed, "CAT—YOU UP HERE?"

No answer except for the echo of her voice off the walls of the school building and trees.

One of the parents, a woman, glanced up and waved Lynn over. "Lose someone?" she asked curiously with a pleasant smile.

"My sister. You haven't seen a girl up here, have you?" replied Lynn. "Seventeen, looks like me, but shorter. Has blond hair, and is in big trouble when our mom gets a hold of her." In the last year, Lynn shot up a quarter of a foot and towered over her older sister by two inches.

The woman paused, thinking. "A group of kids did wander through here about an hour ago," she said, pointing a finger toward the rear of the school toward the church property, "but I don't remember a blond mixed in with the bunch." She glanced at the man at the next swing who'd stopped to listen.

He shook his head in the negative. "Tell you what, kid. I'm leaving in a couple of minutes. I'll drive around the neighborhood for a bit and see if I can spot her, Okay? What's your sister's name again?"

"I will, too," the woman assured Lynn quickly, helping her child put on his coat.

"Gee, thanks. Her name's Caitlyn. Caitlyn Brennen, but most people call her Cat." Lynn scanned the grounds one last time. "I'd better be heading home, too. I promised my mom I wouldn't be out too long. She'll be worried about both of us."

Lynn trudged down the hill trying to decide where else Caitlyn might be. Walking toward her on the sidewalk were two girls. On the off chance they'd seen her sister Lynn stopped and asked, "Excuse me. Have you seen a girl named Cat? Blond hair, looks kinda like me? She's my sister."

One girl, a short brunette wearing black-rimmed glasses said, "Cat?" She peeked sideways at the other girl. "Nope, no cats. Saw a dog before, though. Didn't look like you." The two giggled.

Lynn frowned. "Funny. No, I was serious. My sister is missing, and I'm trying to track her down. We're new around here. Thanks for the help, anyway." She began walking away.

"Hey, sorry," the brunette said, her smirk vanished. "I wasn't trying to be mean or anything. My name's Trish, this is Val. If we see her, we'll tell your sister you're out searching. What's your name, anyway?"

"Lynn, I just moved in today." She gestured down the hill toward her house. "My sister went for a walk sometime this afternoon and hasn't returned yet. My mom sent me out to find her."

"We'll look. I promise. You moved in today?" the other girl, Val, asked curiously, as she scrutinized Lynn. "What grade are you in?"

"Tenth. My sister is seventeen. She'll be a senior."

"Cool. We'll be going to the same school, then," Trish remarked.

Val said, "We gotta start moving. Our parents wanted us home an hour ago."

"No problem," Trish remarked to her friend. "We have an excuse now, we're searching for cats." She waved to Lynn. "Catch you later, Lynn. If we see your sister, we'll let her know to haul her tail home pronto."

Lynn watched the two leave. *Well, I've done everything I know to do. Better drag my butt home, too, before Mom has the National Guard out searching for us.*

All the streetlights shone overhead as Lynn finished walking down the hill and back to her street. When she entered the house, the first words out of her mother's mouth were, "Did you locate her?"

Lynn read the look on her mother's face. She wore the same expression as the one at her father's funeral. Her voice was grim. "No, Mom, but I met people, a man and a woman. Two girls also. They all promised to look for Cat, and tell her to come home. Don't worry, she'll show up." Lynn tried to relieve the tension building inside the room. "You know Cat. She probably met some girls and started doing cheer-talk." She waved her arms and sprang into the air as if holding pom-poms. "Ra-Ra! Kick 'em in the bootie. We love our quarterback, he's a cutie!" She attempted a split, reached halfway to the floor, and straightened up quickly, face red and hair disheveled. "I told you, I met a couple girls myself on the way back here and sort of lost track of time talking. I bet Cat did the same and she'll walk in the door all apologetic."

Her mother's face bent into a smile, but immediately transformed back into a frown. "I'd better not hear any lame excuses," she fumed, throwing her hands in the air displaying the frustration she felt. Mrs. Brennen glanced at her watch. "Your sister is old enough to know how to ask.... I'll let her have fifteen more minutes. If she's not in this house, I'm hopping in the car and searching for her, and when I find that young lady...." She left the rest of the sentence unfinished with a disgusted shake of the head as she started counting the minutes.

Cat, you're so in for a grounding now. Mom's really pissed. "She probably has a good..." Lynn began. Her voice trailed off as her mother's attention shifted to her. Daring her youngest daughter to say what would be a good enough excuse to explain the aggravation her oldest child was putting her through.

Mrs. Brennen paced, continually glaring at her wrist, her anger and worry mounting. After the allotted time passed, she announced, "I'm gonna go driving around looking for your sister." She said to Lynn, "You stay here. If she shows up, call me, *immediately.* Do you understand? First thing tomorrow, I'm buying you both phones, no matter how much they cost. This will never happen again." She stormed out the front door, rattling her car keys.

Lynn stood at the front window and watched her mother drive off, laid on the couch in the living room, and switched on the TV, trying to locate a program interesting enough to watch and distract her from the worry building inside, clenching at her stomach. She popped up again, and flipped on all the outside floodlights, somehow expecting they would make their brilliance easier for Cat to find her way home. Lynn settled back on the sofa and continued to change channels, unable to think of what else to do. All the stations were strange. She finally decided on a documentary about African elephants, but kept the volume low hoping she'd hear Cat's voice if she were sitting on the stoop or standing in the yard speaking to someone.

When a noise rustled outside on the front lawn, Lynn sprang to her feet and raced to the entrance, throwing the door open wide. "Cat, Mom is so gonna...." No one was there. An empty fast food bag bounced across her line of vision into the darkness, and continued its way along the street until it disappeared from view. "People should learn how to throw their trash in the garbage," she muttered angrily and slammed the door, resuming her seat. The disappointment plus the anger at the bag caused her worry to increase.

The phone rang. Lynn jumped erect, picked up the receiver, her heart racing. "Hello? Hello? Cat, is that—"

"Lynn, has Caitlyn shown up yet?" The caller was her mother.

Lynn was taken aback by the fury and worry in her mother's voice. "No, Mom. Nothing yet."

"I've driven up every street within a mile of our house," snapped Mrs. Brennen, more frustration and concern pouring into her tone. "I'm checking the turnpike, stores, and shops. Call me if she returns." The phone went dead.

Her mother's panic mingled with the apprehension Lynn felt already. Wild scenarios bubbled in her mind. What if some pervert kidnapped Cat and tied her up in his basement? Lynn once saw a television show where the same thing happened and the movie scared the wits out of her. What if she climbed into a tree for some crazy reason? Fell and broke her leg? Cat could've crawled off into the woods by the schoolyard and be lying on the ground right now, whimpering with pain in the dark.

Her parents always cautioned the two of them about talking to strangers until the warning grew automatic and the response was always, "Yes, Mom, Dad. We'll be careful." They'd never given the ultimatum much thought. Cat and she were city girls and knew how to take care of themselves out in public, but assaults, kidnappings, and robberies were all her father and mother spoke about. The reason her parents wished to move to the suburbs, to flee the violence they perceived all around their apartment and on the crowded streets. The terror of everyday life her mother sought to escape in the city had tracked the family to this house.

"I'm being ridiculous," Lynn muttered. "Probably hanging out with some guy in his living room right now, watching TV and eating popcorn." Nevertheless, she discovered keeping still and waiting, doing next to nothing except watching a program she wasn't interested in, was impossible. Instead, she paced along the length of the carpet, once hurrying to Caitlyn's room to see if she'd left a note. Caitlyn's pocketbook was on the bed, wallet on her dresser, including her purse and a pile of loose change. *Wouldn't have gone very far and not brought her I.D. and money.*

Lynn bit her upper lip, trying to decide what else she'd forgotten or where she hadn't searched yet in the house. *Of course, the kitchen. Maybe Caitlyn left a message on the table, or counter. I bet Mom never looked, neither did I.* She hurried down the hallway and rushed over to the kitchen counter, sweeping aside the coffeemaker and sugar bowl, searching for a note under salt and pepper shakers. Nothing. The kitchen table yield the same results.

Lynn resumed her pacing.

An hour later, Mrs. Brennen returned. "I'm calling the police. I don't know what else to do," she breathed hopelessly.

"You think something's happened to her?" Lynn asked anxiously. The impact of what her mother said was awakening new fears already seething in her overwrought mind.

"I don't know." Mrs. Brennen picked up the phone. She dialed nine-one-one.

"Hello? I want to report my daughter missing… My name is Mrs. Joan Brennen, my daughter's name is Caitlyn…Twelve Honeywell Drive…Yes…How long?"

Mrs. Brennen glanced at Lynn, and whispered, "How long has Caitlyn been gone?"

Lynn studied the clock on the wall and made a quick estimated in her head. She mouthed back, "About nine hours."

"Nine hours...No, we haven't checked any of her friends. She has no friends here. We only moved into this house today from the city...No. I haven't called the hospital." Mrs. Brennen pulled the receiver slightly away from her mouth, the muscles in her jaw bunching. "Are you going to help me?"

Mrs. Brennen's fingers shone white at the knuckles as she squeezed the phone, her face shading to red. "Thank you. I will." She slammed the phone down in the cradle, closing her eyes, and pressed her palm to her forehead.

"What'd the operator say?" Lynn asked, watching her mother's face.

"I have to call the hospital," Mrs. Brennen mumbled, fumbling with the phone. "The police are sending someone over. I need Caitlyn's social security number, picture, and write down what she was wearing. I don't remember what any of this...Hello? This is Mrs. Brennen. Has a girl...."

Lynn didn't wait to hear more. *Her wallet.* She raced to Caitlyn's room and snatched the heavy leather folder off the dresser along with Caitlyn's purse. Then she hurried to her own room and scooped up a framed picture of her sister taken the previous spring wearing her cheerleading uniform. As her mother hung up the phone, Lynn was back, out of breath. "Here. I.D., social security card, driver's license, and the picture you took of her at the state lacrosse finals." She dumped everything on the coffee table in front of her mother. She snatched up a pad and pencil, scribbling what Caitlyn wore the last time she saw her sister. "Anything else we need?"

For the first time her mother smiled and shook her head. "No. I think we have everything. Now we sit and wait for the police."

A few minutes later, a knock banged on the door. Mrs. Brennen hurried and opened it. A young uniformed police officer stood there. "Mrs. Brennen? We received a call about your missing daughter."

"Yes, please, come in."

After Mrs. Brennen delivered all the information the officer asked for, he wrote out a report and handed her a copy. "Here's the file number if you need to contact us." He showed her a long number on the upper corner of the paper.

She watched the man hopefully. "Do you think there's any chance you'll find her tonight?"

The police officer's face remained impassive. "We'll send the word out to all the local agencies in the area. Everyone will be looking," he assured her. The officer asked, "Did she say anything unusual the last time you spoke to her? Maybe a quarrel between you and her?"

Mrs. Brennen shook her head. "No. Nothing. We left to eat and when we returned she was—gone."

Lynn shot her mother a sideways glance and said to the officer, "Well, she wasn't happy about moving out here from the city, and she was asking if Mom would let her stay at a friend's apartment for the rest of the school year, but I don't think she was so upset she'd...."

The policeman nodded and made a note in his pad. "Has anyone notified her acquaintances from your old neighborhood? Contacted a boyfriend maybe? It's possible she hopped a train or someone she knows drove out here and picked her up. It's a long shot but worth a try."

Mrs. Brennen nodded eagerly. "I'll jump right on it. I never thought to call her friends from school or the apartment building. Anything else you can suggest we do? Anything at all?"

The officer nodded. "One last thing. If she has a computer or phone, you might want to check her e-mails and any texts she made or received. Always the chance she was corresponding with someone you didn't know about, or an acquaintance may have e-mailed her, and there's no phone number written down."

"No phone," Mrs. Brennen admitted. "I always thought they were too expensive and the girls never needed one before. She has a computer. I…" She looked to Lynn. "Did Caitlyn set up the tower and monitor yet? I don't recall…"

"Yeah, Mom. I stuck the whole thing together on her desk before we left."

"Those are some of the items you can check while you're waiting." The police officer closed his notepad. "Other than what I've said already, I can't think of anything else, Ma'am," the officer said as he moved toward the door. "I've got her picture. This is all I'll need for now. Tomorrow, if you haven't heard from her, we'll start canvassing the neighbors, see if they heard or saw anything suspicious. If you can think of anything else, or she turns up, give us a call, okay?"

"Of course, officer. Thank you."

"I'll grab Cat's pocketbook, Mom," Lynn said. "She keeps her address book inside." She ran and fetched Cat's handbag, riffling through the mass of papers, cosmetics, and pens until she located it. "Here." She handed the book to her mother. She added in a rush, "I'm not going to use Caitlyn's computer. When she comes back and finds out I was in her room and using her machine, she'll have a fit. I know her password, though, and I'll use mine. Okay?" Lynn watched her mother. Mrs. Brennen nodded absently. "I'll start checking her inbox and sent right now and see what I can find."

"Thank you, Lynn." Mrs. Brennen flipped through Caitlyn's phone book until she found names and addresses and got busy.

Lynn sat at her computer desk, checking Caitlyn's mail.

Nothing today, but she sure was busy in the last week. Musta e-mailed everyone she knew. I wonder if...? Let me try trash. Lynn was busy into the early morning. On the chance her mother missed a phone number, each e-mail she replied to ended with "Have you talked to Cat?" She fell asleep at her desk.

Mrs. Brennen hunched over the phone. "Hello? This is Caitlyn's mother....Yes, that's right, Caitlyn Brennen. Is Caitlyn there? No? Thank you anyway. If she drops in have her call me at once." She ran through one page, started on the next. "Hello? This is Caitlyn's mother....Yes, that's right..."

Mrs. Brennen called her daughter's friends late into the night.

***

The next morning, a police officer visited the Baker's house. Mrs. Baker answered the door.

"Good morning, ma'am. We're searching the neighborhood for a missing girl," he handed her a picture, a photostatted copy of Caitlyn. "The daughter of your neighbor." He pointed to the house behind hers. "Have you seen this girl? She went missing yesterday afternoon. Any suspicious people driving around the street you noticed, strangers walking by the houses, ringing on doorbells to see if anyone was home? Anything unusual you recall."

Mrs. Baker pursed her lips while studying the picture carefully. "No. I know new people moved in yesterday, we saw the lights on all night and was wondering what they were doing, but I assumed everyone was busy unpacking. I haven't seen their daughter or met her parents yet. We were here most of the afternoon and evening, and I didn't have anyone come to the door. Sunday, you know. Quiet around this neighborhood. About dark, I guess the time was I did see a few teenagers, girls I think, walking by, but having the school up the street..."

"I know," the officer said. "I patrol this area. Anybody else live here who might have noticed anything?"

Mrs. Baker hesitated and then said, "My husband was with me all day. He didn't mention seeing strangers. I'd have to ask when he returns from work tonight. I have a son, but —"

"A son? Is he around?" The officer peeked over her shoulder into the house.

"No. He's in the army."

"Oh. Well, if you remember anything at all, let us know."

Mrs. Baker shook her head vigorously. "I certainly will, and when we're done here I'll call my husband and ask." She stared at the picture. "That poor girl and her family. I was going to walk over there this morning and introduce myself. Maybe I should wait. They certainly don't need a stranger in the way at a time like this. Maybe I'll stop by tomorrow real quick and see what I can do to help." She held the picture out.

"No, keep the photograph. Show the print around to your friends," the officer said. "I have more." He sighed. "Happens all too often with kids this age even in the best of areas. They fall into the wrong crowd, drugs, alcohol, or simply decide to take off and go on a great adventure. Most turn up eventually. A few...." He lifted his shoulders and dropped them. He said his goodbyes, and walked on to the next house.

Chapter Five

"Mom, I feel stupid dressed like this." John's parents had driven to the army base to watch their son graduate from basic training, took him out for lunch, and then brought him home for a five-day leave before he left again to start advanced training. Both his parents insisted John wear his full dress uniform while home, at least when he went out in public, and planned to show him off to their friends and neighbors later in the week. "The idea behind taking leave is so I *don't* have to be in uniform." John rubbed his chin, feeling the stubble of a beard already bristling on his cheeks. "I don't even plan to shave unless I have to."

John's father sat in his recliner, reading a book, the television on. He smirked at John as he listened to his son gripe. His mother walked out of the kitchen into the living room and lightly brushed a speck of white lint off John's label and straightened his uniform jacket with a tug. "You look so handsome, though," she exclaimed, standing back and inspecting him from head to toe. "And I'm sure all your friends want to see what you look like all dressed up."

John tried to suppress a grin and finished buttoning his jacket. "They'll think I look like a G.I. Joe jerk," he grumbled. "I'm supposed to be meeting the old gang right now at the diner for breakfast," he checked his phone, "and I'm late. Gotta go."

"While you're here, I want to introduce you to our new neighbors, the Brennens, who moved in behind us," his mother said as he started for the door. "Nice woman. Tragic, though. Her husband died before they moved in. She has two daughters. Her eldest daughter went missing as soon as they arrived. First day, in fact. Her younger daughter's name is Lynn. She's been combing the area ever since, poor woman."

John froze, his hand on the doorknob, refusing to acknowledge his mother's remark with more than a slight nod. "If I have the time. Got a lot of catching up to do in five days, you know."

"Oh, which reminds me," his mother added, refusing to allow John to leave. "I need you to crawl under the house."

Coldness clutched John. He swung around and said slowly, "Why? What's the matter?"

"I smelled something rotten." Her eyes shifted to her husband with a glare. "I think there's a dead animal in the crawlspace, but I'm not sure. I searched the whole house thinking a mouse died under one of the couches, walked around outside looking, and saw nothing. The crawlspace is the only other place the odor could be coming from. Your father claims I'm smelling things."

The coldness inside John changed to panic. "No one checked under there yet?"

John's father shifted in his recliner uncomfortably and placed his book down. "The odor vanished after a couple of days," he said matter-of-factly, "and I never smelled anything anyhow, and I took a peek around too, but make your mom happy and do a quick look-see. Maybe a cat crept in there or a raccoon. Won't hurt to search and scooting under and checking only takes a couple of minutes."

John relaxed and said to his mother, "Probably dad's ratty old chair. I bet he dropped part of a meatball hero in between the cushions, but don't worry. Before I leave I'll nose around and see what I can find." He glanced at his phone for the time again. "Oh, gee, I gotta go. I'm late."

The mention of the neighbors caused a surge of curiosity inside John. He drove around the block, slowing as he passed the Brennen's home.

The white siding shingles were dingier then he remembered. The hedges in front of the picture window needed trimming. Yard could use a good raking to collect the autumn leaves gathering in the corners blown from the fall winds. The house showed people lived inside, but barely, as if the building waited for better times to arrive. The inhabitants preoccupied by other business. John's first impulse was to knock on the door, introduce himself and offer his assistance in a yard cleanup. He felt guilty. The small signs of neglect his fault. The inattention a direct result of what he'd done to the homeowner.

Don't go there. Never grow close to these people. Best to stay away and forget what happened.

John sped up staring straight ahead, and drove down the street.

Charlie, Billy, and Herbie waited for John in the diner parking lot when he arrived. Charlie, the oldest, shot John a thumbs-up sign and yelled, "About time you showed up. If this is the way our military conducts battles, I hope you soldiers don't sleep through the war." The three boys hurried over.

Herbie broke out in a grin as John stepped from his car and scanned him from the cap to his shoes. "Cool." He gave his friend a nod of approval as he admired John in his dress uniform.

Bill slapped him on the back. "Let's move inside." He clasped his hands together and rubbed his fingers. "The wind is freezing out here."

As the four hurried to the diner, Bill asked, "The army makes you march in this weather, must be brutal."

"Well, yeah. What do you think?" John said. "My Company Commander took us on a five mile hike a week ago. I jumped in a trench, broke through the ice in the bottom of a hole and landed in freezing water." He laughed. "You know you're in the military when, right?"

Herbie said, "Tell us all about your great adventures in the army." He fingered one of the medals on John's uniform as they paused at the diner entrance and searched for an empty table. "What's this for, sit-ups?"

John touched the decoration with a smirk. "Nah, for shooting a gun," he replied as his friends and he found seats in a corner booth. John studied his chest. "Received one for throwing a hand grenade too." He flicked another medal. "The army hands you a medal for everything you do, as long as you don't kill yourself while you're doing it. No big deal. Got a ribbon, too, for completing basic."

Charlie hunched forward and asked, "So what do the sergeants have you doing besides shooting and marching?"

John shrugged. "Oh, you know. A lot of different classes, PT, first aid, communications." He laughed and added, "Sorta the same as Boy Scout camp but the drill instructors scream at us all the time, makes everybody do push-ups, and wakes you up in the middle of the night for guard duty."

"You shoulda gone to college after you graduated," Charlie said. "Preston isn't the greatest, but man, you should see all the pretty girls." He smiled wickedly. "Classes are okay, too."

"After I finish my enlistment in the army, I'll be attending, don't you worry," John assured him. "Three years, in and out, all benefits included." He said to Bill and Herbie, "So how's the old high school doing? Anything new? How's the football team looking this year? We going to State?"

A waitress walked over. The four ordered coffee and she left menus and silverware. "Coulda used you," admitted Bill, "but we're doing alright for so early in the season. Only lost one game out of three so far."

As their coffee arrived, three girls entered the diner and sat opposite John's booth two tables away. John was busy pouring creamer and sugar into his coffee when he heard hysterical laughter.

All four young men glanced over at the table where the three girls huddled. "What the…?"

The girls giggled madly, the one in the middle holding up an oversized comic book in front of her face, while the other two leaned in to read with avid interest. John thought he recognized the one on the right, a petite girl wearing dark-rimmed glasses perched on her snub nose, and long, raven black hair. "Herbie, isn't the girl over there you sister?"

Herbie cocked his head taking a fast scan of the girls and nodded, returning to fixing his coffee. "Sure is Trish, alright. Hanging out with her friends. Why?" The girls continued to laugh, oblivious to the people glancing at the three in amusement, while they pointed at the pictures exchanging excited whispers and squeals.

John peered closer at the cover of the book. The shiny surface portrayed a costumed woman wearing a mask, battling a multi-legged demon, but the woman looked—strange. An eruption of giggles started again as the girl in the center flipped a page. "What are those kids reading?" he asked, his face screwing up, half-perplexed, half in glee.

All four boys watched the girls now with unusual attentiveness, smiling, the laughter infectious as another couple in a booth glanced over and chuckled. Herbie snorted and guffawed, "Oh, new comic book hero the publishers started printing this fall for the new season. Everyone under sixteen is reading the magazine. Ah— Spidergoat Babe she's called. There's a Saturday morning cartoon out on her too, toys, and commercials. I heard next year the comic book people are talking about making a movie if the interest holds."

"Spidergoat Babe?" John shot Herbie a dubious expression as if he thought his friend was putting him on. "You gotta be kidding me, right?"

Charlie crossed his arms on the table and leaned toward John. "No, the comic is for real, I swear. Not just kids either. People are reading the books on campus, too. I even heard a rumor they're incorporating a few issues into Contemporary Lit beginning the spring semester. She's an ex-soldier who was sprayed with Nano bots and spidergoat DNA. The enemy captured, raped, and left her bleeding in a bunker until the Special Forces rescued her. The chemicals covered her skin, entered her system, and changed her body."

John shook his head, still finding the explanation hard to believe. "What the heck is a spidergoat?"

"I guess you don't do much science in the army," Charlie said. "The biologists take a goat, inject spider DNA into the animal and the goat produces spider webs instead of milk."

"Now I know you're stringing me along," John scoffed.

All three of his friends were smirking at him. "Serious," Herbie said. "Go on line, do a search. You'll see."

"I will, just to learn what kind of idiots you guys are." John studied his menu. "I think I'm going to have the blueberry pancakes. Anyway, if she was sprayed with goat DNA and bots, I'm surprised the chemicals didn't kill her."

"She's a superhero," Bill said and chuckled. "They never die. You know how comic books are. How else can you change into the ultimate rescuer of us poor mortals?"

"Anyway," Charlie continued, "Now every time she gets mad, she develops goat horns on her head and an udder on her belly."

John found it hard not to laugh aloud. "She gets horny, huh?" he quipped.

"On the cartoon version she even has a theme song." Charlie started singing off-key in a deep bass voice,

"Spidergoat, spidergoat, does whatever a spidergoat does."

John attempted to ignore his friends. They wouldn't leave him alone. "Think I'll order ham and a stack of those pancakes."

"She sprays acid milk from half her udders, spider webs from the other half and swing on the threads," said Bill, his teeth showing from his smirk. "Wanna know what her catch phrase is when she squirts a villain in the eye?"

John took a deep sigh and placed his menu down. "Sure. This should be good." He took a sip of his coffee.

"Udder you like this."

All four doubled up chuckling, John tried to contain his laughter, but burst out the loudest of all, coffee spraying from his nose and mouth onto the floor. His friends banged him on the back as they continued to laugh hysterically. The three girls stopped their giggling and stared at John in surprise, the girl in the middle with an amused grin.

John gazed into the face of Caitlyn.

Their vision locked. A spinning sensation spiraled in John's mind as he fell into those eyes. She raised one brow and regarded him, a tentative smile flickering on her lips.

John broke away from her stare, an electric shock of fear shooting through the back of his neck into his brain.

The girl can't be her. She's dead. How could Caitlyn return from the grave? He hastily picked up his menu and pretended to study the selections, his face blanching.

"What's the matter buddy, not funny?" Herbie asked as he scooped up his menu, running his finger down the breakfast items. "You were laughing, now you look like you've seen a ghost."

"I feel like an idiot," John lied. He tried to control his voice. "I sprayed coffee all over the diner. Everyone was staring at me like I was a mental defective." He took a deep breath and peeked over the top of the menu. The girls had disappeared behind the comic book again, heads bobbing in conversation. "Who's the blond with your sister," he casually asked. "The one in the middle. I don't remember ever seeing her around here before. Someone new in town?"

"Huh?" Herbie peered at the girls. "Lynn something-or-another." He paused trying to associate the face to where she lived. "You don't know her?" he said at last as he recalled the location of her home. "She's your neighbor, for Pete's sake. The house behind you."

Lynn, Caitlyn's sister. John remembered she spoke of a younger sister, so did his mother. He relaxed. The dead were not revisiting him from the grave after all. "Oh, no. Never met the neighbors back there. My mom told me new people moved in, but I've been in the army, remember?" He lowered his menu to mouth level so he could see over the top, and still act as if he was debating which selection of dishes he wanted for breakfast.

As he studied Lynn, he realized she didn't look exactly like Caitlyn. Close, but the differences were in the details. True, the shape of her face was the same, but her nose was straighter. Lynn's honey blonde hair was the same as Caitlyn's, but tied back in a ponytail instead of a pageboy cut. If Trisha's size was any indication, she was taller than he remembered Caitlyn being and not as skinny, giving the impression of maturity the dead girl hadn't shown.

Caitlyn said her sister was tall. Jeez, at first glance I coulda sworn they were the same person. Handed me the fright of my life. I hope she doesn't think I was checking her out. The last thing I want is for her to walk over here and introduce herself. I don't need another Caitlyn. He tried to picture the dead girl in his mind, and then shook his head, as if attempting to empty the thoughts. *It never happened.*

"I'll bring you up to date," whispered Bill. "Her sister went missing the day they arrived." He threw a glance in the direction of the three girls. "Was supposed to be a senior this year, but got pissed off at her mother and ran away, I hear. Rumor says she took off with her boyfriend from the city, the two are doing drugs and living in one of the burnt out buildings you see down by the river when you ride along the expressway."

"I heard they hopped a freight train and are out west in the desert, living on a commune with one of those crazy religious cults," said Charlie judiciously. He stuck up one hand in a pledge, palm out. "You know how rumors go, though. This is what I heard from reliable sources."

"Barracks rumors," John corrected his friends. "Gossip circulates all the time in the army. Everyone has a different version of what our next training mission will be, and they're usually wrong, or so exaggerated you wouldn't recognize what the original story was. I've heard the tales a thousand times."

"You shoulda heard one version going around, and the story was so far out no one believed the rumor was true, but people are still spreading the gossip." Charlie's lips arched upward. "She was a lesbian, and came out of the closet, told her mom she was bringing her girlfriend to the senior prom this year, and her mother threatened to throw her out of the house if she did or told anyone else. That's why she left. She's living with her girlfriend in Ohio somewhere on a twenty-acre farm."

Herbie stretched back in the booth, arms crossed against his chest, and cleared his throat. "You all have the story wrong," he announced importantly. "Let me tell John what really happened. Lynn was over at my house hanging out with Trish, and she was talking to my mom. I heard the whole story. What went on was, the mom and Lynn ran out for pizza. When the two returned the sister, Caitlyn's her name, I think, was gone, disappeared."

John asked, "Do the police have any idea where she really is, and leads? I mean, her mom must suspect someone, right? She couldn't just vanish into thin air."

John's overwrought mind felt sure Herbie would say the cops knew of a suspect in the area, were close on the kidnappers' trail. An arrest was only a matter of time before the police solved the mystery of the missing girl. He waited tensely for a reply.

Herbie regarded John indifferently and cleared his throat. "Her mother combed the neighborhood, called everywhere, and finally notified the police. The cops searched—nothing." He raised his hands when he saw John still listened to his story intently. "The police have a nationwide alert out for her, so far no leads. The authorities even checked the woods using search dogs. I saw Lynn and her mother and a group of cops in a long line walking through the woods up by the schoolyard. Lynn and her mom have been doing the social media stuff, you know, posting her description online."

The tension in John's body ebbed. He felt calm enough to joke, "Alien abduction maybe? Any UFO's reported in the area around the time when she disappeared? Crop circles?"

The three young men chuckled. Charlie made a comment about operations and alien babies.

"Her mother's kinda cracked up," Herbie said, as he picked up his menu, plainly finished with his story. "I think I'll have blueberry pancakes too. Haven't had those in a long time."

"What do you mean, cracked up?" John asked. "My mother didn't say anything."

"I don't mean nutso," Herbie hurried to say. "Sticking flyers up on all the telephone poles in town, passing 'em out at the mall and stores. My dad said he saw pictures of this Caitlyn in a restaurant he and my mom ate at the other day."

"She even handed me one when I was at the sporting goods store," Bill said. He reached into his jacket and withdrew a folded square of paper. "Here—" he gave the flyer to John, "—take a look."

John unfolded the leaflet and smoothed the paper on the tabletop. A black and white picture of Caitlyn smiled back at him with big, bold letters underneath saying, "MISSING," right below that, "HAVE YOU SEEN MY DAUGHTER?"

On the bottom was a brief description of the girl, the date she vanished, along with a telephone number to call.

In a detached voice, John said, "Pretty." He glanced over to the other table where the three girls were busy ordering something to drink. For the briefest of moments, the memory of what Caitlyn looked like when she was alive flashed through John's mind in stark clarity. He muttered, "This Lynn looks a lot like her sister."

"Don't start thinking up any ideas," Herbie joked. "She's the same age as my sister. Fifteen. Jailbait. You don't want to wind up in prison, do you?"

"Huh?" John returned to reality. "I didn't mean….What do you think I am," he exclaimed, aghast, "a child molester?"

"Watch out, Herbie," Charlie said, "Next thing you know he'll be chasing Trish; he hasn't dated a girl in two months, remember? He's horny and need some loving. You'd better watch out yourself."

The waitress walked over to take their orders. John muttered to his friends, "You're both perverts. There's plenty of women in the army. Why would I have to return here to rob the cradle?" He snatched Herbie behind the neck between his thumb and forefinger and shook his head. "Or you?"

Invisible fingers clutched at John's throat. The last thing he wanted was to become involved with Caitlyn's mother, sister, or Trish, for that matter. How could he speak to any of these people, look Mrs. Brennen and Lynn in the eyes and pretend nothing ever happened? *No*, he resolved. He'd never known Caitlyn.

***

"I'm going out for a while," Mrs. Brennen called from the kitchen, throwing on her jacket and slipping her gloves on. She scooped up a stack of papers from the table and tucked the bundle under one arm. "Keep the doors and windows locked and don't answer if anyone knocks and you don't know who the people are."

"Mom." Lynn's mouth bent into an upside down U as her mother entered the living room. "Trish and Val are stopping by this morning. We're walking up to the diner to hang out."

Concern passed over Mrs. Brennen's face. "The diner? You have a long walk. I could drive all three of you there, maybe wait and have a cup of coffee myself until you're done chatting with your friends. I could —"

A desperate note entered Lynn's voice. She knew what her mom feared. "*Mother.* I'm in a group of people, it's the middle of the morning. I'll be fine." She eyed the papers clutched in her mother's arms. "More flyers?"

"A few of the ones on Twenty-Third Street blew away in the rain yesterday. I noticed the posters were missing when I was driving from the grocery store last night. Then I was going to take a trip to the harbor and check there. I'm sure the restaurants will allow me to place one in their foyers if I explain why." She gave Lynn a cheery smile. "You never can tell who might remember something important, or tell someone who tells someone else." She paused, undecided what to do about Lynn. "You have your phone on you? Call and let me know when you leave the house and arrive at the diner, okay? If you go anywhere else, I want to know, too. Don't make me have to search for you."

Lynn nodded her head vigorously, her ponytail jumping up and down. Constant communication was her mother's top priority since Caitlyn's disappearance, along with flyers, of course, and calls to the police. Even when she left for school in the morning, standing at the bus stop waiting for pick up, and after the driver dropped her off in the afternoon at the corner, her mother was there before her, or demanded notification via Lynn's new cellphone.

Mrs. Brennen took a deep breath. "Fine, keep the door locked until your friends show up, and don't let anyone enter the house you don't know." She stepped to the door. "You realize you could ride along with me and help. I'm sure Caitlyn will appreciate the effort when she —"

"*Mom.*" Lynn grimaced. "I've put up pictures, passed out flyers, walked through every woods around here for miles by myself and along with groups of searchers. A couple more leaflets by the water aren't going to make any difference." As soon as Lynn spoke, she knew she was wrong. She saw hurt in her mother's face, but the frustration over her mother's attitude was driving her to the point of madness. What else in the world did she want? Everyone was doing everything in their power to find Caitlyn.

Mrs. Brennen bit back a caustic remark. "Well, we have to keep trying," she said finally.

Lynn realized she must do something to help her mother's anxiety. "While I'm waiting, I'll jump online and post more pictures," Lynn promised quickly. "We'll reach more people, and spread the news farther than the posters will, okay?"

"Thank you," Mrs. Brennen said quietly. She hugged her flyers closer to her chest. "I know this is hard on you, but it's all we have." She walked out the door calling behind her, "Remember, lock the door and call."

Lynn's eyes moistened as she heard her mother drive away. She locked the door, and rushed to her computer, copying and pasting Caitlyn's picture and description on every site she could uncover. Pain stabbed her heart, compressing until she couldn't breathe. She knew her mother was taking Cat's disappearance hard, worse because of the death of her father. Her mother refused to believe nothing else was possible to do, even though the police assured her every jurisdiction in the nation was on the alert and searching.

Lynn realized she'd posted the same picture on the identical website four time and gave up, issuing a tired sigh. Ambling into the living room, she sat on the couch and switched on the TV, flipping channels until she found *Spidergoat Babe*, her favorite Saturday morning cartoon.

Not as good as the magazine. Oops, almost forgot, I promised to bring the comic to the diner. She sprang up and hurried to her bedroom again, rustling around in the bottom of her clothes dresser and took out the comic book she'd hid there so her mother wouldn't see what she read. The front pictured a half-naked woman, long horns popping out of her head and enormous udders hanging from her stomach. If her mom ever saw the cover, it would guarantee a lecture, confiscation of the book, and a grounding to last the rest of the school year. Lynn wandered back into the living room and settled down, thumbing through the pages while she waited for her friends to arrive.

When a knock echoed on the door, Lynn checked the peephole. The top of Trisha's head was visible. She threw the door open wide. "Hi, guys. Come on in."

Trisha marched in as Val trailed on her heels. "How you doing girl, ready?" Trisha asked. She ambled over to a wall mirror and examined her lipstick carefully in the reflection, finally puckering her mouth as she blew herself a kiss.

"Yep, waiting on you." Lynn waved to the comic book folded on the coffee table. "See, I told you I bought a *Spidergoat Babe* comic." She issued a low whistle. "Boy, you should check some of the pictures inside. Sure does beat the cartoon."

Trish stood on her toes and peered into the kitchen. "Mom home? I guess not, or you wouldn't be leaving the evidence laying around where she could spot the cover."

Val sat on the sofa and snatched the comic book, eagerly flipping pages. "I don't believe you found this."

Lynn said to Trish, "Thanks for reminding me, I gotta call her and say I'm taking off." She took out her phone from her pocket. "Hi, Mom. Leaving now....Yes, I will....Bye." she shoved the instrument back in her pants.

"Your mom makes you check in everywhere, doesn't she," Trish commented, clearly indicating by her expression she thought this was the oddest behavior she'd ever heard about in her life. "All my mom says is don't walk into the house pregnant."

Val's head snapped up, eyes wide. She slapped her hand over her mouth to keep from laughing.

Lynn shifted uneasily. "Yeah, well, you know. She's still freaked out about what happened. I don't like calling all the time, but I can't really blame her." Lynn grabbed her wallet off the coffee table and snatched the comic book out of Val's hands. "Hey, you're drooling all over the pictures." She rolled the magazine up and stuffed the mag in her waistband, heading for the door. "C'mon, let make some tracks. I don't want to know about Trish getting pregnant and I'm hungry."

When the three arrived at the diner, the girls saw all the booths occupied by late morning visitors. Lynn hesitated at the doorway for a second and then weaved her way with Trish and Val through empty chairs until she found a table out of the way where they wouldn't be bothered. Directly opposite their seats in a booth, four young men busily talked, not paying any attention to the diners around them. Lynn withdrew the comic from her waistband, held the magazine up so Trish and Val could see and read along. The three studied the pictures intently, paying special attention to the male villains and naked demons Spidergoat Babe fought on each page.

Val snickered and jabbed her finger at a male villain. "Do you think boys really look so huge without their clothes on?"

"Oh, stop putting on the act, Val," Lynn replied. "You've been to the beach. What do you think?"

"But I mean not wearing their..."

Trish remarked, "You can't really see anything anyway. His cape is covering all the good parts."

"How'd you manage to buy this anyway?" Val asked Lynn. "I thought you had to be eighteen and show ID."

"My mom and I stopped at a comic book store so she could ask to leave her flyers on the counter and tape one up in their front window. When no one was looking, I stashed this one in between two others I was buying." Lynn shrugged. "My mom never noticed. She was busy talking to the clerk. He scanned the prices and never checked the covers. Stuck 'em in a bag. My mom paid and we walked out. Simple."

Val said excitedly, "Lynn, turn the page, I'm finished reading this one."

Lynn dutifully flipped to the next side. The three girls paused to scan the dialogue.

Trish released a high, tittering giggle and blushed red, covered her mouth, and bent closer to the comic for a better look. "Do you see what I see?" she whispered to Val and Lynn in awe, jabbing a finger at the bottom of a panel. "The cape isn't covering anything on this one."

Lynn studied the picture critically, her mouth open. "I don't believe they actually printed this in a book where kids can —"

An explosive guffaw ricocheted around the diner. Lynn dropped the comic and all three girls looked to see what the noise was.

One of the four boys, a young man in uniform, sitting opposite their table, sputtered and coughed. His friends laughed and pounded him on the back. As he glanced around his eyes locked on Lynn's. She gave him a tentative smile back, unsure if she knew him or not. A flicker of recognition flashed on his face as his features transformed into horror. He hastily reached for his menu and studied the writing intently.

The recognition, fear, and sudden retreat left Lynn bewildered. Who was he? She was positive now she didn't know the boy, for sure, she'd remember. She did know one of the other boys in the group, Herbie. She held up the comic again so the young man couldn't see her and whispered to Trish, "The boy who was coughing, over there in uniform talking to your brother. Who is he? Do we know him? I don't remember ever meeting him around here before, but he acted as though he recognized me."

Trish did a quick peek over the top of the magazine. "I know him, but I don't think you do. He's John Baker. The people who live behind you? He's their son. John's a friend of Herbie's from high school."

Lynn thought back. She'd met Mrs. Baker a few times when the woman walked over to see her mother. "Oh, yeah. I remember his mother talking about him when she stopped to ask how we were doing. Nice lady. She offered help in case we need any searching for Cat. I'm convinced I've never met him now, though. Odd, he acted as if he'd seen me before and I scared him."

"You should have used more eye-liner," Val said. "You wouldn't spook the boys so badly. Maybe blush." The girl cocked her head and surveyed Lynn. "You're as pale as a ghost."

"Oh, hush, Val," Lynn replied, refusing to allow herself suckered into a makeup discussion.

Trish studied Lynn's face critically. "Some mascara wouldn't hurt either."

"Will both of you cut out the cosmetic talk?" Lynn said. "I asked a serious question."

"Maybe your mom handed Mrs. Baker a flyer of you and your sister?" suggested Val. "She passes out pics to everyone, right. Probably his mom showed the photo to him, and that's where he recognizes you from."

"Maybe," Lynn said, dubiously. "She does have photos of us in the same picture. In fact, she gave one to the police, but why…?"

"I had a crush on him in seventh grade," Trish said. "Every time he stopped by the house to see Herbie, I'd tag along hoping he'd notice me. All they wanted to do is talk sports." She crossed her arms on the table and whispered to Lynn and Val confidentially, "Once we played football and I was on the opposite team. When he tackled me, I loved his arms around my waist and we rolled on the ground. I giggled like crazy. I'm over him now, though. Moved on to new meat. He never did take the hint." She nudged Lynn. "You can have him if you want him."

"Trish-a." Lynn punched her friend in the ribs. "Like I'm going to chase some boy I've never met."

"Ouch. Hey, you hurt." Trish rubbed her side. "No problem, girlfriend. If you want, I'll take you over and introduce you to the whole bunch. I know all those boys, they're friends of Herbie's, and you can check out John at the same time. I mean, you guys are next door neighbors and all. If you don't like him, take your pick."

Lynn peeked over the magazine and hurriedly covered her face again. "Oh, no. I'd be too embarrassed. He'd think I was coming on to him." She shaded pink at the thought.

Trish shrugged and pointed to a panel of Spidergoat Babe. "Well, lookie here. See? If you want to be a superhero, you can't be self-conscious at all. She certainly isn't. See what she's doing now? I think the old Spidergoat Babe is enjoying herself."

Lynn and Val followed her finger. "I guess she is, but I'm no superhero," Lynn replied looking down at her shirt. "If I had boobs like her I'd flaunt both, also. Too bad I can barely pass the pencil test."

All three girls giggled and said in unison, *"Udder you like this."* An eager discussion arose about bra sizes, which girls at school padded theirs, and who needed to.

Before Lynn switched her attention to who Trish and Val gossiped about, she took one additional scan of John, deciding to ignore him. *He does look hunky in his uniform, though.*

Chapter Six

"Caitlyn…. I mean Lynn, did you print out more flyers as I asked you to do for me?" Mrs. Brennen paced nervously in the living room while struggling to push her arms through the sleeves of her sweater. "I don't have all day."

"Finishing up right now, Mom," Lynn yelled from her bedroom where the printer chattered away spitting out sheets of paper. She scooped a stack from the tray and stuck a heavy rubber band around the pile, carrying the bundle into the living room, and handed the newest batch to her mother. "Here, hot off the machine," she said. "New heading, different font, same but different picture. I used the one we took at the lake before Dad died. You're all set to go."

"Thank you." Mrs. Brennen thumbed through the pile apprehensively. "I hope these will be enough. The weather's been so terrible. So many have blown away, and I think kids may be ripping down more. I'm glad today is nice so I can check."

Lynn had long since given up hope her mother would slow down in her quest to locate Caitlyn. Lately, though, her mom sometimes confused her with her sister. Lynn was sure her mother was preoccupied, but still, when she heard her mother call her Caitlyn, it was—unnerving.

"Mom, She's been missing for three years. No one looks at the flyers anymore. I'm surprised the neighbors haven't complained. The posters are scattered all over the street. Why don't you take the day off and relax for a bit? Cat won't mind, I'm sure." Lynn understood her mother's grief, but she was taking her sorrow to the extreme, even to the point of refusing to allow Lynn to store Caitlyn's clothes in the basement and changing her bedroom into a guestroom.

"Nonsense," Mrs. Brennen replied. "Why the other day Mrs. Baker asked me if we'd heard any word from your sister, or if the police unearthed new leads on her case." She snapped her fingers. "Oh, I almost forgot. The Baker's are throwing a welcome home party for their son John tonight. He was discharged from the army." She added seriously, "Poor boy, he was hurt in the war, you know, but at least he's alive. Mrs. Baker invited both of us, if you want to go. All his friends will be there. You'll probably know some of the people." She clutched her papers tighter. "As for the neighbors being mad about our flyers, she told me to bring a stack along and leave the notices on a table in case anyone wants one." Mrs. Brennen nodded, having made her point. "Now remember, lock the door when I leave and call if you go anywhere."

Lynn felt her jaw muscles tighten. Equal parts of sadness and anger washed over her. "I'm eighteen. I know what to do. In a couple of weeks, I'll be attending Easton. You don't expect me to notify you every time I walk from class to class across campus, do you?" She flashed a smile at her mother, trying to soften her words and tone of her voice.

"You're six months older than Caitlyn was when she vanished," her mother retorted firmly, "and no. I'm not asking you to call every time you change a class at college. You're among a group of people, they have security on campus, and it's daylight." Her mother smiled sweetly at Lynn. "A call when you arrive, and a call when you leave will be fine, and no more arguments, young lady. I'm still your mother. I worry." She glanced at the clock on the wall. "Oh, you've made me so late, standing here talking. I still have to food shop, too." She hurried out of the door muttering, "I'd better not see any kids ripping down my posters." She called over her shoulder, "I'll be back. Remember what I said."

After her mother drove off, Lynn strolled to her bedroom, picked up a recently purchased college algebra text off her desk from a stack of equally new books for her other classes. She lay on her mattress, kicking her feet in the air and thumbed through the pages. She'd been over every square inch of Easton's campus, knew where all her classes were held, even gone as far as researching her professors for published works online. Lynn was ready for the first day of school and she knew it. *Maybe even take a few summer courses. I could compress four years into three.* The doorbell rang interrupting her thoughts.

Trish strode into the house as Lynn hurried down the hallway. "Hey, bitch," Trisha said with a laugh. "See? You forgot to lock the door. That'll show you. I coulda been an axe murderer stopping by to chop up your body. What's happening?"

"Back to yah, slut," Lynn replied to her best friend. "I'll know better next time. Never can tell what will wander in. Mama is always right." She hip-bumped Trish. "Nothing much. Spent most of the morning helping Mom do flyers. She wanted a new design, and fonts. Forced me to put on my artist hat and think creative. Now?" She hooked a thumb over her shoulder. "Going through our textbooks, trying to get a handle on the work. I don't want to look like an idiot on the first day of school if the professor asks me a question."

"I don't believe the girl with straight A's and two scholarships will have much of a problem," Trish replied. "I still don't understand why you didn't apply to one of the Ivy League Schools. Preston is so….Preston."

"Even with scholarships, those universities are expensive," Lynn replied. "I didn't want to leave my mother all by herself. She'd go nuts if she couldn't make sure I was safe every day. Besides," she threw an arm around Trish in a hug, "how could I leave my BFF?"

Trish smirked. "Grown accustomed to my bad ways, huh? I'm rubbing off on you." She wandered into the kitchen, Lynn following, and immediately walked to the refrigerator, rummaging through the contents until she discovered a can of diet soda. Trish had long ago discarded any hope Lynn's mother would release her friend from the mania the woman displayed. She'd taken the mission upon herself to guarantee Lynn enjoyed the best high school experience circumstances would allow, without the two of them being thrown into jail. "Uh, as long as I'm in here, you want a soda?" Trish called out.

"No thanks, I'm fine," Lynn replied.

Trish continued to browse. "Found celery. Now, let's see…." The girl pulled open the bottom drawers. "Got cream cheese?"

Lynn drew back, her lips flickering, watching Trish's plump rear sway back and forth as she dug through a lower compartment. "I don't think —"

"Never mind. I found what I'm looking for." Trish straightened up, arms full of soda, vegetables, and silver packages of cheese. She dropped her plunder on the table and made herself comfortable in a chair.

"Do you want something to eat," Lynn asked.

"No thanks. I'm not really hungry," Trish replied spreading cream cheese on a stalk of celery. "I'm on a diet. I want to look my best for college. Hence the veggies." She crunched down and popped her soda open.

"Don't your parents feed you at home?" Lynn asked, amazed, as her friend finished the first piece of celery and started on a second stalk applying a thick layer of cream cheese with a butter knife.

"Of course," Trish replied, not at all offended by Lynn's remark. "You have to remember, though, we have a Herbie still living at our house." Trish frowned slightly.

"The boy's grown four inches during the last three years and put on fifty pounds, all of it out of the 'fridge. Potato chips have become an endangered species in our home. So has the dip. Which reminds me…" She looked around.

"Sorry, we're out," Lynn said quickly.

"Not chips, silly. Are you going tonight?"

"Tonight?" Lynn paused, trying to think. "I don't recall we made any plans. Is this one of your schemes? Don't forget college starts next week. We can't be hiding from the police."

"No, I mean to the Baker's party for their son. Mrs. Baker invited your family, didn't she? They asked the whole neighborhood—my parents, Herbie. Everyone. I might even show up if you promise to go with me." Trish showed Lynn a wicked grin. "Lots of cute guys will be there, I bet."

"My Mom did say we're invited," Lynn replied. She hesitated and added cautiously, "Gee, I don't know, though." Lynn peeked out the kitchen window to the next yard. The Bakers were busy stringing outside lights and hauling out aluminum folding tables from their garage. She turned and leaned against the sill. "I've never actually met their son—seen him a few times around town when he was home." She giggled. "I remember when he hacked all over the diner."

"See? You know him," Trish said brightly. "You're neighbors right? Even have something in common. John trying to spray us using his coffee mouth when we were kids." Trish waved her can of soda toward the window. "Half of Easton will be at the party. All his old friends who graduated from high school with him."

"Well…."

Trish took a long sip of her drink. "Tell you what. Throw some makeup on your pretty face. When I'm ready I'll stop by and pick you up. We'll check out the party, the guys, and if nothing is happening, we'll do a movie or something—mall running, maybe. How does hanging out for a while grab you?" She waited expectantly for an answer.

Lynn grimaced and stepped over to the table. "I guess a cameo won't hurt. If I show up, I'll make my mom happy, and if we leave, she knows we're together. Maybe she'll be too busy to bug me every five seconds about where I am. Mom said she was bring posters." Lynn gave a vigorous nod as she made a decision. "Sure, why not. We'll rock the party."

Trish rose and tossed her empty soda can in the trash. "Catch you in a while, girlfriend," the girl said. "Oops, forgot." She grabbed another stalk of celery and held it up like a sword. "Snack for the road."

After Trish left, Lynn wandered to the kitchen window and stood gazing into the Baker's backyard. The guest of honor balanced precariously on a stepladder while fastening a line of colored lights onto a hook attached to the house. *Does have a nice ass. Be fun to meet him if he's not a total jerk. Handsome with his short hair.* The young man climbed down the ladder and surveyed his handiwork critically, his gaze checking the string of lights around the yard to assure himself they hung correctly.

His eyes stopped, fixing on the house behind his. Lynn stood framed in the kitchen window.

***

Three hours later, Trish and Lynn sauntered along the garden path. People already gathered around the barbeque in the Baker's backyard, drinking, talking, or making suggestions as they watched Mr. Baker flip hamburgers and hot dogs over the hot coals.

"There's your mom and my mom talking to Mrs. Baker," Trish said. She scanned the crowd. "I don't see John or my brother anywhere." Trish checked the rest of the faces, centering on a tall boy wearing a blue hoodie, a big "Easton College" printed on the front in bold white letters. He stood in a group of young men who spoke to each other muttering an occasional low laugh. "Him we know," Trish said to Lynn. "Remember? He was on the basketball team last year. Dated Val for a while before the two broke up in the spring. He goes to Easton now." She put her finger to her mouth. "Ron, I-don't-remember-his-last-name. Oh, yeah—Billings, I think it is. I double-dated with him and Val a couple of times." She grabbed Lynn's wrist and made a beeline for the group. "C'mon. Let's mingle."

Trish dragged Lynn behind her, waving a hand in the air. "Hey, Ron, what's happening? Where is everyone?"

"Hi." His vision rested on Lynn and then roved over the rest of the gathering. "You see it." He hooked a thumb at the two boys standing alongside him. "George—Larry." The two nodded and murmured greetings.

"Oh, you remember Lynn, right?" Trish jerked Lynn forward.

"Uh-huh." He smiled briefly with a nod. "Val's friend, right?" He asked, while searching behind the two, "Val here?"

Trish turned solemnly around, looking for their friend while shooting Lynn a wink. "Nope. Val said she was on a hot date. Been hanging with this guy for a while." She noted the expression of disappointment and a hint of jealousy on Ron's face. Trish made a note to inform Val later. "Where's John—my brother? How can you have a party when the main attraction and his sidekick aren't here?"

Ron waved to the front of the house. "A bunch of the guys ran out to pick up more soda, beer, and ice. Should be back any second, in fact," he explained.

Trish wiggled her fingers at him. "Well, talk to you later, I expect. Probably see you on campus, too. We start Easton next week." Trish swung away, Lynn flanking with a quick smile on her face at the young men, and hurried after her friend.

"Why'd you stand there like a dummy?" Trish asked as the girls wandered through the people toward the barbeque. "Three cute guys and you couldn't speak to one?"

"I barely know Ron and I've never met the other two," Lynn retorted in a whisper. "I thought this was supposed to be a cameo, in and out. You didn't say a word about trying to pick up boys." She handed Trish a sideways glance. "At least I didn't come here to."

Lynn and Trish stopped at the grill and grabbed hotdogs from a stack on a foldout table where paper plates, napkins, buns, mustard, and ketchup stood, alongside potato salad and baked beans. Lynn noticed a pile of flyers, the topmost displaying the picture of her lost sister, and winced inwardly to herself. An older man behind Lynn looked curiously at her, glancing from the leaflets to her profile.

"My sister," Lynn explained quickly before the man said anything and examined her closer. She spun away, saw Trish saunter toward the drinks and rushed after her. The girls fished around in a galvanized washtub containing half-melted ice until they located anything marked diet. "Let's take off," Lynn said. "People are staring at me. Everyone thinks I'm Caitlyn."

"Well, maybe you're right," Trish mumbled around her hotdog, "mostly old folks here. I thought there'd be more hunkas. Let's tell our moms we're leaving and catch a movie."

Trish's mother, Mrs. Baker, and Mrs. Brennen were still in animated discussion, standing by the garden, but watching the rest of the people mill about in the back yard. Occasionally Mrs. Baker waved to people, called out their names and then returned to her conversation with the two women.

"...he was medically retired and discharged." Mrs. Baker said, holding a plate of potato salad. "Poor boy has headaches from the concussion and such terrible nightmares. Last night we heard him screaming in his bedroom, but when we ran upstairs, he was sound asleep. After we woke him up, he didn't remember a thing."

"Such a shame," Trish's mother exclaimed. "Will he be alright? He's such a nice boy."

"The doctor's at the V.A. say he'll be fine as far as the nightmares are concerned," Mrs. Baker explained. "They're not so sure about the headaches. The physicians are prescribing medication for the pain when the throbbing becomes too bad, and for the dreams. We'll have to see—they told me it all takes time."

"Terrible, simply terrible," Mrs. Brennen murmured. She took a sip of soda and shook her head, spotting Lynn and Trish walking over. "And here are the two I've been looking for," she said, swinging her head in the direction of the girls. "Where have you two been?"

"Oh, we've been here for a while, Mom," Lynn replied, crossing her fingers behind her back. "Mingling, and talking to people, but we're about ready to take off now. Trish and I are going to see a movie."

Before Mrs. Brennen responded, Mrs. Baker exclaimed, "Oh, no, you can't leave now, my dear. You haven't met John yet. I'm sure he will want to meet you, I've told him so much about your family." Mrs. Baker raised on her toes, searching the crowd, "In fact, I think he's here now." She went on, "You see, you must stay, if only for a while."

Six young men marched into the backyard through the breezeway, John and Herbie in the lead, totting bags of ice and cases of beer and soda. Laughing and shouting greetings, the group headed straight for the washbasins by the barbeque where they restocked the dwindling supply of beverages to the cheers of the people standing around.

Mrs. Baker waved. "John—John, over here, dear. There's someone I want you to meet."

Her son signaled back, and said something to the others. He hurried to his mother. Lynn swung around to watch him approach.

John froze.

***

"When you're finished stringing the lights, I need you to go to the store and buy more drinks and ice." Mr. Baker kicked the two washtubs containing beer and soda. The ice he'd filled each with earlier in the afternoon was already melting, and his wife informed him more people than expected were stopping by for the party. He wanted to guarantee they didn't run out of drinks. "I don't know how many people will attend, but we can always use the extra. Beer and soda won't go to waste."

John climbed off the stepladder. "Sure thing, Pop," he yelled. He stood, arms folded across his chest, checking the outdoor lights to make sure all the bulbs worked. Next, he examined the backyard carefully, to see what else needed doing for the party before he left.

The bushes required trimming. Weeds and small trees sprouted among the flowering plants. In the corners along the fence, leaves piled a foot high with dead sticks from the overhanging oak trees. *Dad should have hired a gardener while I was away. This place is a mess. I see I have my work cut out for me between school and trying to readjust to civilian life.*

The ivy planted as a groundcover by the neighbors behind his house had crept under the chain link. John groaned inwardly at the job he'd have ripping the plants out. He scanned the rest of their yard, trying to estimate which side of the fence appeared better.

A silhouette outlined the upstairs kitchen window. John glanced away and swung his attention to the barbeque grill where his father laid out his utensils for cooking, and his mother busily stacked paper plates and napkins. *Wonder if the Brennens are coming tonight.*

On his few trips home during his stint in the army, he'd never visited Mrs. Brennen's house or met the woman. He dreaded any confrontation where the subject of her missing daughter might arise. Her daughter—he thought her name was Lynn he might have seen once or twice around town with Herbie's sister, Trish, but he wasn't sure. Herbie would be here, his mother too. Maybe Trish would attend. John hoped the Brennens didn't. He'd never be able to look either one in the eye without guilt written all over his face.

"Hey, buddy." Herbie strolled into the backyard accompanied by four of John's friends. "I've brought reinforcements. Need any help?"

John released an immense sigh and said, "Nope, and I see the troops have arrived after the battle is over and the victors have taken the field." He waved to the rest of his friends. "Hi, guys. Thanks for the offer, but we're all finished except for the eating and talking."

"Don't forget my drinks and ice," Mr. Baker yelled, and waved a spatula. "People should be arriving any minute and I don't want to scramble after I'm sitting and relaxing."

"Oh, yeah." John flashed his father an okay sign. He asked his mother, "As long as I'm running you need anything? More paper cups, plates, napkins?"

His mother surveyed the foldout table. "No, dear, I think I'm set here. Don't be long."

John wiped his hands on his pants and said to his friends, "You people want to go with me to the beverage distributor? Only take a couple of minutes."

Herbie yelled out, "Rode trip, I'll drive." He saluted Mr. Baker and said, "Be right back, Mr. B. Your son is in good company."

The boys left and John shouted at the top of his lungs, "Shotgun!" as the gang piled into Herbie's car.

After John picked up the supplies for the party, Herbie took the long way back, swinging by the harbor, and splitting a six-pack of beer, while John relaxed in the passenger seat relating war stories.

"Lots of dead bodies?" One of his friends asked in a hushed voice.

"Sometimes, depending on where you were stationed," John admitted, thinking of his days in the desert as he gazed at the boats in the water. He chuckled. "Almost got killed myself. The enemy knows when we have formations and eat. The suckers wait until we're all together and then lob in mortar rounds." He performed a flying motion using his hand over his head, his fingers cupping downward. "*Whomp*. One knocked me ten feet into a cement wall and I landed on my ass." He rolled up his sleeve displaying a long scar to his friends. "Put a big rip in my arm, too." He sighed and snuggled deeper into the car seat, taking a long gulp from his can of beer. "Best thing was, though, meeting other guys from different countries. My battalion sent us to England for training. Work all day and drink all night. A whole bunch of us, Brits, Irish, even had a detachment from Lithuania in the barracks."

"Lithuania?" Herbie asked, puzzled. "Are those people on our side? I thought they were like, Russian or something? I didn't know we're allies."

John emptied his beer in one swallow and shrugged. "I guess so. Anyway the Lithuanians drank like Russians." He held his hands wide. "*Big* glasses of Vodka." John chuckled to himself warming up to his story. "A whole group of us did a beer walk in London." When his friends showed puzzlement he said, "You know. Hit a pub, buy a drink, ask the bartender to sign your card proving you were there, and hurry to the next bar. See how may signatures you can have in one night."

"Sounds like fun," Herbie said.

"We had a blast," John agreed. "Although we sorta staggered to the last few pubs and had to go to work the next morning. Talk about hangovers." His phone started ringing. "Uh-oh, we'd better hurry," he said after looking at the screen. "Mom's texting me. We're late. Geez, I hope the ice hasn't melted all over the trunk."

The backyard was crowded with people now, all waiting for John's return. People yelled his name in greeting, and a few hooted at the group's tardiness, as the young men carried cases and bags to the barbeque shouting apologies to Mr. Baker. John heard his mother calling his name from a group of women and looked over quickly, waved that he'd heard her, as he poured drinks and ice into the tubs his father had waiting. He straightened with a groan, grabbed a bun and hamburger from a stack on the table, put a squirt of ketchup on, and wandered over to the people where his mother impatiently waited for him.

A woman John didn't immediately recognize stood there alongside Herbie's mom and Trisha. Lynn stood beside the four. For a brief moment, déjà vu hit John as he gazed at the slim, blond girl who watched his approach, a flicker of a grin on her face.

Oh my God, she and her sister look like twins. Small breasts the same as Caitlyn, too. I like girls who have small breasts. He groaned inwardly. *What am I thinking? This is horrible. No way. How am I going to do this?*

"Uh, hi." He nodded briefly to the gaggle of women and shifted his attention back to his mother, keeping his sight firmly fixed on her face, but trying to appear as if he were not ignoring the rest of the people in the group. "You needed to see me?"

"Yes, dear." Mrs. Baker tipped her head. "I wanted to introduce you to our neighbors. I don't think you ever met these two, but you've heard me speak about the Brennens. This is Mrs. Brennen and her daughter, Lynn."

"Uh, yeah, I remember you talking about the people who moved in." He glanced at the grass, his vision switching to Trish and Lynn, and quickly centered on Mrs. Brennen's chest. "Nice to meet you, finally," he muttered. John shuffled his feet. "Haven't really had a chance to reacquaint with the old neighborhood, you know," he explained, extending his hand to Mrs. Brennen while trying not to stare at her face. "So many people moving away and new people arriving. My mom says you're good friends already." He shifted his feet nervously and stepped forward, shaking Lynn's hand. "I think I've seen you around town hanging with Trish. Glad to meet you." He stood awkwardly, not knowing what to say next, and afraid to say anything about Caitlyn. *I'm acting like a complete jerk. Calm, I gotta stay calm. Why should they suspect anything?*

To change the subject, he grinned at Trish. "Hey, Trish, how's everything going? Haven't seen you in a long time either. Sorry I missed your graduation party. Herbie told me it was quite a bash. What's next on your plans?"

Trish smirked back. "You should have been at my friend Val's party. We had even more fun. Gonna be a freshman this year at Preston," She wrapped her arm around Lynn's back. "Me and my BFF. I hear you're starting too. I'm catching up to you, you know. If you don't watch out, I'll be a senior and you'll be a junior."

"Still have to buy my books and find a map of the place," John admitted. "Missed orientation and the last time I was on campus was for a play on a high school trip four years ago. I'll probably be late for all my classes the first week unless I leave a trail of breadcrumbs from building to building."

Mrs. Brennen said to John, "My Caitlyn would be a junior now too. She'll have a lot of catching up to do when she returns. I brought flyers in case you want to pass out a few to your friends." The woman smiled foolishly, nodded to the rest as if waiting for Mrs. Baker, Trish's mother, and John to agree and rush for the table to distribute the papers in the town.

A sensation the same as scurrying bugs ran up John's neck. No one else said anything. He mumbled, "Ah, yeah. I guess so." He tried hard not to stare at her.

Lynn winced, her lips compressing into a hard, straight line. "We'd better move if we're going to catch the movie," she said to Trish. To John she added, "Nice meeting you. Probably see you at school if we're all freshmen. We'll have classes together." She snatched Trish by the sleeve and said to her mother, "I'll call you, Mom, when the movie's finished."

Herbie wandered over and shouted to his sister as Trish walked away, "Don't bother to say hello to your big brother!"

Trish swung around, laughing. "Hi, big brother. Where's the five bucks you borrowed from me last week?" She stood grinning, waiting, not expecting an answer, but happy she thought up a quick retort for Herbie in front of all his friends.

Herbie winced and he mumbled, "Me and my big mouth." He called back to Trish, "Catch you later," and turned to Mrs. Baker, ignoring the two girls who whispered to each other and giggled. "Mrs. B., I have to steal your son. Can't monopolize the host, you know. I want to introduce him to some of the guys from Preston."

John watched the two girls walk away and said to his mother, "Gotta go. My public awaits, and I'm the person everyone came to see." He nodded to Mrs. Brennen. "Nice to meet you."

The haunting thought of the expression on Mrs. Brennen's face plagued John as he shook hands with people and made small talk. The idea of attending classes alongside Lynn troubled him even more. How could he see her every day, possibly forced to speak with her, and not be reminded of what happened?

He excused himself and made his way to the barbeque. His father was still busy flipping the last of the hamburgers and turning franks. John plunged his hand into the freezing ice water of a washtub and rummaged around pulling out a can of beer. He flipped the tab up and drained the contents in one swift gulp.

"Better slow down, son," his father advised. "Still have the rest of the day ahead of you. It's not even dark yet."

John slapped his father on the back. "I'm okay, Pop. I've had a long three years and now is the time for me to relax. I have a lot of catching up to do."

Chapter Seven

The smell of falling autumn leaves filled the air. A chill wind blew, sending a crispness of excitement through the college campus as new and old students alike hurried to the opening day of class.

John rushed also, but not from excitement. So far, the day was a kaleidoscope of confusion and tardiness, wrong turns and backtracking, and his newest objective had proved not to be the exception.

The red brick building was old and ivy covered, exactly as he'd always pictured the institutions of higher learning would be. The lecture hall felt hot and stuffy, though, and he'd become lost walking from the parking lot and arrived late to class. Students occupied all the seats in the room except for the first two rows where the absence of bodies was conspicuously noticeable. John enjoyed the dubious privilege of walking down the aisle and interrupting the professor while he lectured, thereby receiving a glare from the teacher, as John mumbled an apology and assumed a seat. He hunched low, secretly glancing right and left, while still trying to pay attention to the front of the class. He hoped to see a friendly face, or at least someone he knew among the other freshmen staring straight ahead with avid interest to the lecturer.

After the professor finished his talk for the day, John joined the throng of classmates shuffling out of the room like a herd of bawling cattle into the hallway. He tried stopping to check his schedule, obtained a bump from behind by students exiting adjoining rooms, who all seemed to know where their next classes were. After repeated jostling, and being stepped on by mistake, his fellow pupils swept him outside into the bright sunshine and fresh air as if being delivered from hell.

John came to rest on the pavement, more disoriented than ever, and cradled his books in the crook of his left arm while holding his schedule in his hand. He held up the map of the campus using the right, attempting to figure out where his next class was and how to arrive there in the quickest possible time without becoming lost again.

If I can read a damn elevation map and not drive the wrong way in the desert, why can't I decipher little footprints drawn on this thing? I'm a freshman, darn it all, not a PhD. A snake crisscrosses over itself less times when it's curled up than these tracks do on the paper.

He snorted in disgust when he realized he held the map upside down and tried to flip the paper around one-handed. He succeeded in dumping his books and notebook in a heap all over the pavement.

"Hey, sailor, lonely?" Lynn strode up to him, smirk on her face, a pile of books similar to his clutched in her arms. The girl wore a white sweater with a big P on the front and appeared serenely happy and not at all confused. "You look like a lost puppy who can't find its master," she joked.

The relief of seeing a familiar face outweighed the fact this was the last person he desired to meet anywhere, anytime. "I'll say more like a lost kitten left out in the rain." He glanced over Lynn's shoulder. "Where's Trish? I thought you two would be together today."

The girl's lips bent down ominously. "The rat. At the last minute Trish managed to swap her schedule around to late morning and afternoon classes so she could sleep in late." Her eyebrows knitted together in thought. "Her brother musta clued her in on how to switch lectures. I couldn't and I tried."

"Wish Herbie told me how to change my classes, too," muttered John in disgust. "I've got fifteen minutes to go somewhere and I don't have the slightest idea where the heck I'm heading." He bent over, picking up his books in aggravation, still trying to study the map he held.

Lynn snatched the schedule out of his grasp and read the paper, pursing her lips and nodding. "We both have the next lecture together, English one-o-one." She handed John back the paper. "Follow me. If we hurry and don't stop to smell the flowers, we can still make the class on time." Lynn spun on her toes and walked briskly along a concrete path where students strolled in small groups, talking. John watched her stride away, mouth open, and then hurried to catch up, juggling books in both arms. "In fact," Lynn continued as John came abreast of her, "I think we have all our classes together." She cut off on a side path, which angled toward a newer building in the distance displaying a fountain in front spitting water in the air. "You didn't see me but I was in the lecture hall with you, way in the back where I could hide and the teacher won't notice me." She glanced at him sideways. "I was in your math class, too. I don't think you've make it to any of the sessions on time, have you?"

Chagrined, John admitted sheepishly, "Yeah, well, that's me. Day late and dollar short John. Hopefully, I won't attend my funeral on time either." He knew he was speaking in clichés and felt like a jerk doing so, but he was ill at ease, yet at the same time comfortable chatting to Lynn, but he didn't know what else to say. The girl was so easy to talk too, acted as if they'd been friends forever, just like...but—*What if I say the wrong thing? Should I bring her sister up?* He shook his head and concentrated on the building ahead. The death never happened. "Doesn't the hall grow any closer the longer we walk toward it?" he joked. "The administration should lump the freshman into the same building or provide us with roller skates or a guide."

"Well, like the man said, 'Half-a-league, half-a-league, half-a-league—*Onward.*'" Lynn sang the last word in a high, clear soprano, "Or something along those lines from what I remember," she added.

"A-plus for English," John said, as Lynn and he joined a mob of freshmen trampling up the stairs into the building. "Probably my fault," John admitted. "I'm still used to the army, being marched everywhere." He spotted a sign listing room numbers in black print marked with arrows aiming in different directions. "We're this way," he said, pointing to the left.

"Let's take two chairs together," Lynn suggested. "We won't feel so lonely, then." They walked into a hall, and Lynn spotted two seats on the aisle, halfway between the front and the back. She grabbed John's arm. "Right here, this is the perfect spot." Lynn steered him into one and sat beside him. "If the lecture's boring," she whispered confidentially, "we can text each other and tell jokes. It'll make the time pass faster and we'll still appear to listen."

Against John's better judgement, he shrugged, giving his assent, head adverted so as not to offer Lynn a false impression he was interested in her, and tried to concentrate on what the teacher said throughout the lesson. Nevertheless, he couldn't keep his mind off of her, and the situation wasn't made better by the occasional nudges Lynn gave him in the side when the professor made a particularly funny comment or a dramatic remark.

After they'd finished classes for the day, John walked Lynn to a nearby student parking lot at her insistence. "This one's mine." She gestured to a new, bright canary yellow convertible parked in the corner.

John issued a low whistle in admiration as they strolled over. "You sure won't lose your ride in a crowd," he said, running his eyes over the sleek lines of the car, thinking of the used rust bucket he'd picked up second or maybe third-hand from a car lot after being discharged from the army.

"My mom bought this for my graduation," Lynn said. "Oh, thanks for reminding me, I have to call." She reached into her back pocket and took out a phone, hitting a number with her thumb. "Mom...? Yeah, all finished.... No, no problems. In fact I met John....You know, John Baker from next-door....Yeah, him. We have all our classes together so you don't have to worry. He walked me to my car and I'm together with someone I know." Lynn placed a hand over the phone and said to John in a loud whisper, "Mom says hi." She said to the phone, "Trish? No. She changed classes at the last minute. I forgot to tell you....Yeah, I'm on my way home now. See you in a while." Lynn slipped the phone back into her pocket and said, "Love this car, but the engine sure drinks gas."

"Uh, mine, too," John admitted, confused about the call he'd heard. He asked, "You phone your mother everywhere you go? What, she doesn't trust you?"

Lynn reclined against the door of the car, staring down. "Mom expects me to," she replied. Lynn examined her sneakers with a thoughtful expression. "You see, my sister...."

John cringed inwardly and his eyes glazed over, wrenching his gaze from her face. "I understand," he mumbled at last. "My mom told me all about what happened." John studied her sneakers, too.

"Calling's really no problem." Lynn raised her chin and hurried to say, "I've been checking in for so long, it's a habit I suppose by now, and the calls keep her from not worrying if anything's happened to me. That's one of the reasons I asked you to walk me here. This way I could tell her I was with a person we know, since Trish ditched me on the first day." Lynn stood upright and rose on her toes, surveying the parking lot and students scurrying between the cars. "Where are you parked?"

John released a long, shuddering sigh, relieved the conversation changed. He swung in a wide circle, searching, and waved off into the distance. "Other side of the campus. I didn't know where to park and was afraid I wouldn't be able to locate my car when I was finished, so I parked by the entrance as I drove in. First lot I saw and I figured the lecture halls were near Administration. I didn't realize there'd be so much walking to the buildings, and the classes were so far apart."

Lynn opened her door. "Hop in," she offered, slipping behind the steering wheel. "You did me a favor, I owe you one. I'll run you over. The front lot is on my way out anyhow. No problem, really."

John made a big production of studying the sky. "No, I think I'll walk, but thanks for the offer." He realized how attached he was becoming to Lynn in the short hours he'd known her and wanted to stop growing any closer. The situation was wrong. The day accompanying her to their classes, and to the parking lot was nice, he'd forgotten Caitlyn, now Lynn's call to her mother brought back the horror of what he'd done all too clear in his mind. "I've learned the best way to explore a new territory is by walking the terrain. One day I'll need to navigate this campus by myself without help. I don't want to appear like a fool carrying a ball of twine in my pocket, running a string from building to building with the name of my classes attached to knots at each stop." He shook a finger at her. "You owe me a solid though. Don't forget. One day I'll collect."

Lynn gave him an absent smile. "Oh, okay. Walking is up to you, cowboy. Exercise never hurt anyone. I tell you what. Remember where this parking lot is and park here tomorrow. It's close to all our classes. Whoever arrives first waits for the other." Lynn watched him keenly and when the girl saw him hesitate, added, "It'll make my mom feel better knowing someone she trusts is accompanying me to class so I'm not attacked by the other students now Trish isn't with me."

She's not going to let this go, is she? "I suppose so. Yeah, sure, why not. Be on time, though, okay? I received enough glares from the teachers today. I don't want to make lateness a habit." John flashed her a smile to let her know he was joking, patted the car door, and gave Lynn a quick salute. She waved back, started her engine, and drove off, leaving him standing in the lot, staring at her retreating taillights.

When Lynn's car disappeared, John slumped. He wandered through the parking lot and hurrying students toward the main entrance deep in thought. He supposed the idea wouldn't be so bad conducting Lynn from class to class. Afterwards to her car when the school day finished. In fact, this might be a small way of repaying the Brennen's for the horrible thing he'd done to their family.

Would Caitlyn have been this way after the two of them knew each other for a while? They'd only talked for such a very short while. If he hadn't....Lynn was nice, and he already held strong feelings for her. He couldn't let himself become too attached to this girl. What if something happened while they were together? What if he said the wrong thing? Did the wrong thing? He couldn't avoid Lynn, but maybe after a while if he didn't speak, ignored her, she'd catch the hint and leave him alone. Lynn and he attended the same classes, though, knew the same people, and lived next to each other. He didn't want to hurt her feelings or make her mad at him. The circumstances weren't her fault. Lynn was innocent. He was the bad one in all of this. His fault—all his fault.

A car beeped at him. The driver waved angrily for John to move off the street and out of harm's way. He'd walked into the middle of the road by mistake while thinking. John stepped back onto the sidewalk and realized the main entrance was in sight. Taking firm steps, he hurried to his car and resolved to play the relationship casually. Yes, Lynn and he were neighbors, had mutual acquaintances. He saw no reason why they couldn't be friends. He would keep his mouth shut, avoid close contact, and pretend the past never occurred. Indifference to her physical appeal, bright and bubbly personality, was his best weapon. A false impression, true, but one he hoped would keep a distance between this girl, her dead sister, and himself.

***

"You should have seen the expression on his face," Lynn told Trish on the phone. She doodled on a pad, trying to draw a picture of a wet dog and gave up. "I called him a lost puppy. He looked so abandoned and confused I wanted to pick him up and cuddle him right there on the pavement."

Lynn hear Trish giggling. "Not so mad at me now for changing my courses, are you?" Trish said, swallowing down her laugh. "You've been meeting him in the parking lot every day though for the last week you said, right? Is he the new thing for the fall season? Has he brought you home to meet his mother?"

"Oh, Trish, give the drama a rest, will yah? I've met his mom a hundred times and, no, he hasn't 'brought me home to meet his mother'. As for being the new thing this year," Lynn rolled on her bed onto her back staring at the ceiling, legs crossed. "Gee, I don't know. Yeah, maybe. He's cute and all, makes me laugh the way he acts and his funny expressions, but he's so shy. Hardly says a word to me unless I work at getting him going by concocting a smart-ass remark. You know what I mean. Sometimes I have the impression he doesn't like me as more than an acquaintance."

"He's probably preoccupied concentrating on his class work," Trish scoffed. "Remember he's been out of school for over three years. This is a relearning experience for him, and who knows, Herbie tells me John's on meds, too, from the war. He might be a little zoned out."

"He doesn't act like he's on drugs," Lynn said tapping her teeth with her pencil as she thought. "At least not in class. If I didn't know better and wasn't walking right beside him, I'd say he didn't know I existed."

"Oh he knows you exist, sister," Trish said. "Herbie tells me he talks about you all the time when they hang out. Asks him if you've been over our house, what you said; if you mentioned him, or are you dating anyone."

"Really? He acts so withdrawn when we're together. It's as if he's somewhere else, or thinking of someone else."

Trish paused. "I know John Baker. He's anything but shy, or at least the John Baker I use to remember," she declared firmly once she digested this piece of information. "Hmm...." Lynn pictured Trish stroking her chin as she thought hard, eyes narrowed in concentration, hatching one of her plots. "Okay, sister, I've devised a plan for you."

"Oh, great. Just when I thought I was safe," Lynn replied. "What are we planning to do, kidnap the dude and hold him hostage until he agrees to go on a date with me?"

"Almost, but I like the way you're thinking," Trish replied. "I saw on one of the bulletin boards the school is hosting a play this Friday night. Some off-Broadway group from the city making the rounds of all the college campuses in the area. Why don't you ask him if he wants to take you?"

"I don't know. Pretty obvious, don't you think?"

"No problem," Trish said, her voice sinking low into plotter mode. "Buy two tickets. Tell him I bailed on you at the last minute and now you're stuck holding an extra one. Your mother won't let you go by yourself, especially at night, and would he *please* take you? As a friend, of course. It'll snap him out of the college routine and loosen him up some. Who know, maybe you'll get a kiss out of the deal at the end of the evening. If not, *then* we can attempt your kidnapping idea."

Lynn grimaced, thinking this sounded exactly like one of Trish's hair-brained schemes, which usually got them in trouble when they were in high school. *She is a sneaky one, but sometimes her plans worked out. What the heck, I'll try her idea.* "Might fly," Lynn replied, rolling onto her stomach, reviewing in her mind the possible mishaps that might occur. "What happens if he doesn't want to go, or already has plans for Friday? I told you, I don't think he's so much into me. I'm stuck holding two tickets for a play I have no desire to see."

A long-suffering sigh whistled out of the phone. "Well, worse case, I'll go with you. I don't have anything happening for Friday night anyway. We'll call the evening a girls' night out, maybe have pizza afterwards so watching a play isn't a total waste of time. How's my idea sound to you? A plan?"

"I think I'll have more fun hanging out with you instead of John if he doesn't speak to me," Lynn replied.

"This is a win-win for you anyway, sister," Trish replied. "Both ways you see a play, go out on a Friday night instead of staying home doing schoolwork, and there's always the change of pizza afterwards. Oops, have another call. Talk to you later."

With many misgivings, Lynn purchased the tickets. Friday afternoon she called John, acting as apologetic as possible.

"Hi, John? Yeah, it's me. Say, I have a favor to ask you....No, not really, and what I need isn't anything illegal." She tittered. "I bought two tickets for a play at school for me and Trish for tonight and she bailed on me at the last minute, said something important came up....You saw the poster? Yeah, that's the one. I was wondering if you'd go with me. I don't want to waste the ticket....Please? You know my mom will freak out if I tell her I'm going by myself at night, and I don't want to lie to her and I haven't seen a play for *ages*....You will? Great. You are one marvelous friend....No, I'll pick *you* up around six. You're the one helping me out, and I'm imposing on you enough already, and thanks. You are helping me so much....Fine, I'll see you then."

Lynn shut off the phone, heart pounding, out of breath. An expression of triumph crossing her face. *Wasn't so bad*, she admitted to herself. She pulled the ruse off like a pro. *Took some nudging, but now to see if all this plotting was worth the effort.* Lynn hoped the play wouldn't be a dud. She'd need all the help possible to break John out of his monolithic self and see if the two of them really clicked.

Lynn showered, dressed in her nicest outfit, dabbed perfume behind her ears, and gave her teeth an extra brushing. When six o'clock rolled around, she jumped into her car with fingers crossed and drove around the block. *Here goes nothing.*

John was waiting on his front stoop when she drove up.

"Hi." He hopped into the passenger seat, drew the seatbelt across his chest and buckled himself in. Breathing a sigh of comfort, he made himself comfortable in the bucket seat as he stretched out his long legs.

"Hi, yourself," Lynn retorted driving away from the curb. She glanced into the rearview mirror and said, "I want to thank you again. You're really a lifesaver."

John scanned the inside of her vehicle. "First time I've been in here," he said, making small talk. He leaned forward and touched the dashboard. "Look at all the gadgets." He reached out for a button.

"Don't push anything," Lynn cautioned in alarm. "I don't know what half of these controls do myself. If you mess around, I may have air conditioning blasting in October and never know how to switch the heat back until

July." She weaved through the back streets heading for the main highway. "Hope this play is good," Lynn said. "I'd hate to drag you out on a Friday night and you not have a good time."

John stared at the buildings passing by and said, "Well, to tell you the truth, I've never actually seen a play except once. I mean a real one. When I was in elementary school, they'd have one every year, if you want to call those plays." He looked at her quickly and said, "I was in one when I was in the third grade. 'The Wizard of Oz'. I starred as the Cowardly Lion." John issued a low, menacing growl and hastily swung to the window again staring out into the night.

Why doesn't he ever look at me for more than a few minutes? Am I so ugly? "I'm sure you were a magnificent lion," Lynn replied, concentrating on the road.

Unexpectedly, John asked while gazing out the window, "Do you ever think about your sister?"

This was such an odd question out of nowhere it took Lynn a moment to realize whom he was asking about. "You mean Caitlyn?" she replied, startled. "Sure, sometimes. Why?"

"I don't know." John concentrated on an auto dealership they passed displaying all the new cars parked outside on the lot under the lights. "What type of a person was your sister? I mean, not like a sister, or maybe that too, but—nice? Not nice? Did she have the same type of personality as you?" He groped for the right way to express what he wanted to know. "Smile at your face one moment and then stab you in the back the next?"

Lynn braked for a light, considering what John asked. "I guess we're about the same. Cat always enjoyed doing things—band, cheerleading, hanging out in crowds and celebrations. I'm more the studious type. I'll attend parties and enjoy myself, but I'm not the center of attraction like my sister was. I never saw her being catty or talking about people behind their backs, if that's what you mean. We had our fights, I guess all siblings do, but she was always there for me when I needed her." She added wishfully, "I wish I were there for her now whatever has happened to her. I loved her."

John didn't reply. From the way he asked, Lynn received the impression he really didn't need to hear an answer.

The turn for the entrance to the college appeared on their right. Lynn snapped on her blinker and swung into the broad road, slowing and following the looping street to the assembly hall. John said, "I'm sorry, Lynn, about your sister. I am so sorry."

Lynn's forehead wrinkled concentrating on pulling into a parking space. She shut off the car. "I am too, but you have nothing to feel apologetic about. It wasn't your fault Cat disappeared." Lynn hit the door lever and stepped out. "C'mon, let's grab a couple of good seats before they're all gone and we have to stand."

Chapter Eight

John slapped his math book shut and studied the equations scrawled across the computer screen. No matter how long he stared, the numbers still didn't make any sense. He'd been going over the same pages for the last hour with the same results—nothing. The more he scrutinized the figures, working the problems over and again on paper, the less meaning the symbols held. Each time he arrived at a different sum and the amounts all appeared to be correct. He silently cursed whoever invented college algebra and forced unsuspecting students to learn it.

He'd begged off two campus parties, one he was sure would have been a blast and a half, to sharpen his skill in his poorest subject. To make matters worse, math was one of his best classes in high school, the one subject he never worried about, and the thought irked him he couldn't figure this stuff out. Everything was easier then. Nowadays concentration was harder, more distractions, the urge to be out and doing real work rode on his back like a horseman in the saddle, digging spurs into his side, demanding he run faster. The ever-present throbbing in his head, lurking in the background waiting to start anew at a moment's notice, began again. The numbers blurred before his eyes. Without thinking, he popped a pill, finished the beer sitting on his desk, and tossed the empty in the garbage. *No wonder I'm still having nightmares. This math stuff is a horror. If I ever meet Achimedes on the street, I'll bash him over the head using his lever as a club.* He ripped the tab off another can of beer and regretted not taking the night off as he scrolled his mouse backward, starting at the beginning of the chapter again.

His phone chirped. With a groan, he scooped the instrument off his desk, studied the screen in surprise, and answered. "Hello? Lynn? What….I hope you're not asking about math, I'm drowning over here in numbers and brackets. If I never see an *a* times *x* or a *y* squared again….I think I remember hearing something, or maybe seeing a note…." *She wants me to take her to a play? Why in the world….* "….Oh, I see. Sorry to hear you were stuck, but last minute changes happen. Gee, I don't know. I have so much studying to catch up on. Reason I'm sitting here in the first place banging my head against a wall instead of enjoying myself on a Friday afternoon."

John glanced at the closed book on his desk and the scrawl of numbers across the computer screen. The equations made less sense now than they did before Lynn called him. The urge to escape the workload staring him in the face and relax won out. "I wouldn't want to cause your mom to have a fit. She'd tell my mom and there, where would I be. The bad boy on the block….Sure, why not. I'm going crazy here spinning my wheels and not traveling anywhere fast….How much do I owe you for the ticket…? It's up to you. Should have Trish pay for one. She's the person causing all the last minute headaches, right? What time do you want me to pick you up…?" John laughed. *The poor girl sounds so desperate. Lynn must really want to see this play. Hope the show is a good one. I wouldn't want her to be disappointed. Oh, Trish, what you put your friends through.* "No problem. You're the excuse I needed to push off this work until tomorrow. I'd feel guilty now if we didn't go, and it'll be fun to have a night out for a change. I'll be waiting in front of my house for you."

John shut off his phone and leaned back, his tension—which condensed into a lump on the back of his neck all afternoon—vanishing as if the pressure never existed. He reached out, switched off the computer with a sigh of relief, and leaned back in his chair. *Better start cleaning up.*

As the hot water from the shower beat on his head and back, John debated how he should act tonight. It would be impossible to ignore Lynn, show her polite nods and grunted replies as if he were concentrating on the work ahead as he usually did during the school day. They weren't hurrying to class and pretending to pay attention to the lecture of a teacher, or discussing the possibilities of what the next professor might say or do. This was a date, even though among friends. Lynn and he were going out by themselves. The last thing he'd plan to do with her.

The relief John felt vanished. The tautness in his neck exploded anew, threatening to awaken the sleeping ache in his head while his mind was still in a turmoil. He threw on his pants and shirt, taking calming breaths, doused himself in a handful of aftershave, and rubbed on a good layer of deodorant, suspecting he would need the help before the evening was over.

John surveyed himself one last time in the bathroom mirror. He placed a grin on his lips, which belied the fact he was nervous as hell inside. *You did a good cowardly lion before a hundred kids. Let's see how you perform tonight when the pressure is on.*

The sky blazed in red light, streaking the clouds into ribbons, as the sun settled for the night. John thudded down on the stoop watching it vanish as he waited for Lynn to arrive, indecision racing through his mind. He checked his phone for a message. Maybe Trish changed her plans again and Lynn decided to take her instead. All his problems would unravel then. He'd already resolved to push his studying off until tomorrow, and could still make one of those parties. The night wouldn't be a total loss after all.

No message. With the sun now hidden, the air blew cold. John drew his coat closer around him, searching the street for the headlights of Lynn's car.

Lynn drove up promptly at six o'clock. Summoning a wrenched effort of will, John blanked his mind, shifting into the same mode he'd used preparing for combat missions. *No worries. I've gone out with girls a million times. I'll survive this fine.*

As John slipped into the passenger's seat, a stray breeze wafted the odor of Lynn's perfume to him. She smelled like roses. John fought the urge to lean over, sniff her neck and kiss her. Instead, he pretended to study the dashboard of the car. Lynn drove a brand new vehicle containing all the newest gadgets. He marveled at the lights glowing in the dark as if rubies, sapphires, and emeralds were sprinkled in gay profusion across the console and onto the doors. Even the floorboard shined with a pale blue radiance. After commenting, he switched back to the window and stared out into the night, trying to think.

Lynn was Lynn, not her sister Caitlyn. What happened that day, happened. Nothing he could do would change the events of the past.

I wonder how different Lynn is from her sister. I only talked to Caitlyn for a short time. She was nice. Even her crazy mother isn't so bad.

Maybe I should have stayed in the army. Sure, the government would send me overseas for another tour of combat. After all, I didn't have to accept their medical retirement. Lots of people in my position stayed in. Combat was not so bad, not like on the television where the troops hit the beach carrying blazing machine guns, fire and artillery blowing up all around you. I could head over to one of my friends from the military. They'd told me to stop by after being discharged. I would find a job. Settle down. Relocating would mean not seeing my family very often, but what the heck, I'd only visited my parents a few times over the last three years anyway.

John asked Lynn about Caitlyn, but only half listened, her reply confirming what he already understood. She was a nice person who didn't deserve to die. He recalled many things in his past life he'd like to do over again if he could, the kids in school he'd been mean to, Caitlyn, the enemy he'd destroyed in the war. Was one so different from the other? Wrong was wrong. He'd have to live with the consequences of his actions. Running away would solve nothing.

As they walked into the auditorium, John painted on a good face, determined to enjoy himself and make sure Lynn did too.

The play was surprisingly enjoyable. Off Broadway? Off the wall, the show should have been touted as on the handbills. Pirates sailing into the gutter searching for "Pieces They Ate," sewer rats, and items so gross John didn't even wish to think about. The show put a totally new spin on the phrase toilet humor, and the play was a musical, too. The actors sang off-key and one slipped and fell during a scene, but the mistakes only made the production more humorous. Lynn placed her head on John's shoulder and cried softly when the ship's cat fell overboard and disappeared in a ribbon of sludgy grey water. They both laughed when kitty reappeared out of the prop sewage, wiping toilet paper off his ears, and drawing a fish skeleton out of its mouth. It sang the theme song, "Pieces They Ate," as he crawled back aboard the boat and shook himself vigorously, spraying the first three rows of the theater in silver confetti from a hidden blower.

John nudged Lynn and whispered, "I hope the ship isn't bombed from above by those bats. Wouldn't that be a laugh?"

Lynn giggled and held his bicep tight, pointing a shapely finger at the stage. "Is that what I think it is crawling across the deck? Oh my God, this play is so gross, the show is hilarious."

The play was three hours long. As they tumbled out of the auditorium, red-eyed from laughing and wiping tears, John exclaimed, "Fantastic. We gotta do this again sometime." He craned his neck and looked toward the stage, "Are all plays this good?"

Lynn choked back a laugh and gasped, "The college runs shows every month during the year. I hope the plays are all as funny as this one was, but we'll have to wait and see. I'll check the bulletin board next week and take a peek at what the school has scheduled next."

They continued to stroll out into the parking lot, chuckling and repeating lines from the show to each other pretending to be the actors on the stage. They reached Lynn's car and John asked, "Do you want to stop and have something to eat?" He tried to make his voice as deep as the pirate captain had from the play. "Pizza? A burger? We catch some mighty fine tidbits in these waters, you know, ma'am."

Lynn replied in the high squeaky voice of the female lead, "Why, Captain John Widdlebottom, I'd be delighted to dine on whatever is placed before me by you and your crew."

"You have the spirit, matey. We only feast on the grandest cuisine of," he paused, his eyes twinkling, and both sang together, *"Pieces They Ate."*

John patted Lynn on the back and his voice returned to normal. "The night is too early for me to go home yet, and if I do, I'll be tempted to glare at my math book." He gave a fake shudder, grimacing and baring his teeth.

"Me too." Lynn gazed at the bright stars with a contented sigh and inhaled the crisp autumn air. "It's too beautiful a night to sit in our rooms and do nothing for the rest of the evening. We have all Saturday and Sunday to put our noses to the grindstone and let our chins be flattened." She peeked sideways at John. "Pizza?"

"I'll buy. You paid for the tickets."

"You have a deal, matey."

Lombardo's, pizza palace extraordinary with award-winning hot wings, was crowded as usual for a Friday night. Besides food, the restaurant provided twenty TVs and doubled as a sports bar. There was also a game room included for those who wished for a fun time of play on the weekend. Even through the dark oak doors the rhythm of music and the babble of voice assaulted John's ears as they drove into the packed lot and found a spot to park. John took a deep breath and held Lynn's hand, walking up to the entrance. "Ready?"

"Yes." A group of teenagers burst through the door talking excitedly. Lynn and John jumped out of the way as the entrance slammed in their faces. "I think."

John swung the door open and the blare overwhelmed the two. They stood helplessly, searching for an empty table while people swirled around them.

"Hey, John—Lynn, over here!" Herbie stood in the middle of the throng, making a frantic hurry-on motion from a table halfway across the restaurant. Trish sat with her brother, waving as energetically as he did. John signaled back and latched onto Lynn's arm, hurrying to their friends.

"What are you two doing here?" John asked as they dropped across from their friends.

"No dates," Herbie replied shrugging as if this was a normal occurrence. "Friday, the loneliest day of the week when you don't have someone to love." He patted Trish on the hair. "I figured I'd take the little sister out and show her how the big boys roll."

Trish frowned and shook his hand off her head. She said innocently to Lynn, "You two out on a date?"

"Oh, no. We decided to stop in and have something to eat after we left campus from seeing the play at school." Lynn looked Trish in the eye, "Which someone was supposed to go with me and bailed."

"Yeah, what gives, Trish?" John asked. "I thought you were going to the play, and then I got a call from Lynn saying you couldn't because something more important turned up."

"Oh, uh, I was bailed on too." Trish's forehead wrinkled. "This guy I've been seeing called and wanted to take me out tonight. After I told Lynn I couldn't see the play, the rat told me a relative died, and he needed to leave town to attend a funeral." She glared at the tabletop. "I bet he has two girlfriends and I was the loser. I'll never date him again."

Plates and napkins littered the table. John eyed the dirty dishes and asked, "You two eat already?"

Herbie shook his head. "Nope, we scooted in here as the other people left. In fact—" a harried waitress hustled their way "—here comes our hero now."

The woman swept the plates away and dropped menus. "Sorry," she said, out of breath, "short on busboys tonight. We're running behind. Drinks?"

John said to Herbie, "Split a pitcher of beer? I'll buy the first one." His friend nodded. "Girls? What do you want to drink?"

"I'll have beer," Trish said quickly.

"No way," Herbie exclaimed. "Mom and Dad would kill me if I brought you back to the house drunk." He said to John, "One of the drawbacks of living at home. Can't bring drunks. The rent's free, though, and so is the food. Guess the good and bad even out."

"I'll have a diet soda," Lynn decided. "All I need is to walk into the house and have beer on my breath. If my mother smells alcohol, I'll be in the dog kennel for the rest of my life."

John nodded in approval. "Your mother would never let us go out together again," he agreed. The note of concern in Lynn's voice for her mother's reaction relieved John. This wasn't Caitlyn. The small differences between the two became more apparent the longer he was with Lynn. He said to Trish, "Catch a clue from the pretty girl." He hooked a thumb in Lynn's direction, "Diet soda."

Herbie made a big production of studying his sister's hips. "Wouldn't hurt," he commented.

Trish punched him in the shoulder. "Enough. I'm the perfect weight for my height and age."

Lynn ignored bother her friends and flashed John a small smile. "Why, thank you, sir, for the compliment."

He returned her smile with a wink. "Gotta take care of my matey, right?"

Trish looked from John to Lynn, perplexed. "Matey? Did you two see a play, or go for a boat ride?"

Lynn chuckled. "Capt'n John and I are now glued to the hip by *The Pieces We Ate*."

When both Trish and Herbie acted confused, Lynn said to Trish, "I'll explain later."

The time was well past midnight when Lynn dropped John off at his house. "I had fun," he said, before stepping out of the car.

"Me, too," Lynn agreed. "I'm sorta glad Trish was bailed on and we met up with her and Herbie later. Tonight was like a double date, which wasn't a date, if you know what I mean."

"Yeah. A bunch of friends hanging out. Best time I've had in a long while," John agreed, half wishing the evening would continue. He tried stretching the conversation to make their night together a little longer.

Lynn bent forward gazing into John's eyes. "I want to thank you again. I really appreciate you helping me out like this, and taking me for dinner afterwards."

John rubbed his chin, thinking. "You know, it's ridiculous us driving two cars to school every day, and then trailing each other home after classes. Did you want to start carpooling? We could take turns, switch drivers every week. I don't know about you, but using my car half the time will save me tons of money on gas."

"I was thinking the exact thing myself," Lynn agreed quickly. "I didn't want to appear pushy about riding together, but using one vehicle instead of two will allow us time for extra study, bounce questions off each other also when we have a test. If nothing else, at least we'll have someone to talk to."

The faint fragrance of Lynn's perfume still clung to her. She leaned closer, not saying a word.

"Well, gotta go. I'm glad you called me." John debated in his mind if he should kiss her goodnight.

Don't go there. It's too early.

He stuck his hand out. "Have a good night. I'll talk to you tomorrow."

***

"Hi, Mrs. Brennen. Is Lynn ready to leave?"

Mrs. Brennen swung the door open wide. "Oh, hi, John. Yes. Come on in. I'll let her know you're here." Mrs. Brennen walked into the living room, John in her wake peering over her shoulder searching for Lynn. He made himself comfortable on the couch while she yelled down the hallway, "John's here, Lynn." She walked back and headed into the kitchen saying to John, "Where are you two off to today? Some great adventure I imagine, right?"

"Uh...." Lynn and John's carpooling during the week spilled over onto Saturday mornings, and extended into a custom of jaunts somewhere in the country, and then breakfast, or brunch, at the diner afterward. During the late winter and early spring, their favorite spot was usually the harbor, where, weather permitting, they'd watch the boats and speculate about the people who owned each craft. After heavy snowfalls, John and Lynn drove through the countryside, gazing at the snow on the trees and hills, sometimes stopping for a quick snowball fight or sliding on an icy stretch of water. Lynn conceived the plans, sometimes plotting with Trish during the week to locate the most fun places to visit or see. John was happy to explore the surrounding towns and villages or investigate wherever Lynn desired to venture.

"You'll have to ask your daughter, Mrs. Brennen. Your guess is as good as mine," he said ruefully. "Lynn is the master. I am but her humble servant and follow where she leads."

"And this is the way it should be," Lynn said as she strolled into the living room. "Men are less than the dust beneath the feet of women."

"Lynn, what a terrible thing to say," her mother gasped, with a smirk.

"It's okay, Mrs. Brennen. I'm used to the slurs by now." He said to Lynn, "Where are we going today? Gonna tell me before we arrive or make me guess?"

"I thought we'd take a walk along the water."

"The harbor again?" John asked, surprised. "We went last Saturday. Finally running out of places to go?"

"Of course not, silly. The beach on the south shore. I want to drive over to the ocean and watch the waves crash on the sand." Lynn was dressed in a heavy fur-lined jacket, jeans, and boots. Thick leather gloves poked from her pockets. "I haven't been there since summer, and I don't think I've ever seen the shore covered in ice and snow. The waves must be fantastic." She sat next to John, shoulder brushing his.

"You'll catch your death of cold," Mrs. Brennen exclaimed hurrying from the kitchen and drying her hands on a dishcloth. She frowned, surveying her daughter, and chided, "I have enough trouble worrying about Caitlyn. I don't need you catching pneumonia and getting sick."

Inwardly, John groaned. *Please don't start in. I don't need this so early in the morning.* He nudged Lynn imperceptibly with his knee, hoping she'd understand the gesture and leave before her mother fell into one of Mrs. Brennen's talks about her missing daughter.

Lynn didn't take the hint. "I'm wearing a heavy coat, sweatshirt, and warm pants, Mom. I'll be fine." The girl withdrew a wool cap from her coat pocket and waved the hat in the air. "See, I've covered all bases. Anyway, most of the time we'll be in the car except for the actual walk, and it's not going to be so long. I want to look, not swim."

Mrs. Brennen said to John, "You know, my Caitlyn is two years older than Lynn. Would catch a cold if she didn't dress properly for the weather. Never listened to me when I told her what to wear. Always arguing she knew what was best, but when you meet her you'll be amazed what a wonderful person my daughter is."

John cringed deeper into the sofa cushions and bumped Lynn harder with his knee. "Yes, Ma'am. I'm sure Caitlyn is a great girl."

Lynn took the hint this time. She stood. "We have to start rolling, Mom. The ocean is a long way from here, and if we don't hurry, we'll never get back for a late breakfast. See you this afternoon." She asked John, "You ready?"

He shot off the couch. "Guess so. Mrs. Brennen, don't worry, I won't lose this one. She's a keeper." He strode to the door and pushed Lynn outside.

"Sorry about my mom doing her Caitlyn talk," Lynn said as they hurried into John's car. "I know you don't like talking —"

"It's not I don't like speaking to your mother," John said as he drove away from the curb, "but—" He groped for the right way to express his thoughts. "Every time? You'd think she'd give her speech a rest by now. Your mom acts as though your sister will walk through the door any minute and nothing is amiss. 'Oh, yes, by the way, this is my daughter, Caitlyn' sort of thing. She acts creepy."

"My mother is not creepy."

"I didn't mean…."

Lynn released a huge sigh. "Well, maybe the way she speaks sometimes is kinda strange, but Mom doesn't behave like she's not in touch with reality most of the time. I know Caitlyn's not coming back, you know the same thing, but can you blame her for hoping? I still wish my sister would return, too. It's sad to think I'll never see Cat again. Sometimes, when I'm at the in between place between sleep and awake I hear her voice talking to me. So young." Lynn leaned back in the seat and closed her eyes. "I even wrote a poem one day in English class. I was debating whether to submit it to the school newspaper, but then I thought the verse was too private to share among anyone. Maybe one day I'll rewrite the poem into a song."

"A rose, cut from the vine.
Wind blows, pedals fly.
Too soon, it has died."

"So beautiful," John murmured. He glanced at Lynn. Her eyes were wet.

His eyes were moist, too.

The corners of John's mouth bent down. He swung his attention back to the road and concentrated on the driving. The expression on Lynn's face made it plain he was entering fruitless territory and not a place he desired to venture on a Saturday morning.

Deep in their own thoughts, John hit the expressway, cut off onto the parkway, and took the ramp to the causeway. Sullen grey-green water swirled around the pilings as the car crossed the bay with the ocean pictured in his front windshield. A gale swept across the road, pushing his car dangerously close to the railing. The parking lot of the seashore appeared deserted except for a dozen widely scattered vehicles drawn haphazardly close to the sand. He circled the vacant asphalt and drove into a space abutting the beach, and near to the concession stand, already thinking of a hot drink for Lynn and him after the walk finished.

Steam vented into the cold air from the lunch bar, curling into the leaden sky, while flocks of seagulls circled overhead mewling their plaintive cries and dive-bombing a dumpster behind the building, searching for a free meal.

John zipped his jacket up to his chin and drew the hood over his head for good luck. He took a deep breath. "You ready to do this?"

Lynn took out her woolen cap from her pocket and jammed the hat over her blond hair, checked the buttons on her coat, and slipped on her gloves. "Let's."

John hit the door handle and tumbled out of the car. A frigid blast of air smacked him in the face, snatching the breath from his mouth. Lynn shrieked as the air clutched at the exposed part of her hair, twisting the long strands behind her into a yellow lasso. "We must be nuts," he yelled over a gust of the wind.

"I know." Lynn reached out a hand and took his, tugging him forward over the curb onto the beach. "Let's look at the water," she laughed.

Lynn pulled John toward the surf, their feet sinking into the soft sand as they ran, kicking up grit behind their feet. Lynn stopped abruptly, John standing by her side as the two confronted the ocean.

Waves crashed on the shoreline, reaching fingers out to engulf their feet. Grey clouds overhead whipped across the sky in a race, obliterating the light from the sun, while sand picked up by the wind peppered their cheeks.

They plodded across the beach, dancing out of the way of the surf when water threatened to drench their shoes. "The ocean is so awesome and scary," Lynn yelled. She pointed far out where a sailboat made a choppy way across the silver water. "How would you like to be on one of those going anywhere you pleased?"

"I'd love too, but not in this kind of weather," John shouted back to make himself heard. "I'll wait until the summer arrives when the air is warm enough to breathe." He scooped up a flattish pebble and flung the stone along the top of the water. He achieved two skips before a swell swallowed up the rock in its maw.

They walked a hundred yards along the shore and then swung around, marching back up the beach toward the car. As John walked, he watched the turbulent combers destroy their tracks in the sand.

"It's as though the ocean doesn't want anyone to know we've been here," he remarked. John glanced to their rear. The footsteps left behind also disappeared under the pounding of the waves.

Lynn squeezed John's hand and swung both high in the air as they trudged along. She began to sing, *"...and hand-in-hand, on the edge of the sand, they danced by the light of the moon, the moon, the moon. They danced by the light of the moon."*

"Is that another song you made up?" John asked.

"A poem. 'The Owl and the Pussycat'. My dad made Caitlyn and I memorize the words when we were kids. I—Oh, look. Pretty." Lynn dropped John's fingers and bent over, picking up a sea scallop shell the size of her hand, half buried in the sand. "This one goes into my collection," she announced, shoving the prize in her pocket. "Mission accomplished. Let's scoot outta here, I'm freezing."

As the two hit the curb, Lynn halted. "Wait a minute." She searched around in the sand and located a large stone as big as her thumb.

"What are you doing?"

"You'll see." Lynn scooped sand into a wall against the curb leaving a hollow inside and placed the stone in the middle. She stood and nodded in satisfaction. "There. The waves won't wash this away, and everyone will know someone was here."

"Until a kid steps on your castle," John agreed, "but at least, we'll remember. C'mon, I'm freezing."

They hurried to the car. John started the engine and switched the heater to high. "I'm numb," Lynn exclaimed. She took off her gloves and blew on her fingers. "The wind whipped straight through my clothes. See my hands? The skin is white and wrinkled from the cold."

"I think the next time we return will be in the summer," John agreed. He took her fingers and rubbed the palms and the back of her arms vigorously. "This is nice once, but laying in the sun and getting a tan is a lot more fun."

Before they left John made a quick stop at the concession stand. "I'll buy us some coffee," he said, stepping out of the car, "keep us warm on the ride home."

"Light, sweet and hot," Lynn yelled after him.

He returned balancing two take-out cups, juggled both in one arm as he cautiously opened the door and slid behind the steering wheel.

"Oh, goodie. Gimme." Lynn reached for one cup. "My face is frozen and your heater sucks." Her cheeks had changed color from white to red from the cold wind and sand, but her eyes sparkled.

"My mechanic says the heater works, but the coils emit mellow heat." John reached the cup toward her. At the same time, the clouds parted, and a ray of sunlight shone through the side window lighting up the back of Lynn's head, transforming her blond hair into spun gold. John stopped, gazing at her.

"Here, I'll warm you up." He leaned forward and kissed her lightly on her cold lips.

Lynn's eyes opened wider in surprise, mouth twitching upward. "I'm really cold," she murmured. "Better heat me up one more time."

John kissed her again, a long, lingering kiss.

Lynn flowed into his arms, the coffee forgotten.

This woman is wonderful.

***

"So, are you going to sleep with him?"

"Trish-*A*." Lynn pictured her friend laying on the bed, on her stomach, legs kicking in the air, munching potato chips as she talked on the phone. "We kissed once. It's not as if I let him go any farther. He never even tried moving to second base."

"One smooch, a long time waiting to happen, sister," Trish mumbled. Lynn heard a crunch. "You guys have been hanging out for months. It's about time he gave you a lousy kiss. You should have won a home run by now."

"Are you eating?"

"Yeah, why?" Lynn heard another crunch. "They have ridges. Tastes good. Could use some French onion dip, though. My mouth is dry and I'm too lazy to walk to the fridge. Don't know if Herbie left me some, anyhow."

"I thought so. I'm no virgin, but I don't sleep with every guy I date, and certainly not after one kiss. You know I'm not a tramp. It happened, may not ever occur again, who knows?"

"Uh-huh. I hear wedding bells in the future. Better run to the drug store and buy protection in case John forgets to bring his own or doesn't carry any." Trish said meaningfully, "'It happened', could happen again. You know what people say, 'A stitch in time saves nine months walking around holding a big belly."

Lynn pulled the phone away from her mouth and stared at the instrument in disbelieve, gaping. "I don't know why I stay friends with you," she gasped at last. "You have an evil mind and say the darnest things."

"I have a sparkling personality," Trish replied. "Everyone loves me no matter what I say or do. Besides, the same spur of the moment thing happened to me once or twice. Make sure you have a ring on your finger and then babies, not the other way around. I'm too young to be an aunt."

Lynn began to say she was too young to be a mother and changed her mind. "You're a good friend. I'll keep your advice right where I put all your other comments, helpful or not."

"Just saying." Lynn heard another crunch.

"Talk to you later, girlfriend." Lynn switched off her phone, shaking her head at the conversation with Trish.

She smiled.

Chapter Nine

"I don't know if my mom'll go for the idea." Lynn studied her friend closely. "This isn't another one of your hair-brained schemes, is it?"

Trish sat cross-legged on Lynn's bed, a wicked smile on her face. Lynn rested opposite her in a similar fashion, biting her lower lip. "Nonsense, I made the reservations last fall before you and John ever hooked up together," Trish scoffed. "My family and I went camping up there for the week, during the Thanksgiving break, remember? The place is beautiful, mountains, the lake. All the trees changing color. We stayed in the lodge, but I reserved a campsite for us, big enough for three tents. I figured me and my boyfriend, Herbie and his girlfriend, you and whoever you wanted to bring. John is an add-on."

Lynn was still a city girl and camping under the stars certainly sounded like fun to her. She'd never slept outside before, and been dying to do something, anything, even if her vacation was a couple of day trips into the city to drop in on her old friends, explore the haunts of her childhood, and visit her former schools and teachers.

"You'll back me up on this, right?" Lynn said earnestly to Trish. "My mom will shoot me down for sure. I know she won't roll over and say yes without handing me an argument. I'll be told good girls don't go camping unchaperoned alongside boys. Sometimes I think she's living in the nineteenth century."

Trish brushed her bangs out of her face. "Don't worry. Right behind you. I have your back. I never let a friend down."

"I don't need you behind me unless you're able to hold me upright. I want you by my side so I can make sure you don't run away when the fireworks start."

"Funny." Trish uncrossed her legs and hopped on the floor, extending a hand to Lynn. "Might as well get the advice over and finished. C'mon, let's ask before you chicken out on me. I think your mom has dinner ready, anyway. Smells great and I'm hungry."

Mrs. Brennen was in the kitchen cooking supper for the three of them. Lynn and Trish took seats at the table and watched Lynn's mom stir away at a pan. "Don't start snacking," Mrs. Brennen warned, "dinner is almost ready."

"Smells great, Mrs. B. What are you making?" Trish asked.

"Beef stroganoff. Have to stir in the sour cream for the gravy and we're all ready to eat," Mrs. Brennen said over her shoulder. "Lynn, start setting the table, please."

Lynn jumped up and grabbed plates from the cupboard. "Oh, Mom, by the way, I almost forgot, Trish asked if I can camp with her this weekend." Lynn put the plates down, found napkins and silverware, not daring to look at her mother while waiting for a reply.

Mrs. Brennen dropped her spoon on the edge of the pan and watched Lynn placing knives and forks by the plates. "I don't know. Two girls all alone...."

Lynn folded the napkins carefully. "Oh, the two of us aren't camping alone," she assured her mom. "Trish is bringing her boyfriend, Herbie's taking his girlfriend, and, I think, John might be coming along too."

"You're bringing boys with you?" Mrs. Brennen's tone made Lynn cringe. Lynn shot Trish a pleading glance.

"Don't worry, Mrs. B," Trish spoke up. "Boys in one tent, us girls in the other. The lodge is a swell place, canoeing, horseback riding if you want to try. I cleared it with my parents already. I think there's even a zip-line.

Fresh air, sunshine, swimming. My parents and I were up there last fall."

Mrs. Brennen frowned, debating in her head. "I don't know. You said camping is okay with your parents? Where is this lodge anyway?"

"Fine with them. The place is upstate in the mountains. We drive up Friday, stay Saturday, and return Sunday. If you want, you're free to join us. Tent might be crowded, but I can always dig up another sleeping bag. We'll make room if you want."

Lynn glared at Trish. Mrs. Brennen chuckled. "Me? Sleep on the ground? With my bad back and old bones, I'd be in the hospital for a week afterwards, and the last thing I need is sleeping in a tent alongside a bunch of giggling girls when I need a good night's rest." The woman sighed, and returned to the beef stroganoff. "I suppose you can go. I trust John, but separate tents, and I expect a phone call at least once a day. Understand?" She placed the dinner on the table along with a big bowl of egg noodles and bread. "Okay, girls, dig in. I suspect this will be the best meal you'll have until you return." Mrs. Brennen took in each girl by eye. "Remember, no one buys the cow if they can get the milk for free."

"Mom." Lynn blushed red and scooped noodles onto her plate, passing the bowl to Trish, embarrassed to look up. Out of the corner of her eye, she saw her girlfriend snickering.

After Trish left, Lynn busied herself compiling a list of everything needed for the trip, and spent an enormous amount of time hunting through the garage searching for her sleeping bag, which she hadn't used in six years since a slumber party at a friend's house. Lynn had about abandoned hope when she discovered it in a cardboard box marked "Misc," which lay forgotten in a stack of other boxes unpacked during the move from the city. She lugged the bag to her room and prepared for sleep.

Lynn lay in her bed, staring into the darkness, tired and excited at the same time, thinking of the camping trip and what John and she would do and see.

I wonder if this will be the night, the first time John and I make love? Alone, by ourselves, the perfect chance. He'd always been the ideal gentleman, and except for long sessions of kissing had never tried anything. At times, Lynn wished they'd go farther, and thought about the warm, sensuous pleasure of their naked flesh rubbing against each other, their warm bodies tightly pressed together, but in the past she was content to let events take their natural course.

Now Lynn wasn't so sure she wanted to wait any longer. The occasion was right, and this was the best setting one could imagine.

I want this man.

Lynn fell asleep dreaming of John's chest hairs brushing against her nipples.

***

John and Lynn tracked Herbie's car as the two vehicles weaved through heavy traffic. Towering buildings and factories loomed on either side. "Where are all these people heading?" John hunched over the steering wheel and snarled as another car cut him off on the expressway through the city.

"Same as us, I suppose," Lynn replied as her foot searched for an imaginary brake pedal on the floorboard. "This is Friday afternoon and everyone is escaping the city for the weekend. Don't worry, we're farther out than in now. Be patient. We'll be on the thruway before you know it."

Traffic thinned to an occasional vehicle in the distance as the cars traveled north. John relaxed, and soon mountains and forest replaced houses and factories. Two hours later, they pulled off onto a side boulevard and from there onto a single lane road winding up into the hills. Herbie stopped before a large stone building and Trish hopped out of his car. "Be right back," the girl yelled to John and Lynn. "Gotta sign in and get directions."

Trish returned a few minutes later and handed Lynn two brochures. "Follow us to the campsite," she said jumping back into Herbie's car.

"This paper says to watch out for bears," Lynn told John reading the brochure. She flipped the leaflet over. "Has a map on the back, too, detailing the different sites and hiking trails."

"Right now I have to watch where Herbie's going," John replied. His friend took a cutoff along a narrow lane, burning rubber.

"We have rattlesnakes, too," Lynn said.

"Great. No lions or tigers? In the desert, I had to worry about scorpions."

"Nope. No scorpions either, and I think dire wolves went extinct a long time ago. Maybe mosquitoes and bees, though, and ants. There's always ants." Lynn flipped the paper over again. "Hope Trish picked an area near the water," she remarked as John drove passed a lake. "Oh, look, canoes and paddleboats."

Herbie zigged onto a dirt road and John zagged after him, passing three camping spots containing green tents set up in a semi-circle. The two cars pulled into an open space, which included a picnic table, fire pit, and a water spigot. Herbie stepped from his car as the rest of his passengers piled out of the doors. "This is our new home for the next few days," he called to John. "We've reached the spot."

The site Trish picked couldn't have been better for people who wanted privacy. Secluded from the rest of the campers by a screen of trees, the six possessed a view of the lake on one side within walking distance of the dock and boat rental. On the other side, not far away, were the toilets and showers housed in a beige building. Trish sauntered over to Lynn and waved in triumph. "Well, what do you think? Did I do good, or did I do good?"

Lynn broke out in a grin, making a slow circle, surveying the area. "This is wonderful. Just like our own little hideaway."

John nodded his approval. "For once you didn't screw up, kiddo." He shouted to Herbie and Trish's boyfriend. "Let's erect the tents, canopy, and explore before the sun sets and we lose the light."

Trish announced, "Dinner is hotdogs and beans for tonight. If anyone goes fishing tomorrow, we'll add pan-fried bass to the menu, otherwise we eat hamburgers and chicken. Lynn and I made plenty of peanut butter and jelly sandwiches for lunch and snacks if anyone wants a quick meal."

They set up the campsite. Lynn laid out their sleeping bags side by side in the tent. *Same as a double bed. Good for snuggling, and....*

After the tents were assembled, food unloaded, and canopy strung, the six set off toward the lake, discovering a dirt hiking trail winding around the shore, which led to the docks and boats.

"Oh look, horses," Herbie's girlfriend, Vicki exclaimed as two people rode toward their group on the path. They made way to allow the riders to pass. She waved and the people waved back. Vicki took out her map and studied the different paths as the six continued to walk. When the group hit a cross trail she announced, "This way to the stables." She said to the rest, "I love horses. Anybody else want to take a stroll and look?"

John shook his head. Lynn said, "I want to see the boats and lake."

Trish said, "Have fun. We'll meet you at camp and you can give us a report."

The four continued to wander along the path until they spotted the dock and a wooden building marked "Rentals—bait and tackle" on the outside. John and Trish's boyfriend Rick checked prices, and then John and Lynn strolled to the end of the dock looking at the lake. Lynn glanced sideway at John, his eyes squinted, dark brown hair fluttering in the breeze, a hint of five o'clock shadow marked along his chin and cheeks.

I wonder if tonight will be the night?

"What do you think? You guys want to rent a boat? The time's kinda late." Trish stood behind the two looking at her phone. "If not, we're heading to the tents and build a fire, break out the food, and start cooking."

John said to Lynn, "Well, it's up to you. I'm easy either way."

"Uh..." She searched the sky, saw the sun was way past its zenith, and realized they'd missed lunch. "Well, the time is late, and I'm hungry."

Trish did an about face and hooked her hand through her boyfriend's arm. "C'mon, hunk of burning love. I'll demonstrate how we made supper in the Girl Scouts." She took off at a brisk walk, dragging him along.

John and Lynn strolled slower. Lynn's phone rang. She checked the screen and exclaimed, "Oh, gee. I forgot, my mom. Hi, Mom.... Yeah, we made the trip to the place safe....Right now? Walking around looking at the lake and boats, going back to the camp to start dinner.... Beans and franks.... Well, we are camping.... I'll have to see. I think I packed carrots....I will. Talk to you tomorrow." Lynn shoved her phone into her back pocket and said to John, "Mom says hi, and to tell you to make sure I eat right."

"Double portions of beans for you then. Plenty of fiber and you can forget the rabbit food."

"Thanks, but remember you have to sleep in the same tent beside me tonight. You know what everyone says about beans," Lynn joked. *Oh God. Stay away from the beans.*

When Lynn and John returned to the camp, Trish already had a smoky fire burning in the barbeque pit, an empty pot in front of her. "I have the Boy Scout out finding us some sticks to roast the franks," she announced. Trish fumbled with an opener trying to fit the utensil on a big can of baked beans, squishing her mouth to one side, perplexed. "The manufactures make these tools more complicated than a microwave," she muttered, as the utensil slipped off the top of the can and fell into the dirt. "Why don't these darn things have instructions printed on the sides?" Trish held the opener up and searched the handle. "Not even in Spanish," she murmured sadly. "I give up." Shrugging, the girl held the beans out to John with a smile. "Here. You were in the army. This calls for a professional."

John smirked, squeezed the opener onto the lid, and, with a few quick twists, opened the can. Without saying a word, he handed it back to Trish. "You are awesome," she exclaimed, dumping the beans into the pot. "There, now we're cooking."

Herbie and Vicki still hadn't arrived when dinner was prepared. "I'm not waiting," Lynn announced, threading her hot dog on a long stick. "My stomach is growling."

"Me neither," said Trish. "You snooze, you lose. I slaved over this big pot of beans all day. I'm famished." She reached out and stirred the pot of beans warming on the side of the fire. "My work is done here."

The two missing campers sauntered in a half an hour later. Herbie commented as he grabbed a paper plate and hot dog, "Horse people and horse talk. How can you have so much discussion about dog food on four legs?"

Vicki was in the middle of jabbing her frank with a stick. She stopped and glared at him. "You we can do without. The horse talk stays. You'd better learn to enjoy barn discussions if you want to ride this cowgirl tonight."

"She got you a good one, Herbie. Giddy-up— giddy-up."

"Watch out, buddy. I think your girl is wearing spurs."

Herbie winced and hung his head down, refusing to reply to the humorous remarks from his friends. Vicki patted him on the knee. "Don't worry. You're okay. I have to break you to saddle, that's all. I'm sure my Herbie will do fine."

Trish stood and stretched. "I'm heading up to the bathrooms and grab a shower before the hot water is shut off for the night. I smell like smoke, and I think the clerk at the desk said they turn the boilers off at nine." She turned to Lynn. "You coming with?"

"I'll grab my towel." Lynn sprang up and ran to her tent.

"Me, too, I guess," John sighed. Rick nodded.

Herbie held up his plate. "Still eating. We'll be along later."

The bathrooms were clean and the water still hot. Lynn and Trish relaxed and let the shower wash over their bodies.

"So, tonight will be the big night?" Trish asked, scrubbing under her arms.

Lynn felt her pits. Nubbly, but passable. So were her legs. "I don't know. Maybe. I wish I knew how to get John started."

"Put his hand between your legs."

Lynn giggled. "I couldn't do that."

"Well, on your boobs, then. Letting him start at the top is almost the same thing. He'll understand the hint."

Lynn tittered hysterically and choked out, "You're right. It's almost the same thing. No. Now stop trying to make me laugh, will you? You're going to make me pee all over myself."

An impish expression crossed Trish's face. "How about falling to your knees, ripping his shorts down, and shoving his junk in your mouth."

"Ewww." Lynn stared at her friend in horror. "Where do you think up all these things?"

"Oh, like you never have," Trish replied, smirking.

"Well, once," Lynn admitted, "but I was worried all the time he'd, you know, in my mouth. He kept complaining about my teeth scratching him, and I had to fight the urge to bite. It wasn't a fun experience for either one of us."

Trish finished rinsing off and dried herself. "You'll figure out a way. If not tonight, then tomorrow. You'll be alone sleeping together for two days."

"You're right," Lynn replied with conviction, toweling herself off and attempting to devise plans in her mind and dismissing each as quickly. "I'll think of something."

"At least, did you bring protection in case he didn't?"

"I tried," Lynn said. "I went to the drug store, but I was too embarrassed to buy any. I never realized there was such an assortment. I pictured myself standing at the checkout counter and people seeing what I was buying, and…" Lynn shuddered. "What if someone said something, asked if I enjoyed that particular brand? Anyway, I finished my period three days ago. I'm safe."

As the two girls put their clothes back on Lynn hear Trish mutter, *"Rookie,"* out of the side of her mouth.

They passed Herbie and Vicki sauntering to the showers. "Any water left for us?" Herbie asked.

"Plenty for you two. Might even be hot," Trish replied. "Did you see the boys? They weren't waiting for us when we finished."

"Already at the site," her brother replied. "I guess you guys took too long. The party has started."

John and Trish's boyfriend sat at the picnic table, cans of beer in front of the two. "Thought you fell in," John said. "What happened to you?"

"We're girls," Lynn retorted, sitting next to him. "We wash more than our hands and face."

"You ready for one?" Trish's boyfriend asked, tossing her a can of beer. "Get it while the ice is still cold."

"Thanks." She popped the top open.

"Lynn?" John made as if to offer her a can.

Do I want to get drunk? What if tonight's the night? I don't want to pass out on him. "Uh, I'd better not," Lynn said. "If I have one, I'll want another." She looked at Trish. "You remember what happened last time I drank too much, at Val's graduation party? I don't want a reoccurrence of the misery I went through."

John asked, intrigued, "And what exactly happened. I never heard this story."

Trish folded her arms on the table and bent forward. "Let's put it this way. I spend an hour in the bathroom kneeling beside Lynn holding her hair out of the toilet. What was coming out wasn't a pretty sight, and talk about the smell." Trish wagged her head. "I think you were still nauseous the day after, weren't you?"

"For two days," Lynn admitted, "and I lost ten pounds. Couldn't keep a thing down. I told my mom I caught one of those twenty-four hour viruses. I never want to experience being sick like that again."

"Oh, I see." John nudged Lynn with his elbow. "Better drink the soda, then. Bathrooms aren't so close and I'm not holding hair while you barf all over the tent, or me, or outside in the bushes. With my luck, I'd step in the gunk. Messy."

"Okay, enough vomit talk. Just the thought is making my stomach upset, and I'm feeling stupid enough as is."

Herbie and Vicki returned and dropped on the bench next to Trish and Rick. "What did we miss?" Herbie asked, taking two cans of beer from the cooler and handing one to the girl.

"Talking about Val's graduation party and what fun we had," Trish said. "You shoulda tagged along. A lot of people you know were there."

"Hey, you reminded me. Did you guys hear about Ron Billings?" Herbie said suddenly.

"Ron Billings?" John said, puzzled. "Who's Ron Billings?" He looked at the others. They stared at Herbie.

"He's in jail for murder."

The light of recognition showed in Trish's face. "I remember him now." She nudged Lynn. "We met him at John's welcome home party." Trish said to John, "Tall guy, played basketball at our high school. Goes to Easton with us."

John nodded slowly. "Yeah, I think I recall his face. Didn't talk to him though. Seen him around campus. He's two years younger than I am and we never played on the same high school teams."

Lynn said, "He was arrested for murder? Oh, gosh, that's terrible. Who'd he murder?"

Herbie bent forward and said eagerly, "Don't know the guy's name, but the way I heard the story, Ron went to a frat party, drank more than he should have, wound up fighting another guy over a girl. Ron goes out to his car. The kid walks out with some friends. Ron throws his ride in reverse and runs the guy over—*twice*. Backed over him and then hit the gas and drove forward."

"Wow." Lynn looked from Herbie, to Trish, to John. "I don't know him, but he didn't act like the sort of person who'd…. What's going to happen now?"

Herbie leaned back and took a long swallow of his beer. "Don't know. What do you call the crime? Vehicular homicide? Premeditated murder? Probably throw him in prison for twenty or thirty years is my guess for killing someone."

"Geez." John ran his fingers through his hair, face pale. "He's what, twenty years old? Twenty-one? When the police let him out of jail he'll be an old man, his whole life over for one stupid mistake." He said shakily, "Don't let me get in a fight with you tonight, Herb. Lynn, take away my car keys. I can't waste the rest of my life sitting in a prison cell." He gazed at Lynn and winked, "I have too much to live for now."

Lynn asked, "You think he'll really be locked away for thirty years?"

Herbie shrugged. "Who knows how the courts work these days? Concurrent sentencing, consecutive sentences. I mean, he did kill the kid, a whole bunch of people saw him. Maybe he'll plead insanity."

"Whatever happens, I wouldn't wish trouble like the one he's in on anyone," John said, full of sincerity. "The only thing I know is I'm happy here hanging with you guys."

"Best years of our lives," Trish said, raising her can of beer. "Life don't get any better than this."

"Big news," Herbie said. "I applied for an internship at this small computer company and was accepted." He raised his can also. "This time next year, I'll be a junior engineer, bringing in the big bucks."

John said with envy, "Lucky you. Now I know who to ask when I need a loan. Congratulations." He reached over the table and shook Herbie's hand.

"No loan yet, my friend," Herbie denied. "Unpaid intern. I work three days a week. Probably have me running for coffee and sweeping the floor, but at least I'll be there so I can impress people."

"You're working for *free*?" Trish said, unable to believe what her brother said. "Don't let Dad hear you say they're not giving you a check. He'll hit the roof and tell you to clean the gutters on the house if you want to work for nothing."

"Which reminds me, buddy," John put in, "I could use help scooping out wet leaves from *my* gutters. Pop's been bugging me for months to dig out the ladder and climb up on the roof."

"Both of you are a riot and a half," Herbie retorted. "You'll see. This place is transforming into the Silicon Valley of the East," Herbie continued. "All sorts of companies moving in. Any luck at all, the company will go public, I'll receive a big chunk of stock cheap, and I'll retire at thirty. I hear identical deals occur all the time."

By the early morning hours, the campers ran out of topics to discuss, drank their fill of beer and soda, and were sick of eating hot dogs and beans. As Lynn and John strolled back to their tent, Lynn notice John walked with a noticeable list in his gait. They crawled into the tent and John placed a sloppy kiss on her cheek as she changed into pajamas, crawled into his sleeping bag and rolling on his side. Soon a gentle snoring filled the tent.

Well, tonight was a bust. Fun evening, but this isn't how I wanted the night to end. Lynn slipped into her bag and pulled herself close to John, spooning him with one arm draped over his waist. She lay there running plans across her mind. *Tomorrow will be the day. How do I break through John's gentlemanly behavior and make sure we do it before the partying starts? How do you seduce a man without him knowing?* Lynn nodded to herself.

I know how.

***

After a late breakfast of eggs and bacon the next morning, the couples parted company, Herbie and Vicki to the stables for horseback riding, Trish and Rick carrying fishing gear and tackle box to see what was in the lake to catch for supper.

Lynn opted to swim first and then canoeing afterwards. John was dubious. "Maybe swimming this afternoon after the lake warms up." He blew his breath in the air producing a puff of steam. "The water is still cold. You'll freeze your backside off."

Lynn stretched, reaching her fingers into the air and arching her back. "Nonsense, the weather is perfect. A quick dip in the water will start our blood flowing. Let me put my suit on." Lynn disappeared into the tent and emerged seconds later in a white bikini. "What do you think?" she asked posing, spinning around slowly so John could see her body from all sides. "I've been afraid to wear it on the beach and have all the people stare at me, but this is the perfect opportunity to show off my itty-bitty bikini."

John understood why she'd been reluctant to wear her suit on a public beach. The two small pieces of material revealed everything while still being legal. Her normally small breasts were pushed up and bulged, while the thong at the bottom disappeared between her cheeks.

Confusion filled John's mind. Lynn was behaving strange, for Lynn, that was. Last night her passion while kissing left him breathless, her squirming and pushing against him erotically as the two lay on their sleeping bags while he pretended to sleep. John's restraint was stretched to the limits. The only thing stopping him from attempting to make love to her was the ever-present memory of Caitlyn screaming for help when he ran his hand up her thigh.

John issued a low wolf whistle and said, "You sure you'll be warm enough in that?"

"I'm bringing a heavy shirt and blanket for afterwards to wrap myself in if I'm cold," Lynn assure him, taking his hand. "C'mon silly, don't be a chicken, let's swim."

The water *was* cold. John stayed in for a few minutes and Lynn not much longer. She ran from the lake blowing hair out of her face and hugging herself. "Oh my, you're right. The water's freezing." Lynn pushed her chest out toward him and commented innocently, "See, the lake made my nipples all pointy."

John looked. She was right. The sheer material of the top showed she was very pointy indeed. He wrapped a towel around his waist so he wouldn't be embarrassed. "Here," he said gruffly, tossing her the red flannel shirt she brought. "Better wrap yourself up good before you catch cold."

"Thanks." Lynn draped the shirt over her shoulders and stepped close to him, placing her arms around his neck and pressing her body hard against his. "I'm still cold," she said. "Rub my back and warm me up."

Even through the thick fabric of the towel, John knew Lynn felt the bulge pressed up against her stomach.

What does Lynn think she's doing? Is this a game she's playing?

He rubbed her back briskly. "Ready for the canoe ride now?"

"Oh, yeah. I've never been in a canoe before, have you?"

"A long while ago. Canoeing merit badge at Boy Scout camp," John said as he kept his attention straight ahead. "I think I still remember how."

While John rented the canoe, Lynn browsed the small shop. She returned holding a brown plastic tube. "Coconut lotion, for later. I don't want us to have a sunburn while we're out on the water." John nodded, paid for lotion and rental, and strolled to the dock searching for the perfect boat. Lynn trailed, tucking the lotion into the elastic of her bikini bottom and carrying the blanket.

John discovered a canoe to his liking, instructed Lynn to sit in the bow and selected a paddle for her. "Now remember, no standing," he coached, "You don't even have to stroke if you don't want to. I'll take care of everything." He held the boat steady while Lynn shimmied in and settled on a seat in the front. John squatted on the stern rest and untethered the canoe. "Here we go," he said as he launched their small craft.

"Oh, this is marvelous," Lynn exclaimed as they glided along. "I feel like a pioneer exploring the new frontier for the first time. Look, little fishies." She pointed into the water where minnows sped above the lake grass. "I see turtles, too," Lynn announced, jabbing a finger at a half-submerged log where a snapping turtle basked in the sunlight. "Not a bad idea," she murmured. "Think I'll catch a tan while we're here." Lynn stretched out facing John, placed her feet on the next seat, legs wide, and took out the suntan lotion. Kicking off her flip-flops, she examined the exposed top of her breasts critically and asked John, "Do you think my chest is red? My breasts feel warm." She squirted lotion on her fingers and massaged her top slowly.

"Uh, yeah," John stammered as he attempted to paddle while watching Lynn spread more cream on her inner thighs and rub the white lotion up and down her legs. "Oh, shoot." The canoe struck a fallen tree, barely visible lurking beneath the green water. The craft teetered wildly as John paddled over the log. "Keep your mind on business, dummy," he muttered.

"Maybe you're tired," Lynn said, waving toward the shore. "I see a beach over there. Let's stop and take a break. I need you to rub lotion on my back anyway."

"Yeah, sure." He paddled to shore, running the canoe up on the sand, and then jumping out and pulling the craft the rest of the way. Lynn spread the blanket on the sand and laid on her stomach.

"Spread the lotion on my back, John," Lynn asked as she snuggled into the blanket on her forearms. "All over."

The sun was well up. John dabbed the white cream onto Lynn, starting at her neck and working toward her hips. He stopped at her exposed cheeks, undecided if he should bypass the firm, soft flesh.

Lynn glanced at him with a smirk. "Don't be a coward. Ain't nothing down there planning to bite you, and I certainly don't want a burn on my bottom."

"I guess not."

The odor of the coconut mingled together and enhanced the womanly scent of Lynn's skin. John felt himself growing hard again as his thumb and fingers slid along Lynn's cheeks and the back of her knees.

"Your hands feel good," Lynn breathed, "so warm and strong."

John struggled, suppressing the urge to lay next to her, sweep Lynn up in his arms, and make love to her, whether she wanted to or not. He found himself leaning forward, his hands caressing her ribs and back.

What am I doing? Wrong. This is wrong. I killed her sister.

He inhaled deeply, and received a nose full of coconut and Lynn's smell. With superhuman strength, he blanked his mind. "Almost noon. We'd better be paddling back and see what the others are up to."

Lynn sighed, rolled over, and sat up, hugging her knees. "I guess so. Whatever."

"Did I say something wrong?" Lynn's tone plainly indicated unhappiness about something.

Lynn stared at her knees. "No." She looked up. "I want to eat lunch, anyway, and then take a siesta. All this fresh air and sun is knocking me out."

No one was at the campsite when Lynn and John arrived. Lynn broke out peanut butter sandwiches and soda for the two of them, and both sat at the picnic table, munching.

"As long as no one's here yet, I think I'll grab my nap," Lynn announced after finishing lunch. "You might as well stretch out and relax, too," she said to John. "Who knows how long we're staying up tonight talking again. Once Trish starts yacking, you can never shut her up."

They crawled into the tent, the inside dark and warm. John lay on his back, Lynn next to him. "Oh, I forgot." Lynn took off her flip-flops, stretched over John to drop her footwear in the corner. At the same time, her warm, hard breasts brushed across his face.

Without thinking, John kissed each one, and then reached up and enfolded Lynn in his arms, drawing her close onto his body. Lynn squirmed down until her lips nestled into the crook of his neck. "You know you've been driving me crazy all day, don't you?" John whispered. Still holding her, he rolled until they lay side by side locked together.

"Making you nuts was the general idea," Lynn breathed softly and nibbled on his ear. She rubbed her naked foot along the inside of his legs and applied her lips to his neck.

John moved his hand up her side, fingers slipping under the top of her bathing suit to cup her breast. Lynn moaned in pleasure, kissing him on the lips and reaching behind herself to undo the tie. She pulled off the top and then the bottom, drawing John on top of her.

All thoughts of the outside world disappeared from John's mind in a blaze of love and lust. This beautiful woman in his arms, so eager and willing, was all he knew.

As they coupled, her hips arching up in desire, passion engulfing him, all thoughts of Caitlyn vanished.

Chapter Ten

The mall bustled, afternoon shoppers eagerly prowling from shop to shop seeking new treasures. Lynn and Trish weaved through the people, glancing in the windows as they strolled the concourse. Trish searched for help wanted signs, looking for a job. The girl industriously checked off names on a pad of businesses she'd already applied to.

"He hasn't said anything yet?" Trish halted before a novelty store, scrutinized the odd items for sale and the shelves beyond through the plate glass window. Trish checked the list, saw the name already scratched off with a scribbled 'on-line' and grumbled under her breath.

Lynn sighed and shook her head. "No. Let's stop a minute and rest. My feet are killing me." She dropped on the corner of a fountain and slipped off her shoe, rubbing her instep and wiggling her toes. "I thought he might ask after graduation last week, or at least mention something in the offhand way he has. John and I were both so relieved the grind was over and we received our diplomas, but...."

"Well, what's he waiting for?" Trish tucked her pad away, took out a compact from her purse and dabbed on lipstick, studying herself in the small mirror. "Do I look pretty enough to hire?"

"You're adorable." Lynn surveyed her friend, dressed in a smart blouse and skirt, from earrings to shoes. "If I owned a business, I'd hire you on the spot and stick you in the window as advertisement." Her eyes stayed on Trish's new black footwear. "I like those, but how can you walk and no fall over?"

"Practice," the girl declared. "Lots of prancing around my room, and pretend interviews in the mirror."

Trish crossed her legs and studied her feet. "I also have a high tolerance for pain and I'm not afraid of heights."

A silence ensued before Lynn ventured to say, "Too bad we have to look for jobs."

"Well, sister, we knew school would end eventually. What do you call this, adulting?"

"I guess I'll have to include Mr. Piggy in finding a job too," Lynn pouted. "He'll be terribly upset about working. He enjoys lying in bed all day." She chuckled. "He *thinks* his job is to sit on my pillows and protect my bed. Certainly wasn't happy when I started dating John. I think he was jealous, but I'll never get rid of him. He's my faithful buddy, always there when I need him."

Trish bit back a remark about Lynn's stuffed toy and returned to the subject of John. "Well, what's he waiting for? Does he need a signed proclamation with your name printed on top?"

"I guess until he finds a job," Lynn said. She scanned the stores on the opposite side of the concourse, searching for any windows displaying help needed signs. "We've talked about marriage, but you know, in a joking sort of way. He's so serious when it comes to responsibility. If he feels he can't support a wife, he's not about to say anything definite. He's old fashioned, thinks the husband has to be the sole breadwinner."

"Not in this day and age, sister, but for Pete's sake, you've been dating for four years. After so long most couple are engaged, or at least talking seriously about marriage. Unless you two want to live together and see how playing house goes. I know you've engaged in making love, and don't deny you two haven't been sneaking around into his room and yours," Trish added when Lynn looked away quickly, giggling. "I bet you and John have investigated every bush on campus."

"Trish, we're two adults, not some sixteen year olds who…"

"Can't he make up his mind? Give him a shove."
Trish grinned wickedly and nudged Lynn with her hip,
almost knocking her friend off the seat into the fountain.
"Propose to him. Maybe he'll figure out you mean
business."

Lynn laughed. "I'd be too embarrassed. Besides,
marriage is a scary step. I don't know if I'm ready yet, and
I know my mother would disown me if I told her John and I
were moving in together without being married first.
Besides, I want to start a career, maybe travel, explore
some of the world I've never seen before. What happens if
I can't find a teaching job around here and have to relocate
out of state? What do John and I do then if he's hired
around here?"

Trish laid a hand on Lynn's arm and said
excitedly, "Let's apply for jobs on a cruise ship. Find us a
love boat and dreamy guys to hang out with and rub our
poor tired feet after work. Sail the seven seas and visit far
off lands. What do you say? I'll sign up if you do."

"I'd love to," Lynn admitted, "but knowing my
luck we'd be in the middle of the ocean and I'd receive a
call for a real job. Do I jump overboard and swim? Tell
them I can't report for an interview for a month? I
submitted five applications for teaching positions. They'd
hire the next person in line. Those jobs are scarce enough to
locate, and a Bachelor's degree doesn't stand up around
here when you're competing against people who have
Masters and teaching experience at private schools."

"True," Trish replied glumly, "and I hear the
owners work the crew twenty-four seven on those ships,
too." She studied the next storefront, an international
woman's apparel shop specializing in sexy lingerie. Trish
rose, took a deep breath, and threw her shoulders back.
"Onward and upward. At least I know about panties and
bras. I've worn both long enough. No sign but asking can't
hurt, right? Should I leave the glasses on and show the

manager my orphan face or—" she took the glasses off and drew the sides of her mouth together in a pucker—"my sexy alluring self?"

"Leave the glasses on," Lynn decided after a pause. "Without them you might find yourself talking to a mannequin. We wouldn't want to give the dummy an impression you're not as bright as it is, right? Besides which, you look like a fish when you do the funny face thing squelching your mouth."

"Quite right." Trish place her glasses back on her face. "The poor little me expression will impress even the hardest employer, and always a good idea to speak to a real person. I'm marching in and filling out an application. Coming with?"

Lynn glanced at the name of the store and ran the company through her mind, trying to remember all the places applied to while waiting for a school spot to open up. "No," she said, "Already did—online, about a month ago. No bites." Lynn didn't mention having Trish for a friend was one thing, working alongside her all day, every day, was quite another. For sure, within a week the manager would fire her or Trish, probably her. "I'll wait here, you go ahead."

"Shop around inside while I'm filling out the application," Trish suggested. "A skimpy pair of black lace panties and matching bra will make John propose fast enough."

Lynn snorted. "First a job so I can afford the prices in there." She added, "Besides, right now shopping for sexy clothing is a waste of time and money. If I make him drool all over me I'd never be able to return the underwear, and John will be too tongue-tied to propose."

"Your loss, you know my suggestions always work—eventually." Trish walked toward the store entrance and called over her shoulder, "Wish me luck."

"Luck," Lynn yelled back.

***

"Good morning, sleepyhead. It's nearly ten o'clock. Are you heading out to job hunt again today?" Mrs. Baker asked John as he wandered into the kitchen dressed in t-shirt and cutoffs. He rubbed his neck, and stood in front of the refrigerator staring blankly at the door. She returned to the kitchen sink full of sudsy water and dirty dishes. "You've complained enough about the time you've spent in school and wanting to work for a change."

John released a yawned. "Been job hunting for the last two weeks," he mumbled, running his fingers through his hair. He fished around in the refrigerator, took out a gallon of milk, found cereal, a spoon, and snatched a bowl from the cupboard. Still half asleep, he stepped over to the table and fixed himself breakfast. "I'm waiting for return calls from the resumes I sent out. Can't do much more than what I've already done unless I find a part time job and quit as soon as I have real work."

His mother finished washing and drying dishes, poured herself a cup of coffee, and took a seat at the table opposite John. "I don't understand why no one's contacted you yet," she said, sipping. "The phonebook is filled with hundreds of accounting firms. Surely one of the companies needs help."

John chewed and swallowed nosily. "I'm being kinda picky right now. Most of those firms headquarter in the city, or are small partnerships with one or two man operations, really only needing help during tax season. I'm looking for a big operation out here in the 'burbs, so I don't have to commute forty miles one way, and I'll still be able to advance up the corporate ladder, if you know what I mean." He took another bite of cereal and mumbled, "Narrows my choices some."

Mrs. Baker placed her cup down. "You're being *too* particular if you ask me. For many years your father—"

The ringing of the phone interrupted her. Mrs. Baker sprang up and answered it. "Hello...? Yes, just a minute, please." She held the receiver out to John and whispered excitedly, "A woman for you, a business."

John snatched the instrument out of her grasp. "This is John Baker.... Yes, I did... Yes, I *can*....Thank you. I'll be there wearing bells and whistles." He hung up the phone, the sides of his mouth lifting. "The firm of Swartz and Cahn wants to interview me today at two o'clock this afternoon. The call could be the one I've been waiting for."

"Fabulous." His mother hugged him tightly. "Are they a good company?"

"Only one of the biggest and best out here," John exclaimed. "I've been told Swartz and Cahn are very selective in the accountants hired, usually don't take on a person unless you have experience working at another firm first."

"Really?"

"Yes, really. The company was top on my dream list, didn't think they'd hand me a second look," he said, a ringing tone in his voice. "But I figured I'd apply anyway for the heck of it. Worse the firm could say is they didn't want me." John saw in his mother's eyes that she was growing as infected with enthusiasm as he was. "If I lock this job up, I'm set for life." John returned his mother's hug. "I gotta tell Dad, he's the one who suggested I apply in the first place. Where is he?"

"Outside, fixing one of the faucets."

John ran outside. He found his father on the side of the house grimly confronting the window to the crawlspace. He looked up at John's approach, issuing a sigh of relief. "Just the man I was hoping for," he said extending a finger toward the window. "I have a mission for you."

The elation flowing through John vanished as suddenly as the feeling appeared. He scowled at the opening. "Turn off the main?"

"Yeah. Two seconds." Mr. Baker held up a wrench and new faucet. "One off, one on. Won't take me more than a minute." He chucked to himself. "Well, maybe two. You know me. I usually don't deal with anything more complicated than a knife and folk." Mr. Baker blinked, and studied the wrench thoughtfully. "How much harder can this be than eating a steak do you think?"

A sickish sensation seized John, but he produced a shallow smile. "No problem, Dad." He dropped to his stomach and wiggled through the opening.

He kept his attention centered on the shut-off, neither glancing left or right as he crawled forward. When he reached the valve, he spun it sharply. "Water's off," he shouted.

His father yelled back, "Stay where you are, I'll have the connection changed in no time flat."

The morning air beneath the house was cool and damp. The faint odor of the undisturbed earth flowed around John as he inhaled deeply. He filled his lungs as he gazed at the cinderblock wall. *Can't smell a thing.*

John, knowing he shouldn't, and against his better judgement, looked toward the corner where Caitlyn was buried. The lump of earth was lower, still higher than the rest of the mounds beneath the house, but blending in among the shadows. He waited for his skin to crawl, heart beat faster, the horror of the past event rushing over him in a wave of guilt.

Nothing.

John was able to survey the grave critically knowing regret but no fear for the first time in seven years.

I'm sorry.

"Switch the water back on. I'm finished," his father shouted.

"Huh? Yeah, okay." John snapped his attention to the job at hand and spun the valve open. "Coming out," he yelled, and crawled back to the window.

"Thanks." Mr. Baker patted his belly. "Your old man doesn't fit anymore. My six-pack has turned into a twenty pound bag of potatoes."

"No problem and you've worked hard to earn your sack of potatoes." John snapped his fingers. "Say, I almost forgot. I came out here to tell you I was called by Swartz and Cahn for a job interview this afternoon at two."

"Yeah?" His father raised his eyebrows in a mark of respect. "Good firm, prestigious. I hope the company hires you."

"Me too," John agreed heartily. "Which reminds me, I gotta take a shower, shave and dress." He dusted off his dirty knees and quipped, "I look like I've been crawling around in the dirt, haven't I." His voice grew serious. "It's a long drive to their office. I don't want to be late for this one. Jobs like this don't waltz along every day."

Mr. Baker nodded his approval. "Always better to be early than late, I always say."

John patted his father on the stomach. "Let's see if this gives me luck."

"Hey, you don't have to rub my belly for luck, buddy. We make our own. You've worked hard these last few years to prove your stuff. Give 'em hell."

Five hours later John returned home, laughing to himself and singing, "I did it. Oh, yeah baby, I did it. Baby, baby, baby." He bust through the front door and commenced a twisting dance on the living room rug.

"Sounds as if someone had a good day." Both his mother and father hurried out of the kitchen, wide smirks on their faces as his parents watched their son perform a spin motion on the balls of his feet as he threw his arms in the air.

"Have me a job," John boasted, too excited to hold still. He stopped dancing and paced around the room, unable to contain his exuberance. "Starting Monday, 30K a year plus full benefits. The company hired me on the spot."

"Tell us what happened," his father urged as he and his wife dropped on the couch. "What did they ask? What did you say?"

John calmed enough to settle next to his parents, but he still rubbed his hands together clasping his palms. "The owner liked me," John said simply as if he still couldn't believe his good luck. "I was interviewed by one of the senior partners, old man Cahn himself. Took me into a back room—you wouldn't believe—big oak wood desk, place looked more like writer's office, books all over, papers in piles, pictures on the wall." John laughed, recalling what Mr. Cahn said. "He asked me about the army, walked to the wall, and pointed to a photograph of him and his buddies in the military. Apparently we were in the same unit, thirty years apart, but…." John stood again and wandered around the living room. "Said I reminded him of himself when he was young—did the exact same thing I'd done, gone into the army and then school. Wanted to know about my medical retirement from the army and said he understood. Also said the firm never hires right out of college, wanted people with hands-on experience in the business world, a CPA, Master's Degree, but he was willing to take a chance on me for old time's sake if I was willing to further my education and certifications." He studied the ceiling. "I'd plan to start back to school eventually anyway. This'll provide the motivation to get off my butt." John stopped walking and said to his parents, "I think I'm going to ask Lynn to marry me."

"*What?*" His parents bent forward and exchanged surprised glances.

"We love each other, been dating for almost four years now." John took a deep breath and stared each of his parents in the eye. "We've even discussed marriage. I didn't want to propose because we were both in school, and who knew what would happen afterwards. Now I have a job and everything is different."

His father leaned back and stretched his legs out, rubbing his chin. "Aren't you jumping the gun, son?" he asked. "What happens if you don't enjoy the job, or the company fires you? What then?"

"We're not getting married tomorrow," John replied, dismissing his father's objections with a flick of his fingers. "Engaged now, maybe in six months we'll tie the knot. Lynn's still waiting to see if she can land a teaching job, but she'll know by the end of the summer when the schools start, and I'll have a handle on this job, and see if I'm staying at the company. One way or the other we'll both be settled in what we're doing. Everything will be fine."

"In any case I suppose we should start preparing for a wedding," Mrs. Baker said, her tone still careful. "Have to tell the relatives, all our friends. This is big news."

John shoved both his hands out, palms forward, and cautioned his parents, "Please, don't say anything to anyone yet. I want this to be a surprise. I still have to buy an engagement ring and figure out the right time to ask her. When I do, I want everything to be perfect so Lynn will always remember."

***

Saturday night Lynn and John attended a play on campus. A remake of *Romeo and Juliet*. Strolling through the parking lot, John recalled the first play Lynn and he attended four years previously, and wondered where did the time go? How quickly events changed; high school, army, college. He was hired for a job and asking Lynn to marry him. Dread and anticipation locked together in his chest, each battling for supremacy and neither winning the battle. He peeked sideways out of the corner of his eye, catching Lynn's profile as she smiled and waved at a few people they knew.

Lynn loved him—he was sure she did, wanted to stay beside him always. She'd told him so many times, but what if she changed her mind at the last minute and said no?

John felt inside his coat pocket for the third time since he'd left his house, assuring himself the engagement ring he'd purchased this morning was still there. The cost nearly wiped out his savings, but the saleswoman swore diamonds were a great investment, always rose in value, good times or bad. More important, this was the ring he'd seen Lynn eyeing longingly one day when he, Trish and Lynn were out shopping and stopped at the jewelry store to browse. He remembered Lynn whispering to Trish in awe, "Now this is the kind of ring I've always dreamed of wearing on my finger. I wonder who could ever afford to buy a rock as big." Lynn stuck her nose so close to the glass case a mark of fog developed on the surface.

Trish remarked, "Keep dreaming, sister, or marry a millionaire. We're too old to start jewelry heists."

John was overwhelmed when the saleswoman took the ring out of the case and handed the large, glittery band to him. As he rolled the piece of jewelry in his fingers, the facets flashed, displaying brilliant colors. The occasional beams of light shooting out from within the gem mesmerized him. He held the circle up close to his face examining the workmanship more intently. Even if the big stone in the middle did not appreciate in worth, wasn't all the salesperson claimed the gems would be, he knew this was the ring to make all of Lynn's dreams real.

Being rich would happen later. Before he attempted to become a senior partner in the firm, Lynn must say yes. Otherwise what good would it do owning an engagement ring and have no one to give the expensive band to?

"Remember the first time we attended a show here?" he said to her as they mounted the steps to the auditorium. "Great play, wasn't it? Sometimes I still hum the theme song to myself."

"Yeah, I hope this one is as good," Lynn replied. She checked the crowd in the large room. "Not a lot of people here yet."

"School's over," John reminded her. "Summer courses only. Let's take seats in the back. Higher up, we have a better view and won't be disturbed." He dragged her into the middle of the very last row.

"Is this a plot to make out with me if the show's boring?" Lynn asked darkly as she took a seat and snuggled to John.

He draped his arm around her shoulder and squeezed her arm lightly. "Maybe, now hush." The lights flickered three times. "The show is about to start."

By the third act, Lynn was crying softly, her head resting on John's chest. "So beautiful. So tragic," she whispered, fumbling in her purse to grab a fistful of tissues.

John reached into his pocket, took out the ring, and held her hand in his. "So are you," he breathed into her hair as he slipped the ring onto her finger. "Will you marry me?"

Lynn froze against him, and then jerked away and studied the ring on her hand in the dim light. Lynn turned and gazed back at him, arms wrapping around John's neck as her lips sought his. After a long minute, she whispered back. "Yes."

Chapter Eleven

John barely heard the account representative talking as the third bank in a row declined him a mortgage. Not really refused a loan. No, but the down payment on a decent house in this neighborhood was out of his reach, and the interest rate was astronomical. He'd thought this part of marriage was simple, no more difficult than shopping for a new vehicle and applying for a car loan. He worked at a good job, had a steady income and money arriving monthly from his VA disability retirement, and Lynn landed a job as a substitute teacher this fall with the local school district.

The representative sitting across from him kept shaking her head and appeared sorry she was unable to help. "I know how you feel," the woman said, shuffling John's application into a pile and pushing the stack back to him. "We have young couples walking in here every day in the exact same predicament you find yourself. The problem is sad. The lending institutes have tightened their regulations, though, after the banking crisis, you must understand. You have no work history with your present employer. We require a minimum of two years' continuous employment, or a down payment of at least twenty percent, and let's face the facts, your bank account won't cover half of what you need. No stocks. No bonds. Neither you nor your wife have any credit history."

"I was in the military. I know the time I was in the army counts toward my credit. I bought stuff and paid everything off."

"Yes," the woman agreed, "but your military service was over four years ago and…"

"I was in college afterwards." *These people don't give you a break. How do banks expect me to have a credit history when they won't let me buy anything? This is stupidity squared—no, cubed. What am I supposed to tell Lynn? After we're married we have to live in a cardboard box? What a great provider I am.*

"I understand you were attending school during the time. We need current credit. Now, if there's a friend, or family member, who'd lend you the money and cosign the loan with you?" John shook his head. He could borrow, but not in the amount he'd need. The woman saw his expression. "Return in a year, save some more money, perhaps find a part-time job, and I'm sure we can work out an agreement then. Okay?"

John mumbled a reply and stepped into the bright sunshine outside the bank. *Save money? How?* Between wedding expenses and the cost of the reception, rings and honeymoon, the zeros he'd accumulated so prudently over the years were systematically being transferred to blue slips of paper from his checkbook, carefully signed on the bottom, and handed over to Lynn on a regular basis. True, she'd saved for her big day, so did Lynn's mother, but not nearly enough for the type of extravaganza John was determined for Lynn to have if she wished a grand wedding and planned for all her life.

Work a part-time job? He was already studying night and day for his CPA exam, with the assurance from the rest of the members of the firm he would fail at least one part of four parts and have to study and retake the examination again. Old man Cahn was hinting he expected John to start working on his MBA. How did this woman imagine he'd fit a second job into the workload already staring him in the face?

Trish, as maid-of-honor, pledged to take care of all the wedding details and honeymoon plans. John agreed readily, but as time wore on, and the girls appeared to accomplished nothing except long sessions huddled in front of the computer with giggles and whispering, he began to have his misgivings. John finally decided it was the anticipation and searching for just the right item that was as much fun for the two as the actual wedding itself.

The details, however, and the constant strain of trying to buy a place to live, were driving John crazy. This refusal added to the face-slap he did every night, and the silent groan he made sure Lynn never heard as he listened to Lynn and Trish planning.

Book a hall how many months in advance? With the economy as slow as it was, John thought he could write a check and rent one the next day. How long did it take to buy a wedding dress? He always entered a store, tried on a suit, and walked out in an hour after alterations. Flowers? Place settings? *More flowers?* Didn't the places supply these things? The halls were asking for enough money. At least they could throw in a couple bouquets of roses. Cruise? Reservations? Airfare? Where did all the details stop?

Lynn explained the whole process to him, and insisted she needed none of these extras. They'd drive over to the town hall, buy a license, and be done with the headaches if John wished.

John didn't, but he was still confused when Trish asked about the type of wedding goodie bags Lynn should buy and what to put inside. "All the same thing, or mix them up?" Lynn put her finger to her lips, and she and Trish vanished behind the computer in his room. An hour later John discovered himself passing over his ATM card number to order a gross of drawstring favor bags.

As he left the bank parking lot and stopped for a light, another thought crossed John's mind, one plaguing him since he'd proposed to Lynn. What about Caitlyn?

True, his presence wasn't necessary to shut off the water to the whole house very often. Most of the connections possessed individual valves. His father knew he was a phone call away if crawling under the house was essential, and even if a stranger were hired to do the work the chances were they'd never notice, never see, what was buried in the dark corner.

Could he take the chance, though? The implications of discovery, the ruin of his new life, if he moved away from the house, weighed on his mind. What would happen if someone stumbled across his crime?

John drove back to work, the problems swirling around in his brain, mini tornados making him dizzy inside. He arrived at his office, sat at his desk, and shuffled through papers until he located an estate account he was working on. A big step, he admitted to himself. He was moving up toward the junior partnership he was hoping for in the future. One of his coworkers passed his cubicle, peeked over the divider at the papers he held. When the man saw what John worked on he gave the newest employee of Swartz and Cahn a thumbs-up and a wink. John smiled back. This was better than punching in numbers for income taxes all day. He returned to the job at hand.

The figures blurred in his vision, refusing to allow him to concentrate.

***

"I like the shorter dress better," Trish said. She cocked her head, critically examining Lynn on the pedestal she posed on, stretched out her legs before her, and dropped one ankle over the other, bobbing a foot and continuing to scrutinize her best friend.

Lynn stood on the raised platform, a three-piece mirror behind her, and revolved slowly in the white wedding dress she contemplated buying. "You think so? I kinda like this one. Old fashioned, elegant." Lynn spun again, the hem of the dress causing a hissing on the floor as the silk brushed the pedestal.

Trish jerked her head in the negative. "Listen, girlfriend, by the time you enter the church and walk up the isle the hem will be black. Even if you carry the dress and change in the waiting room, the gown will still be filthy by the time you make the reception. Trust me on this one. Mamma knows best."

"Are you sure?" Lynn asked, distressed, glancing at the bottom of the white gown.

Trish smiled. "Now if you want to take a walk to my shop, I'm assistant manager now. Twenty percent off and we'll buy you a wedding dress that'll knock their eyeballs out."

Lynn paused. "You sell wedding dresses? I thought the line was lingerie and sexy stuff. When did this happen?"

Trish cleared her throat. "Started this year, and you'd be surprised. 'Hot Brides' it's called. We carry one, uh, a white frilly body suit, including a matching lace petticoat. Comes down to the middle of your thighs." Trish made a cutting motion between her knees and hips. "Garter belt and white stockings thrown in free if you purchase the rest."

Lynn snickered. "What about the dress?"

"That *is* the dress."

Lynn's eyes bulged. "You're kidding me," she gasped at last.

Trish raised her arm up, palm out, snickering. "I swear. I sold one last week. The company even has us passing out a complementary box of garters with naughty expressions written on the outside. You can chuck fistfuls to the guests at the reception. Here..." Trish rifled through her pocketbook, "I carry one to show people." She tossed the band to Lynn.

"'You've tried the rest, now try the best?'" Lynn's mouth opened and closed shut soundlessly, at a loss for words. Finally, she blurted out, "What am I supposed to be, a pizza?"

Trish shrugged. "People buy 'em. Wear the dress and you'll get more than a kiss from John at the altar. I bet couples have done exactly the same thing before."

"Well, not me and John."

Trish stood. "In that case, let's blow this joint. We still have more places to check. We can always return if you can't find anything decent."

Lynn changed into her street clothes and assured the saleswoman she'd return later. *Maybe. A lot more stores to see before I locate the perfect dress for me.* Lynn and Trish strolled into the concourse of the mall and Lynn said, "Don't you have to go back to work?" as the girls passed the store where Trish was employed.

The girl rose on her toes, peered in the window, waved, and kept on walking, swinging her handbag. "Hadta open this morning, start the place running, check inventory, and of course, two delivery guys showed up and I had to help unload and put the clothes on the racks." Trish took a deep breath. "All before I opened the store. The manager is letting me have the rest of the day off since I told her I was shopping for my BFF's wedding dress. Middle of the week, anyway. We're slow until Friday."

Lynn and Trish hit the end of the mall with the big pane glass windows of an international department store confronting the two. "Wanna go in and look around? I've never checked the wedding dresses, but I'm sure they have marriage apparel," Trish said. "If nothing else we can sort through the housewares, see what you like, or whatever else you think you'll need after the wedding."

"I don't believe right now," Lynn replied. "I'm registered at this store already and besides, I'm hungry. Let's grab some food and head downtown and swing by the boutiques. Might be more expensive, but the selection will be better and I want this dress to be right. I only plan on getting married once."

The girls stopped at the food court and ordered hamburgers and fries, discussing plans for the upcoming event.

"We still have to make reservations for our honeymoon," Lynn said, munching a fry. She sucked on her fingertips and then bobbed her hand up and down as if spinning a yoyo, watching mesmerized as the heavy ring on her finger sparkled in the light of the overheads.

Trish viewed her friend, envy and a hint of jealously passing over her features. "One day," she muttered to Lynn, "some guy will slip me one of those."

Lynn read the expression on her friend's face and hastily dropped the hand, picking up another fry. "I'm sure your dream man will ride along any day now," she said quickly. "I was lucky mine lived next-door to me, that's all."

"Never happen," Trish retorted. "Always the bridesmaid, never the bride."

"Maid-of-honor," Lynn corrected. "My bestest friend."

"Which reminds me, have you decided where you want to go on your honeymoon?" Trish asked as she sipped her soda. "When you do, let me know, I'll make all the arrangements, you two have enough to worry about."

"We know we want a cruise," Lynn replied, "but don't know where yet. John has a passport, but I still have to get mine. We've researched and there's so many ships sailing everywhere. I'm thinking the Caribbean, but even so, I'm not sure which islands I want to see, or Mexico. I even read about one traveling through the Panama Canal and up the Pacific coast to California and then up to Alaska. John's no help, of course. A lot of these places he's seen when he was in the army." Lynn dipped a fry in her ketchup, hardly able to keep the amusement out of her voice. "He's such a dear, though. Says 'Wherever you want to go is fine with me'. I think he's spent more money on this wedding than my mother and I combined."

"Any luck on locating a place to live? You said you were hoping to buy."

"Negative on that score, too." Lynn's tone was frustrated. "John's been checking banks on his lunch hour for what type of mortgage we can afford on our salaries, but no luck so far. I'm sure we'll find one to give us the loan we need, but I haven't talked to him this afternoon, however." She smiled mysteriously and sighed. "Who knows? Today might be the day and we'll have a mortgage and wedding dress together." Lynn took a bite of her burger, chewed thoughtfully, and swallowed. "Maybe we'll wind up living in his car. I don't care, we're young and in love. As long as we're together, what does any of it matter?"

"Young and in love don't pay the bills, honey," Trish said. "Better start searching for apartments, talking over backup plans, or buying a bigger car."

Lynn finished eating her burger. "It'll all work out," she said, waving in dismissal. "A place to live once we're married is in the future anyway. Right now I'm concerned by more pressing problems, like what am I going to wear for the wedding?" She stood. "C'mon. Let's take a ride downtown and see what we can find. Otherwise, I might discover myself half naked dressed in your bodysuit and garter belt."

***

"What do you mean, we can't afford a mortgage?" Lynn shoved her coffee cup aside, and hunched over the papers John set before her. She glared at the printouts, and then at John, and back to the papers again. They'd taken seats in a private booth at the diner to have a quiet breakfast and strategize about their upcoming plans. Lynn studied a form containing a long column of numbers printed on the front, frowned, and scooped up another with the same results.

John's lips drooped, brow furrowing, frustration tightening the muscles around his neck. "I'm as unhappy about the answers as you are, hon, but look." He dug four papers out of the pile and laid each in front of her, jabbing his index finger at the bottom of the sheets where a number was circled in red. "This is what our final payment will be, not including property tax, and homeowner's insurance. You know how much we'll be bringing in each month. I have the numbers memorized. We've talked about salaries enough. This is what the interest rate is." He stopped talking and let the numbers speak for themselves.

"This is ridiculous," Lynn sputtered, first glancing at the bottom line of each paper John touched, and then at John himself. "How do they think people can buy houses in this neighborhood when the banks aren't willing to lend you the money?" Lynn stared at the documents, mouth working wordlessly as she added. "Are you sure these figures are right? I can't believe the mortgage departments haven't made a mistake somewhere along the line."

Lynn's bitter words hurt John more than the fact they couldn't afford the home they wanted. "I'm an accountant," he said simply. "I'm sure the numbers are correct." He brushed the rest of the papers out of the way and took her hand in his. "We can, maybe, buy one of those cheese box houses on the other side of town, or rent. I can't think of any other option right now." He fell silent, watching her expression. *Give her a minute. Let her calm down. We can work this out somehow.*

Lynn stared blankly at him and took her hand back, fingers drumming on the table. John added reluctantly, "I hate to rent, though. No equity and we'll never be able to save up enough to buy a nice home around here."

"Renting isn't bad," Lynn commented. "Until my mom moved here to the suburbs, I never lived in a house, neither did my parents. I've seen some nice apartment buildings in town. Never been in one, but we can always look and see what's inside."

John laughed cynically. "The ones you're thinking about are as expensive to rent as paying a mortgage would be, maybe more."

"Oh. Yeah, I guess you're right." Her nails beat harder on the tabletop as she continued to scrutinize the documents with eyes half-closed.

His fingers banged also. "Any suggestions? I've racked my brain until I have a headache."

The side of Lynn's mouth wrinkled up as she shifted her mind into high gear, concentrating on her coffee cup, and some of the tension filling John's body left. He was not alone. Working as partners, they would push through this problem together and reach a solution agreeable to both. He still didn't know how he'd solve his other dilemma.

Lynn's fingers stopped moving. She made a fist and rapped her knuckles on the table blurting out, "We'll move in with my mother."

"You're not serious, are you?"

"Of course I am," Lynn said in a rush. "This is the perfect solution and fixes everything for the time being. Don't you see, I'm sure Mom wouldn't mind, or make us pay rent, but we can help buy the groceries since we'll be eating most of the food anyway, maintenance too, I suppose. Maybe give her something extra so we don't feel like we're mooching. I don't like the idea of leaving her all alone in the house by herself in the first place. Mom's not as young as she used to be."

John cringed. The two of them living in Lynn's tiny room, hardly big enough for herself. The shrine for the sister across the hall, boxes still waiting for the dead girl to

unpack, and Lynn's mother rattling on all day about
Caitlyn, saying, "Wait until you meet my daughter," and
"What a wonderful girl she is." What would happen if Mrs.
Brennen asked him to tag along on one of her daily trips
and hand out flyers? Blandly agree, smile as if he were a
ghoul and stand next to her in a store, knowing Caitlyn
would never return, or refuse those pleading eyes and
happy smile?

Lynn's idea was perfect, but wrong in every detail.
He desperately tried to think up another idea before the
situation was too late and he must agree or devise a better
suggestion. If he couldn't, he'd be pitched into a living hell.

"I have a better answer."

He'd searched for the ideal compromise and found
one. John didn't know why he hadn't thought of this
before, and wouldn't have unless Lynn didn't suggested the
notion first. Her idea solved the housing problem and
eliminated his worries and fears at the same time. "Tell you
what," John said as he banged a fist on the table as
emphatically as Lynn did. "We move in with *my* parents.
You'll have to admit, we'll have a lot more living space
than in your piano box-sized bedroom. We'll have the
whole upstairs for ourselves. Private entrance, bathroom
and shower. We can change the spare bedroom into a living
room if you want, same as a real apartment." John warmed
up to the idea. The more he talked, the better the idea
sounded. "You'll still be next door to your mother anytime
you want to visit or check up on her. I mean, she's over at
my house two-three times a week anyway talking to my
mom, right? What do you say?" He waited eagerly for her
reply.

Lynn hesitated. John could tell what was running
through her mind. Sharing living space with her mother
was one thing, but his mother? And after they were
married, her mother-in-law? His folks and Lynn liked each

other, enjoyed each other's company, but living together might be different.

"Well, what are we doing about the cooking arrangements? I mean, I don't want your mom thinking she has to wait on me or anything," Lynn hedged.

"No problem," John replied with a chuckle. "Worse case, I already have a small refrigerator up there. We'll pick up a microwave, hot plate, and a toaster oven. Coffee pot for the morning, and you'll never have to see them if you don't want to."

"For how long, do you think?" Lynn asked at last after mulling over his compromise.

"Dunno," John admitted. "The company is placing me on bigger accounts every day. Important clients mean promotions, more money eventually. One of the biggest reasons we're refused a mortgage is no job history. A year, maybe two or three and it won't be an issue. If you're called to teach full time," he paused, considering, "the finances will be even better. We should be in good shape, especially after we have the honeymoon over, all this wedding spending is behind us and we make a strict budget to live by."

John heard little rat-a-tap-taps on the tabletop as Lynn drummed her nails again, but this time slower, a faraway look as she speculated about the future. "Sure, but do you think your parents will go for the idea? Your father keeps joking he's glad they're finally getting rid of you."

"You know my dad," John scoffed. "All I have to do is tell Pop he's gaining a pretty girl and that'll convince him us living in my room is a good idea. My parents always planned to rent out the upstairs after I moved out, anyway. This will be the perfect solution for both of us. We save a couple of bucks; my parents make a little. Win-win. Everybody's happy, and at least Mom and Dad have someone they know and trust living in the apartment."

All John's headaches vanished into oblivion. Lynn and he had a place to live until they saved enough money, Lynn was close to her mother without him having to deal with the woman, and most important, he'd protected the secret of Caitlyn's disappearance for a few more years.

Lynn's phone rang, a top ten love song she'd placed on it a week ago. "Mom...? Oh. My. God....Yeah, I'll be right back." Lynn shoved the phone in her pocket, face pale, and body trembling.

"Was that your mom on the phone? What's the matter?"

"The police have found Caitlyn."

Chapter Twelve

Lynn stood, paralyzed, regarding the far wall with a blank stare. "That was my mom on the phone. She needs me to come home right away."

Terror raced through John. "Where did the police find your sister? How? I don't understand…." The intensity of his voice was lost on Lynn. The shock on his face unnoticed. He sat frozen at the table, not moving, in petrified dread of what was happening. *How could the police have located the body? No one has a reason to be searching under the house. I woulda known. This can't be true.*

Lynn burst into motion and snatched her purse off the table, running for the door of the diner. Without waiting to see if John followed, she called over her shoulder, "Some place in Utah. The police discovered a body. My mother was all broken up. Could hardly understand a word she said. We have to go." Lynn kept moving, disappearing out the door.

John leaped up from his seat and strode after her as the two hurried to his car. "Utah?" The fear inside him morphed into confusion. "What would the cops be doing way out there hunting for your sister? A body?" With surprising insight and relief, he realized the police found the wrong person, but his understanding still didn't explain why the authorities were searching in the mountains of the west. Could the hunt for Caitlyn have radiated so far? He'd thought the investigation was halted years ago when the police were unable to turn up any leads.

"I don't know." Lynn rubbed her forehead as she and John jumped into the car. She hunched over in the seat, attempting by will alone to start the car and make the vehicle move faster. "Just drive and hurry."

John pushed on the gas pedal, disregarding speed signs as he weaved in and out of traffic. All the while in his mind's eye, he pictured the mound of earth, police, and flashing lights.

Mrs. Brennen rested in her chair, huddled by the phone on the table, barely glancing up as they entered the house. John saw she'd been crying, her eyes red, a box of tissue beside her, more crumbled up haphazardly on the floor. Lynn raced to her mother and threw her arms around her neck. "Mom, what happened?"

"Lynn. The police, an officer called. I don't know..." Mrs. Brennen stammered in a quivering voice. She gulped and continued, "The man said he'd call back as soon as the police department learned more. A person found a body, out west somewhere, Utah, I think the officer said..." She stopped, rubbed her palm into her forehead, unable to continue.

John hurried to the kitchen window. He stared passed the backyard into the breezeway of his house, still on edge, to assure himself no police waited to arrest him. Not a soul was in sight. The house was quiet.

Of course, this is all a mistake. Why was I so frightened?

"John, help me. Mom's fainted."

"Huh?" he swung around. Lynn bent over, barely supporting her mother who slumped in her chair, eyes closed.

He rushed forward as Lynn fell to her knees under the weight of Mrs. Brennen. *Oh, God, not another Caitlyn.*

"I've got her, Lynn," John said as he dropped to his knees also and held the woman up. He placed his shoulder under her chest, pushing Mrs. Brennen upright in the chair, and held her arms so she wouldn't fall headfirst to the floor. "Grab me some cold water and a cloth," he ordered. John studied the shallow rising and falling of the woman's chest with relief. "I think she'll be okay."

Lynn hurried into the kitchen returning a moment later carrying a bowl and towel. "You hold, I'll wipe, maybe the cold water will revive her," she said. "If not, we have to call an ambulance." Lynn soaked the cloth, wrung it out, and dabbed anxiously at her mother's face.

John watched closely and saw Mrs. Brennen take a long, shuddering breath.

She's alive.

Lynn continued to mop her mother's cheeks and forehead until the woman's blouse was sopped with water. "Lynn, enough. We don't want to drown her," John said. "Hang on. I'm going to move her to the couch." He scooped up Mrs. Brennen underneath her armpits and knees, lifting her gently and carefully carrying her over to the sofa. He laid her down and Lynn stuffed a pillow under the back of her head.

Mrs. Brennen's eyelids fluttered open. "Where—where am I?" Her head twisted, staring at her daughter. "What happened? How did I get over here?"

"You fainted, Mom," Lynn said. "Are you feeling better now?"

"I think, yes, I'm okay." The woman attempted to sit up.

Lynn pushed her down gently. "You'd better rest for a moment. I don't want you fainting again on us. John and I are here, we'll take care of everything."

The phone rang. Lynn sprang up. "Stay right where you are, Mom. I'll answer it," Lynn said as her mother tried to rise off the couch. Lynn snatched the instrument and Mrs. Brennen sank back on the sofa watching anxiously. "Hello...? No, this is her daughter. My mother's resting. Please, tell me what's going on...? Uh-huh, uh-huh, uh-huh. Yes, I understand..." Lynn nodded her head vigorously. Mrs. Brennen watched her daughter's face. John hovered over both, attempting to keep an eye on Mrs. Brennen in case the woman fainted again, while trying to listen in on the phone call. "No, of course not," Lynn said, "we'll be here....Yes. Thank you." She hung up the phone.

"What did they say?" John asked. Curiosity filled him. What connection could a body in Utah possibly have concerning Caitlyn? All that mattered was the police made a mistake and the cops weren't sitting on his doorstep waiting to arrest him.

Lynn took a deep breath, dropped onto the arm of the couch and hugged her mother. "Apparently the police discovered a body on a farm in Utah in a shallow grave," she said. "A farmer saw the corner of a plastic bag sticking out of the earth while he was plowing his field. He stopped and dug the sack up, curious to see what was inside. He found the remains of a girl."

Mrs. Brennen released a deep breath, her eyes filling with tears.

Lynn squeezed her mother's shoulder and continued. "The body was badly decomposed, but matched the general description of Caitlyn. When the authorities searched the remains, the police discovered a crumbled stub in her pocket from the bus station out here. The ticket is what led the cops to believe the body might be Caitlyn. The Utah authorities called our police and they called Mom." She said to John, "Mom calls the station every morning for updates. I guess one of the officers became too excited and notified her before the Utah authorities were sure. The man I talked to on the phone said the investigators are still trying to ascertain who the corpse is. He said they'd call back as soon as a positive identification is made. They're doing an autopsy on the remains right now."

"My baby can't be dead," Mrs. Brennen whispered. Drops of moisture leaked from her eyes as the old woman stared into Lynn's face. "Caitlyn's not dead, is she?"

"Of course not, Mom." Lynn hugged her mother tightly. "The police aren't even sure yet." She said to John, "Tell her."

John patted Mrs. Brennen clumsily on the back while trying to think of something to say. "Uh, of course the girl isn't Caitlyn, Mrs. Brennen—Mom. What would your daughter be doing in Utah, right? And on a bus?" He said to Lynn, "You don't know anyone in Utah, right?"

Lynn shook her head in the negative. "No, of course not. I don't think I even know anyone who knows anybody from Utah."

"You see?" John tried to act as confident as possible. "You and Lynn keep telling me what a wonderful girl she wa—is. Who would hate Caitlyn enough to kill her and bury the body out in the middle of nowhere? Impossible."

"The police said…"

"Police make mistakes too," John replied, nodding to her. He remained upbeat. "How many times have you seen on the news a person is released from prison because the police arrested the wrong man? The officer who called said himself the investigators weren't sure." He added knowingly, "I can guarantee you, when this is all over and finished, the police will apologize for the inconvenience and say the phone call was all a bad mistake. Whoever the police discovered out there isn't your daughter."

Mrs. Brennen said softly, "I'm sure you're right. I don't know why I'm so upset." She dabbed at her eyes and lapsed into silence.

Lynn whispered into John's ear, "Thank you," and stroked the back of his hair.

John took her fingers and kissed her hand.

Lynn and John settled back on the sofa. Mrs. Brennen resumed her seat by the table. No one said a word. All three stared at the phone, waiting.

The minutes dragged by, turning into an hour. When the phone rang again, Mrs. Brennen picked it up. "Yes...? Oh, thank goodness....Do the police know...? Oh, I see. Well, when they learn, tell her parents I'm sorry. Thank you for notifying me anyway. I appreciate the call." She hung up the receiver, breathing hard. "That was the police again on the phone. The body the authorities discovered in Utah wasn't Caitlyn." The old woman wobbled in her chair and recovered.

"Mom, are you okay?" Lynn asked, concern in her voice. She tried to smile and said, "You're not about to zonk out on us again, are you? You handed us quite a scare, you know."

"I'm alright, honey. Tired," she said. "The waiting and suspense, you know after all these years, and imagining my baby was gone." Mrs. Brennen released a yawn and rose unsteadily to her feet. "I think I'll take a sleeping pill and lay down for a while. I'll be fine. Don't worry about me."

Lynn said to John, "Why don't you go back to your house and I'll meet you over there, Okay? I won't be long."

"Yeah, sure." He said to Mrs. Brennen. "See, I told you everything would be fine. Take care of yourself." A thought struck him. "How did the police know the body wasn't Caitlyn? Did anyone say?"

Lynn replied, "Mom sent the police dental records after my sister disappeared, in case," her attention shifted to her mother, "you know." She helped her mother down the hall to her bedroom. "C'mon Mom, let's tuck you into bed and get you comfortable."

John walked back to his house, hurried upstairs to his room and stood wringing his hands, breathing a sigh of relief.

Doubts emerged in his mind. He'd never thought of dental records. What if the police discovered the body one day? The call from Utah, and the quick response from the cops here, indicated the search was still very much alive, no matter how many years passed. Should he sneak into the crawlspace, dig up Caitlyn and smash out the teeth from the skull? Cut off her head? He was thinking crazy, and horrified at the idea he might one day have to mutilate the corpse, but all his old fears returned in a flash. His flesh crawled at the mere thought of touching the remains and gazing on the corroded features of what was once a beautiful girl.

John dismissed the idea. No one located the body, no one would, ever, but misgivings about marrying Lynn sprang up in his mind again. This wouldn't be the last time a false rumor would erupt around her sister. Could he live among the drama of her disappearance the rest of his life? The reminder of what he'd done? Mrs. Brennen's constant search for her dead daughter was bad enough, but what if the old lady died of a heart attack or a stroke if she received another call from the police? Would it be possible for him to comfort Lynn and not confess his crime when he knew he was the cause of her family's grief?

John's head jerked up as the wail of a siren came down the street, stopped by Lynn's house. He raced to her home, vaulting over the fence in his haste, as emergency technicians wheeled a stretcher up to the front door. Lynn stood waiting while waving the people forward.

"What's the matter?" John gasped as he tripped over his feet following the stretcher into the house.

Mrs. Brennen sat on the couch again, pale, gasping for breath. The EMTs fitted an oxygen mask on her face and helped the woman onto the litter.

"As soon as you left, Mom started complaining she couldn't breathe," Lynn said, watching her mother anxiously. "I didn't know what else to do so I called nine-one-one."

"Right choice," John said as Lynn and he danced out of the way of the stretcher. "You ride in the ambulance; I'll drive behind you to the hospital."

John and Lynn stood in the examination room by Lynn's mom while nurses attached monitors to Mrs. Brennen. After a half an hour of asking and answering questions, John's guilt drove him out into the waiting area, where he paced until Lynn waved him to the exam door. "Mom says for you to go home. She's sorry for the trouble she's putting you through."

"Is your mom being ridiculous? I'm staying as long as you do."

How can this woman think like that? I'm the one who drove her into this place.

Hours later, the doctors admitted Mrs. Brennen to the hospital. The emergency room physician explained to Lynn and John, "Nothing serious. Panic attack and stress mostly, but we want to keep her under observation for tonight just to be sure. Your mother should be able to go home tomorrow morning."

"Mom's okay, though?" Lynn checked her mother out of the corner of her eye. Mrs. Brennen breathed normally, sleeping.

"Blood pressure is high, but after a good night's rest, I'm sure she will return to normal," The doctor assured her. "Best thing now is to let her sleep and stop back tomorrow early."

"Doctor's right, Lynn." John placed his arm gently around her. "I'll take you home and we'll rescue her first thing in the morning when she wakes up."

Guilt plagued John as they drove to her house. *My fault, all mine. If I hadn't... First the daughter, and now I almost killed the mother.*

"Drop me off at my place," Lynn said. "I want to make sure everything is shut off and the doors are locked."

John left Lynn at her doorstep, drove to his house and sat in his room thinking. He resumed worrying whether he possessed the right to marry Lynn, his doubts magnified by the hospitalization of her mother. He heard a light tap on his door and Lynn entered. "You have everything secure?" he asked as she dropped beside him on the bed.

"Yeah. Mom would have a fit if I left the doors unlocked. Do you think your parents would mind me sleeping on the couch downstairs tonight? I don't want to start my mother worrying again tomorrow if she learned I stayed in the house all by myself."

"Of course. I'm sure my mom and dad wouldn't mind. You're family now, right?" John nestled close beside her, his remorse and misgivings growing in his mind. To distract himself he asked, "Lucky the cops were able to identify the body so fast. Where'd your mother get the dental records from, anyway?" he said out of curiosity. "Did the police ask for the information along with the pictures when your sister first went missing?"

Lynn's mind still revolved around her mother. "What? Oh, uh, you remember. My father was a dentist." She laughed. "If it's one thing Cat and I had growing up were plenty of checkups, plenty of x-rays, and plenty of records. Mom kept a file at the house and hauled everything to the station." Lynn lifted her lips in a broad smile revealing her gums and teeth. "See, gleaming white and straight. Never a filling or cavity."

You are the most adorable person I've ever met, but I don't know if I can continue to put myself through this and marry you.

"Do you think we should postpone the wedding for a while?" John asked, the fear solidifying in his mind. "I mean, your mom with all the shock of thinking Caitlyn's dead and still not knowing afterwards. Now she's in the hospital and who knows if she'll have a relapse, and then the excitement of the wedding right after. We could postpone a month or two, put the ceremony off until we're sure everything is all right. Wait and guarantee there aren't any more phone calls..."

"Are you kidding?" Lynn said. She poked John in the ribs with a finger, and then draped her arms around his neck, giving him a kiss on the cheek. "No way. By the time the wedding rolls around Mom will be fine. The doctors said so. I'm not about to let you sneak out on me now, John Baker. It took me too long to track you down and catch you."

John returned her kiss, hugging her fiercely to his chest.

Don't let the memory of Caitlyn haunt me for the rest of my life. I love Lynn so much. I want this to happen between us. No more death. Please let this work.

***

A warm sun shone on the cruise ship sailing under clear blue skies, on a smooth sea toward Mexico. A balmy tropical breeze wafted along the covered walkways, cooling the passengers lining the deck, who gazed out over the water, or strolled and chatted among new friends they'd acquired on the trip. Lynn broke away from a group of three women and sauntered to John, perching on the edge of the deck chair next to his. She faced her back to him, having finished the investigation of the boat and boutiques.

"Rub some more of the suntan lotion on my shoulders, hon," Lynn asked, lifting her hair to one side, exposing a neck coloring to red. "When you're in the direct sunlight for any length of time you roast. I think I'm starting to burn." She handed him a brown tube from her pocketbook.

"Sure, babe." John squirted a large glob of white cream in his hand, the smell of coconut flooding his nose. He read the label. *Same brand she used when we went camping in the mountains. The first time we....I know what Lynn's hinting at, I bet.* He rubbed the lotion into her soft skin slowly, a massage starting at the neck and working along the spine to her waist, his thumbs digging into the muscles of her back along the sides until she squirmed and giggled in delight.

"John, you're tickling me," Lynn tittered as she wiggled her body against him.

"There, you've been well basted," he remarked, applying one last rub along the length of her upper torso. "Any other parts and we'll have to take off your top and bottom."

"Humm....Sounds like fun. We could work something out, I'm sure."

He wrapped his arms around her waist and pulled her down on his chest. "I think someone wants to go back to the cabin and get really tickled," he whispered and nibbled on her earlobe.

"How could you ever guess, Mr. Baker."

"I can take a hint, Mrs. Baker."

Lynn and John made love in the small cabin, gazing into each other's eyes, and then dressed for lunch, afterwards taking seats at the bar in the lounge, admiring the décor of the room and people watching.

"Oh, I wish this cruise would never end," sighed Lynn, listening to the soft music playing in the background. "So relaxing, and I've made wonderful friends." She leaned against the bar rail and crossed her legs. "Drifting along and sailing to parts unknown, sleeping late and making love. Wouldn't a life like this be terrific? Trish and I once talked about applying for jobs on one of these ships."

"I hope I was included if you were making love," John teased. "You wouldn't have been thinking of someone else, would you?"

"Of course not. We sailed on a girl's only cruise," Lynn exclaimed. "A job until our white knights rode along, swept us off our feet and married us." She hugged John's arm. "I have mine and we'll float away on our dream ship together."

"Not for too long. Our bank accounts won't absorb the strain of more than one cruise a year," John said. He waved the bartender over and ordered another Bloody Mary, sucking the olives off the toothpick with his lips from his old drink before the glass disappeared. "The price of these drinks alone will cost us more than the entire trip before we sail for home."

Lynn said, "I should have listened to Trish. She asked me if she should order the drink package, said the bundle was a better deal, but..." Lynn pushed her glass forward and another replaced the empty, "who knew? Anyway, we only honeymoon once, right?" She lifted her cocktail in the air. "Let's enjoy ourselves and let tomorrow worry about tomorrow."

"You're right," John agreed, raising his glass also. He sipped the Bloody Mary and watched the people amble across his line of vision and relaxing at the tables. Music played louder and couples rose to dance. "I'm enjoying these drinks, too." He held his glass up to the light and studied the color. "I could become used to these babies. Two and I'm already tipsy."

Lynn hopped down and hauled John to his feet. "In this case I'd better drag you onto the floor and get a dance out of you before you're too drunk to stand." She guided him into the middle of the room and draped her arms around his neck, pressing herself close to him while he wrapped his arms around her waist. "Don't ever let me go," she murmured, resting her cheek against his chest.

"My dad died, my sister disappeared. We had a scare with Mom for a while. I was afraid I'd lose her too. Don't you leave, you hear me? I wouldn't be able to take anymore disappointments in my life."

"Never. You're too precious."

John held her tight. They finished dancing and returned to the bar. He had another drink and Lynn and he strolled back to their cabin and made love again. Afterwards, Lynn vanished into the bathroom. When she came out, John was on the bed, snoring deeply.

Lynn smiled tenderly down at her sleeping husband and spread a blanket over him. "Too much sun. Too much drink. Too much sex," she said softly. "Sleep well, my prince. I love you. Never change."

Chapter Thirteen

"Your company made you a senior engineer? How in the blazes did a big promotion happen? Last week you were a junior engineer." From the corner of his eye, John shot Herbie an incredulous look, raised his bottle to his lips, and emptied the contents in one, swift gulp of disbelief.

Herbie did likewise and released a contented burp as he placed the bottle on the coaster and pushed it to the edge of the bar. As if on cue, the female bartender materialized before John and Herbie. "You ready for two more?" she asked, smiling as she picked up their empties.

John glanced at his phone and then at his friend, who nodded. "Sure, why not." He waved a hand at Herbie. "My friend here received a promotion at work. This calls for a celebration. I'll buy." Two more bottles of beer appeared. The bartender wandered off to the other end of the counter to tend another customer. John said to Herbie, "Who did you have to pay off to win a promotion? Your boss, or does he have a pretty secretary you're dating who takes care of all the paperwork?"

The five o'clock crowd jammed Funzy's. The long bar was packed with imbibers. Herbie raised his voice so John could hear him over the music and rumble of the noisy patrons. "Computers are a fast moving business. If I didn't stay current reading the newest technological journals, I'd have to go back to school or become obsolete." He took a long sip of his drink. "As it is, I see kids graduating from tech schools being promoted over me. I should have been boosted up to a supervisory position two years ago."

"Shoulda studied computers," John mumbled with a wry grin. "I'm earning good bucks, but still waiting to make junior partner. That's where the real money is, in the profits."

"I've been at this working business longer than you have, buddy," his friend reminded John as he swiveled in his chair to address John directly. "You spent three years in the army. Gained you a job, didn't the military? I know you were banged up some, but you're receiving an extra check in your pocket every month. You're behind, but you'll catch up."

John finished his drink and without thinking of the time pushed the bottle forward and another beer appeared. "Not really behind," he remarked. "I mean, I'm receiving raises, being handed more and bigger accounts and all, but a new title wouldn't hurt. Lynn's been bugging me to start house hunting again. Problem is property rates soar faster around here than the money my firm pays me. We can never beat the curve."

"Doesn't enjoy living in your parent's house, huh?" Herbie said knowingly. "Hear it happens a lot with wives in their in-law's homes. I don't blame Lynn myself. If I were a woman, I'd want my own place, too. The impulse is only natural. I think you'd call the desire a nesting urge, if you know what I mean."

John glanced around the bar at the mixed crowd. "Don't say 'nesting' too loud, you'll get us in trouble with the women." He studied his coaster. "As far as Lynn and my mother goes, the two get along fine together," John disagreed. "We take a few meals downstairs at my parents. Sometimes Lynn wants a different type of food. When she doesn't feel like eating what my mom's cooked, she heads up to the apartment and makes her own meal. Lately Lynn's been on a Mexican kick." John thought back to the small, packed refrigerator they owned stuffed full of quick fixed food. "The meal of the day is frozen burritos, hardly touches supper. We go upstairs and she's at the microwave. As fast as she pops the trays in, they're out and loaded with hot sauce."

"Junk food junkie, huh? Trish does the same thing. I call her the queen of the microwave. If my sister ever gets married, the poor guy will never know what a home cooked meal is."

"Lynn too, I guess. I think growing up she didn't do much cooking the way her mother hovers around like she does. I told Lynn all the junk food will rip her stomach up. Of course, she scoffs at me. Next morning Lynn's puking everything up from the night before. I never say a word, but..." John took another swallow of beer, "hubby knows best."

"Yeah, and I bet you were right next to her helping to eat those burritos," Herbie scoffed. He finished his bottle, stood, and announced, "I'm history. Will I be seeing you guys this weekend? Otherwise, I'm calling around for a date. I'm not spending another Friday and Saturday sitting at home watching the television with my mom and dad."

John emptied his beer also. "I'll have to check and see what Lynn is up to. I think she and Trish made plans to go shopping Saturday morning, and then there's this movie we wanted to watch Saturday night. I'll give you a buzz and let you know what's happening. If you have a date, why don't you bring her along and we'll make the evening a night out. Suds and pizza after."

John was in a good mood as he drove home. The alcohol provided a nice buzz and everything was right in the world. Maybe no partnership yet, but advancement would arrive one day. He was sure a promotion was in store for him. He was making nice bucks, maybe not enough to buy the type of house Lynn desired yet, but in another year or two they'd be able to afford their own place. Herbie was right, smart man. Lynn deserved a place to call her own.

"Her own little nest," as John referred to their dream home when he carried her over the threshold—would wipe the worried expression off her face she'd worn lately.

As he stepped through the back entrance to the house and started up the steps, his mother shouted from the kitchen. "John, is that you, dear?"

He paused on the stairs and called back, "Yeah, it's me, Mom. Lynn come in yet?"

"I don't think so. I haven't heard her, or any noise upstairs. Your father and I need to talk to you now in the living room. It's important."

A prick of apprehension stirred in John. His mother never said something was important unless the issue was imperative enough she spoke to him this instant and couldn't be delayed for the general discussion at supper. "Sure, Mom. Be right there." He hurried into the kitchen, and then into the living room where his mother perched on the edge of the couch waiting for him. His father hunched over in his recliner shuffling through a stack of papers and brochures piled on the coffee table before the two.

John took a seat next to his mother, leaning forward as he attempted to see what the titles on the papers they read. The deed to the house sat there, also the survey of the property. "What's the matter? Some trouble about the land? We're not falling into a sinkhole, are we?" he joked. "I thought this only happens in the South." His mind flashed to the crawlspace. "You're not planning another renovation, are you? If so, I opt for a game room containing a pool table and dartboard."

"We're selling the house."

"Huh?" He stared at his dad, trying to comprehend what his father said and not succeeding. He shot his mother a puzzled look. Her features showed concern mingled with anticipation. He swung back to his father and blurted out, "If you sell the house, where are we going to live?"

Mr. Baker took off his glasses and rubbed the bridge of his nose. "Oh, we're not planning on moving today," he assured John, "but we're placing the house on the market. Your mom and I have discussed this for a while now. Property values are up in the Northeast, and the price of condos in the Southeast are down. We're moving to Florida. This is the perfect time to make the jump for our retirement."

It finally dawned on John what his parents were talking about and all the huddled conversations they'd had lately. "Uh, yeah. Swell, I guess. You took me by surprise. I didn't realize you were planning this."

"Your father and I have been thinking of moving for a long time since he retired," his mother hurried to explain. "The cold weather up here in the North, traffic congestion is increasing every day, and the property taxes." She shook her head in dismay. "Every year they jump higher. You understand, right? We're not growing any younger. Time to relax and enjoy ourselves."

John saw the wrinkles lining her face, his father's black hair streaked grey. *I never realized how old my parents look.*

"You and Dad deserve some fun, Mom." He said to his father with sincerity, "You've worked hard all these years. I don't blame you for wanting to take life easy for a change, fish, play golf, have the time to do the things you and mom always wanted to do. Besides, Florida will allow Lynn and me a place to go and stay on vacation."

"I'm glad you feel this way," Mr. Baker said, relief in his voice as he settled back in his recliner. "I know all this is sudden, but telling you now will allow you and Lynn a chance to scout around and buy the place you've been talking about. We didn't say anything before we made a final decision because, well, we weren't sure ourselves what we wanted to do."

John sat back, mouth open, a thousand complications running around in his mind, the ramifications of his parents selling the house entering his thoughts. "I didn't realize..."

"Unless the new owners want to keep you on as renters," Mrs. Baker added quickly. "You'll have to discuss the upstairs apartment with the buyers, whoever the people are. We're advertising the house as a rental space above, or mother-and-daughter, so... but in this neighborhood—" her lips formed a perplexed line "—people rip the old house down to the ground and build new. The location and property is what's valuable. Not the house itself." Mrs. Baker said to her husband, "Remember the place two streets over? For Sale sign on the lawn one day, house disappeared the next, and bulldozers smoothing out the ground and construction crews..."

John barely heard her. His fingers tightened on his knees until his knuckles shone white. A buzzing started in his brain. A grey static mist engulfed him with electric sparks shooting through his mind's eye. He squeezed his eyelids shut, trying to clear his thoughts of the fog. "I'll have to talk to Lynn. See what she wants to do," he mumbled, standing abruptly, his legs weak underneath him. "Think I'll go upstairs now and wait for her to come home. We have a lot of planning to do if we have to move to a new place. Uh..." He tried to think. "How long before the house is sold, you suppose? Any ideas? I'd like to hand Lynn some type of time frame so we can make preparations if we need to."

"The real estate agent we spoke to says usually two months, depending if the people are already qualified for a mortgage or have to try different banks searching for one. You know, then there's a date for signing, etc.," Mr. Baker said. He picked up one of the brochures off the coffee table and held the paper up so John could see the cover. "We've already narrowed our choices to three places, so with any luck we can strike a bargain Monday when we fly to Florida and see the Cowins. One of the places is in the same complex they live in. We'll probably buy that one, but we'll check out the other two, to make sure. Uh," he looked at his wife. "Agent said the house officially lists on the market next week, right, but she may bring select buyers around before then?"

Mrs. Baker nodded in silent agreement.

A feeble grin flickered across John's lips. "Well, Lynn and I will be here to watch the place and let anybody in, in case the agent wants to stop by and show people beforehand. You know our work schedule, right? Tell the real estate lady."

"Uh, hang on," Mr. Baker said. "If you want to help out, I still have a bunch of junk in the basement. Tools, my old shotgun, books, magazines. You know what clutter has accumulated." He reached out and slapped John on the knee. "You hauled most of the stuff down there yourself. If you have a chance, start going through the mess and toss out what's garbage. I'll leave the sorting to your good judgement. It'll be less stuff for me to take when we move."

"Probably most can go, but I don't want to dump the shotgun and tools. They're ancient but still useable."

"Well, anything you find down there is yours if you want the junk, or you can have a garage sale," his father said. "No more hunting or home repairs for me. The bulk of the tools I inherited from your grandfather anyway, and were old when he used the equipment. If you run across any fishing gear—the tackle and rods I want to keep."

John hurried upstairs. *What am I going to do? How can I work this?* All the old problems associated with disposing of the remains scurried through his head, the places for hiding Caitlyn revisited. The thought of locating a home for Lynn and him to live barely crossed his mind in the panic.

The pain in his head returned, feeling like a roofing nail being pounded into his skull. He groped for a bottle of pills on the end table, washed one down with a can of beer from the small refrigerator, and dropped on the bed, face down. He stared at the tiles on the floor trying to think.

His mother was right—old houses disappeared every day. The corpse was sure to be unearthed between bulldozers, workmen, and backhoes. John remembered reading a recently passed ordinance stating when new construction started the homes must connect to the sewer system the county installed, no more cesspools.

When he heard Lynn's steps on the stairs, he was still trying to put his thoughts in order.

Lynn saw the expression on John's face and knew immediately that he needed cheering up. She settled close next to him and placed her head on his shoulder.

"We have to talk," they both said at once.

***

"Are you sure?" Trish scanned Lynn, eyes flashing in excitement, mouth open. She slid closer to Lynn on the bench in the mall and said in a hoarse whisper, "Have you gone to see a doctor yet?"

"No, doctors, I wasn't positive until now. I made an appointment for next week," Lynn said softly, her voice trailing off to a murmur as low as Trish's. "But I've missed two periods, been throwing up in the morning, and"—she laughed—"had this stupid craving for Mexican food. To make sure my suspicions were right I used one of those over the counter tests this morning after John left for work. I'm pregnant."

"Oh, I'm so happy for you." Trish threw her arms around her friend in a tight bear hug. She put a hand in front of her lips and whispered, "Have you told John yet? Your mother?"

"No, no one yet. You're the first."

"Oh, wow. I can't wait to tell everyone," Trish exclaimed, thinking. "This is wonderful news."

Lynn said sternly, "Trish, this is my news, not yours. Hold off until I tell my mother and John's parents first, will you? I wasn't going to say anything to anyone until next week after I see a physician. So hold your horses, okay? But I was going to tell John tonight."

"You mean you haven't said anything to him yet?"

"I told you at first I wasn't sure, and I wanted the news to be a surprise. I even hid the package the test came in so no one would suspect anything, so mum's the word, understand?" Lynn looked sternly at Trish.

Trish nodded her head solemnly. "I promise. Won't tell a soul until you're positive. Let me know right away, though, all right? You know I can't keep a secret for long." Trish's voice fell back into an awed whisper. "What do you think John will say? Think he'll be mad?"

"Trisha, what do you mean, I think he'll be mad?" Lynn's brow furrowed, aghast. "What's he going to do, tell me to take the kid back? He'll be happy, of course, we'll both be happy. We're having a baby."

"Gonna be cramped in your tiny apartment," Trish said. "John cave in yet about house hunting? Newborns are small but babies do take room. Especially when you add crib, playpen, stroller, changing table, those cute little bathtubs. You hardly have any room now."

"He's hemming and hawing," Lynn replied with a smirk. "I know we haven't saved nearly enough money yet, maybe by next year, but we can search around. I have some idea what we are looking for and how much John is willing to spend. I don't know if you've noticed, but contractors are building a new development five miles from here out on the west side of town—the developers already have a model up for people to walk through. When I was out that way last week, I stopped and peeked around. Gorgeous." Lynn paused, a faraway look as she gazed into space. "The houses are farther away from where John works, me too, and I don't know about the schools in the area." Lynn frowned. "A long drive from my mom, also, which I don't like, but the places are so pretty." She shook her head in mock despair. "Decisions, decisions, decisions. Life is terrible playing adult."

"Tell me about being a big person," Trish grumped. "My parents want me and Herbie to move out. Say we're grown now, we should be on our own. I'm expecting to drive home one day and discover my clothing on the curb in plastic trash bags, a big 'See yah' note in black magic marker taped on the outside."

Lynn continued as if talking to herself. "New baby, new house—fairly new husband. Time moves so quickly. Before you know where the years have gone, I'll be a grandma." She said sadly, "Seems like only yesterday Caitlyn and I played dolls and put balls under our shirts pretending we were having babies."

"I use to do the same thing," Trish agreed, "but on top and told everyone I grew big boobs." She hugged Lynn again. "Well, pretty soon you'll have your very own real life doll to play with. Diapers, powder, and onesies," she snickered, "and don't forget those rags for when the baby throws up after you burp her or him." Trish pushed her chest out and said importantly, "I'll be the fun loving aunt the baby always asks for because mean old mommy makes us eat our strained carrots, instead of the yummy ice cream Aunt Trish lets us have."

"You and Herbie will be the godparents, of course. You're our best friends. We wouldn't dream of asking anyone else."

Trish checked over her shoulder. "No wings, but I can fake being the Fairy Godmother. I need a magic wand, though. All I have to do is figure out how to change a pumpkin into a carriage and mice into horses. I'll need practice." She pulled open her pocketbook and peeked inside. "Drat, I left my mice at home."

They both laughed.

"Now for the important stuff," Trish said. "Lamaze lessons for John and you? Natural birth? Breast feeding?" She glanced down at her chest. "Don't ask me to help you with the last, I barely fill out my bra as is, but if John doesn't want to be your coach for Lamaze, I'll volunteer, be there for the birth, too, if you want."

"You're really pushing the best friend thing now, aren't you?" Lynn said. "First let me tell John, and see the doctor. After we've discussed what we're going to do…" She shrugged. "We'll see what happens." Lynn said as an afterthought, "I don't think natural is for me. I'm a wimp when it comes to pain. Keep me drugged up and hand me the baby afterwards. Fine by me."

"Me too. I think when the time arrives, I'll adopt. Bypass the whole delivery diaper thing."

Lynn realized her friend was talking nonsense and the hour was late anyway. She glanced at her phone and sprang to her feet. "Oh, gee, the time is past six o'clock. I'd better start heading home. John will be there already expecting me and wondering what happened."

Trish rose also. "I'll pick you up about nine-ish tomorrow, okay? While we're out, we can check maternity shops. See what type of cute outfits we'll see." Trish patted Lynn's stomach. "You'll need new pants and shirts before long, Mommy."

On the way home, Lynn's head was filled with a kaleidoscope of bottles, babies, and clothes—peace and security in a new house. She kept envisioning herself sitting in a rocking chair, holding a baby, swaying back and forth, feeding the infant a bottle. Lynn parked in the driveway, ran up the stairs, and entered their small apartment humming happily to herself.

John slumped on the bed, face in hands, staring at the floor. *Poor dear, must have had a hard day at work.* She dropped next to him on the mattress, and cuddled close. "I have something to tell you," she whispered.

Her husband spoke softly. "Me, too. We have to talk."

"You go first," Lynn urged as she draped her arm around his waist. *He's really glum. Let him get his problems off his chest, make him feel better for the good news. Hope he wasn't fired at work. Nah—the bosses love him at the office.* "What happened, honey? Tell me what's on your mind."

John was slow in his reply. Drawing a deep breath, which he let out in a groan, he said, "My parents are selling the house. We may have to find a new place to live."

"Oh." *Not so bad. I want to move anyway. This is the perfect excuse. Wonder why he's so upset?*

John smiled weakly. "Maybe the new owners will let us stay for a while. I don't know. We'll have to hold on and see what happens, but this messes up our plans big time. Now, what did you need to tell me?"

Lynn hesitated, debating in her mind whether to delay telling him about the baby until she saw the doctor, or hold off until they went to bed, or if now was the right time to announce the news. *Why not right away? He still looks unhappy, but I'm sure it's the hassle of moving bringing him down. He'll forget all about changing homes when he hears we're expecting.* "I'm pregnant. We're going to have a baby."

John stared at her, not understanding what she meant.

"We're having a baby," Lynn replied, hoping for a reaction. "Remember, I've been throwing up every morning? Morning sickness. I'm pregnant."

The news finally penetrated John's mind. He broke out into a wide grin, threw his arms around Lynn, and kissed her soundly on the lips. "How soon?" He placed his fingertips on her stomach.

"I don't know. I think I'm two months along. I made an appointment to see the doctor for next week," she said, pleased by his reaction. "How soon do we have to move? I hope we don't need to start searching by tomorrow."

John rose and took another can of beer out of the refrigerator. He rubbed his chin, ripped the tab off, and sipped before he replied, pacing in front of the bed. "Depends on how fast the house sells, but packing up won't be in the next month, I'm sure. My parents said usually takes a couple of months. Geez, this complicates matters, doesn't it, though, and the situation was confusing before."

Lynn bit her lower lip. "Time to begin house hunting?" she asked tentatively. "There's a new development across town…."

"I know," John acknowledged, breathing a long sigh as he drank his beer and thought. "I didn't want to tell you, but I drove out there last weekend, to see the model and talk to the realtor."

"So did I, but I didn't talk…"

"Yeah, I figured you'd swing by sooner or later, but I called the agent to meet me, do a walk through and we discussed numbers afterwards. The places are still too expensive for us. I mean, maybe we could manage the down payment, but the money would be tight—real tight. Especially if you have to stop working for a while, and the extra expenses of a baby and all. We might be able to pick up an older house somewhere in town, though, but not around here unless we stumble across a bargain."

The way John walked and the expression on his face told Lynn he was having a hard time suppressing the aggravation he felt having these new problems dumped on him all at once. *John knows I'm here to help, to support. What can I do to make our problems better?*

Lynn spoke up. "I wouldn't mind an older house. I'd rather have new, but a house is a house, right? A place of our own where we can raise our children." She stood and stepped to the window, gazing at the garden and her mother's home beyond. "I think I understand why my parents wanted to move here from the city. Their own yard, lawn, flowers." Lynn walked back to the bed and sat. "You don't know who your parents are selling the house to yet, do you? I haven't noticed—have there been any lookers? I haven't seen anyone…"

John finished his beer and tossed the empty in the garbage, sitting next to Lynn. "No. The house isn't officially on the market yet. Next week, my parents say."

Lynn allowed herself time to worry the problem in her brain. *What do I want? What do we want? Somehow….I know.*

An image stirred in her mind. The answer was standing right before her husband all the time. John should have thought of this himself. The more she mulled over the idea, the better her suggestion appeared. "You know, why don't we buy this house?" She studied John hopefully. "School's right up the street, we're next to my mom's. Your parents might even give us a break on the interest rate and drop the price low enough to afford." Lynn watched John's eyes light up, excitement building inside her. "What do you think? Does buying your old home sound like good idea? Do you know if your parents are expecting the whole amount at once, or will they let us slide with a big down payment?"

John grabbed Lynn by the shoulders, his lips arching upward. He shook her in joy. "I think I'll take a stroll downstairs and speak to my mom and dad right now," he exclaimed merrily, planting a kiss on her mouth.

"You know, if we're buying this house we have to make a lot of revamping."

"Huh? What type of changes?"

"Umm… Your parent's bedroom is fine for now. The space is huge. We can keep the crib for the baby in one section until he or she is old enough to move upstairs so no remodeling there."

"Half of the room used to be my bedroom," John said. "I think having me so close is why my parents were quick to build a dormer on the house. I use to wake up in the middle of the night when I heard their bed squeaking."

"You mean your mom and dad were…." Lynn gasped.

"I don't know. The room was dark and I was about four years old. You can imagine, though, hearing 'Mommy?' 'Daddy?' when you're in the middle of making love. What a great motivation it would be to build another room."

"We'll have to make sure we don't buy a bed with noisy springs then, won't we," Lynn said with a chuckle.

"At least until the baby is old enough to stick into the room up here," John agreed. He added thoughtfully, "Have to check out the mattress first."

"Not in the store," Lynn replied in mock horror. "The employees would kick us out."

"We'll leave new bed shopping for later. Now about these changes. What are you thinking?"

Lynn straightened up and crossed her legs on the bed. "Well, for one, the paneling downstairs has to go."

"Why?" The walls had been the same since he could remember.

"Too dark," Lynn explained, "and you can't change it if you decide you need to. I want to paint, bright colors maybe."

"Uh, okay."

"The dining room, also."

"You want to get rid of the dining room, too?"

"No, silly. How many times does your family sit in there and eat?"

John counted the occasions when he'd eaten a meal in the room. "Once, twice a year? Usually for Thanksgiving when we invite everyone over."

Lynn nodded empathically. "Right. All the wasted space. I want to shove a desk there, also, and my computer in the corner. We can still have the table and chairs, but there's plenty of space. When I sub, sometimes I have to correct papers. I need to sprawl out." She studied the cluttered bedroom. "Up here, I feel like I'm working in a hole."

"Okay, paneling and dining room. Should I start drafting a list?" A smirk spread over John's lips as he pretended to search for a pencil and paper.

"Don't bother. We'll design as we go. One more thing. The family room. We have to build bookshelves." Lynn swept her hand around the bed. Paperbacks piled everywhere. "I still have cartons of books at my mom's house, and those two shelves you have don't cut it anymore." She paused, considering. "I'll be darned if I'm going to walk up the stairs every time I want to read."

Herbie's right. Haven't even bought the place yet and already Lynn's refeathering her nest. "Before we start ripping the place apart, don't you think we ought to talk to my parents first?" He saw the chagrined expression on Lynn's face and threw his arms around her. "I love it when you get excited like this."

"Hey, you're shaking the baby," Lynn chortled happily, kissing him back. "You want to make little Eggbert stupid?"

"Oops." John released her in mock fright and laughed. "You're still a wonderful, wonderful, woman, and you're right, I bet we can work out some type of an arrangement with my mom and dad, too. I'm sure my parents don't need the whole selling price at once. We can make payments the same as a mortgage, maybe even at a lower interest rate like you said than the bank would charge us." He exclaimed rapidly, springing to his feet, "C'mon, let's talk to the folks." He reached out and helped Lynn to her feet. "We can tell my parents about the baby, too. It'll clinch the deal, if nothing else will." He hugged her again, but gently this time. "You've solved all our problems."

***

John was in a great mood as they walked down the stairs. He tugged on Lynn's arm, drawing her into the living room where his mother and father went over the brochures for the condos in Florida.

His parents glanced up as John and Lynn entered. John showed both a broad smile. "We have an announcement to make," he exclaimed, making sure Lynn rested next to his mother on the couch. "We've discussed the moving situation. What would you say if we bought this house from you?" Before his parents replied he said, "We can't afford to pay the whole price, but we've saved up enough to hand over a good down payment, and we'll pay the rest like a mortgage, give you a steady income."

Mrs. Baker shot her husband a quick look. "I don't know," she started. "We were expecting to use the money...."

"Oh, yeah," John added, as if what he was about to say was an afterthought, "Ah, Lynn," John turned to his wife, "maybe you should tell them."

"Lynn?" Both Mr. and Mrs. Baker stared at their daughter-in-law.

Lynn blushed. "I'm pregnant. You two are going to be grandparents."

Mrs. Baker squealed and hugged her. "Oh, that's wonderful, Lynn. I'm so happy for both of you."

Mr. Baker stood and leaned over, squeezing Lynn's shoulders and giving her a peck on the cheek. "Congratulations," he exclaimed, slapping John on the shoulder.

"Oh, we have to go shopping, Lynn," Mrs. Baker said, "I saw the most adorable maternity clothes. When is the baby due?"

"Not for another seven months, I figure, Mom," Lynn said. "I haven't seen the doctor yet, I made an appointment."

"I want to buy you a crib, too," She said. "Don't worry about baby things, and I have to plan a shower. Oh, and you'll need a rocking chair."

"Rocking chair? What heavens for. I'm not that old."

"No, every new mother needs a rocking chair to relax in and rock while holding the baby. It's tradition."

"You're right. I was thinking of a rocking chair driving home," Lynn exclaimed. "I always wanted one when I was a little girl so I could cuddle my baby. In fact, I use to play pretend with my stuffed pig I was a mommy married to a handsome husband." She beamed at Mrs. Baker. "You must have read my mind, and I'll treasure the chair, always, Mom. Thanks."

John cut in with, "Before we get carried away, what about the house?" He looked at his father.

His father's eyes narrowed, mentally counting the money he'd need to buy one of the condos his wife and he were thinking about. He threw back his head and announced, "Can't have my future grandchildren living in the street, now can I? Let's make a deal, here. What kind of down payment are we talking about?"

By the end of the night, John reached an agreement with his parents. Large down payment, but small monthly mortgage at a half a percent lower than the banks would change John. As Lynn and he marched upstairs to their apartment, John felt like shouting to the world, singing, doing a jig. Everything was good and right on earth. He was going to be a daddy, a homeowner, and his secret was safe.

Chapter Fourteen

"Do we have to go?" John complained. He tucked his shirttails in and offered his hand to Lynn, helping her off the couch. "This is—ridiculous."

Lynn smoothed out her maternity dress and scooped up her phone and pocketbook. "She's my mother. We're invited. What do you want me to tell her? No?"

John's forehead wrinkled as his body sagged. "I understand, but, a birthday party for your sister? C'mon, now. She's been dead how many years? Isn't it about time your mom stopped pretending? I don't..." His eyes pleaded, telling his wife exactly what he felt. "Why?"

Lynn released a long sigh and walked to the door. "Mom can't forget. Every week, posters on the telephone poles, calling the police for updates, dropping off flyers at all the businesses in town. I've tried talking to her. She becomes angry. I can sorta understand her point of view. You don't give up hope when you lose one of your own children." Lynn patted her stomach. "Would you forget if this one disappeared? I know I wouldn't. We'll have to deal with my mom. Caitlyn's birthday is only once a year."

"Well, in that case, I'll handle your mother's fantasies in *my* own way." He walked into the kitchen, found a glass, and took out a bottle of vodka from a cabinet. He poured a finger full in the cup and knocked the clear liquid down in a swift gulp.

"I wish you wouldn't drink so much," Lynn said, frowning.

John smiled at her and winked. "I'm dealing with your mother. Let's go and get the party started and over before I have another."

A weight as heavy as a mountain descended on John's neck as they stepped outside. He tried to act cheerful and said, "Do you want to drive around, or should I dig out the wheelbarrow from the garage and push you through the backyard?"

"I'm eight months pregnant, not disabled," Lynn retorted, strolling across the grass to the garden gate as John hurried to catch up to her. "Hear anything from your parents lately?" she called over her shoulder. "How are your mom and dad doing?"

John stepped in front of her and opened the gate. "Fine. Talked to Mom last night after you fell asleep. She's been hitting the stores. Mrs. Cowin has taken her around to all the antique shops. Even joined a bridge club for Tuesday nights and a book club for Thursdays. Dad buying a boat and learning how to play golf. Both my parents said to keep sending the mortgage payment, and they'll be up to visit when the baby's born. Which reminds me, you have to write out a check for my parents this week."

Lynn patted his arm and gave him a cheeky grin. "Keep working, buddy. Now you have two to feed and a mortgage." They walked across her mother's back lawn. "How does it feel to be an adult?"

"I'd rather be home watching Saturday morning cartoons and playing football," John admitted as he opened Mrs. Brennen's back door.

Lynn paused before entering. "Maybe my mother will forget all the Caitlyn stuff when the baby's born. After all, the kid will be a substitute, right? I know my mom, she'll be so busy trying to help me, she won't have time for anything else. This might be what she needs to start looking forward again, instead of behind."

John thought about what his wife said. "You think so? Thata be great." He'd encourage Mrs. Brennen to help Lynn, whether his wife wanted assistance or not. Anything to halt the constant reminder of the past.

"I'm not making any promises," she said, "but we can hope." Lynn walked into the house and called out, "Mom? Hey, Mom, we're here."

John braced himself. *Keep calm, hold your temper. Shoulda tossed down another drink. I can deal with this if I know the nonsense will halt.* He kept repeating to himself, *Smile—be polite. We'll only be here for an hour or so. I've done worse in combat.*

The house felt cold, as if unoccupied except for the relentless memory of Caitlyn peering at John from every corner. Pictures of the dead girl hung on the walls, framed photos rested on the top of the television set and coffee table. Stacks of flyers yet to be handed to the neighbors and strangers were gathered everywhere. The piles marched along the bookshelves and mantle like rows of soldiers neatly dressed in lines ready to stride into battle. Each bundle carried a small sticker numbering a day of the week and different location for the stack to assume the assigned post when call upon.

"In the kitchen, Lynn," Mrs. Brennen replied as they took seats on the sofa. "Be right out in a minute."

Opposite the couch hung an old picture of Caitlyn, enlarged, until the photo seemed to take up half the wall. The girl was dressed in her cheerleading uniform, and stood astride a pyramid of other cheerleaders, all grinning for the camera. Caitlyn balanced, hands on hips, chest thrown out in pride, a haughty smile across her face. John tried not to stare back as he fidgeted at his hands and picked his nails, but the eyes drew him with an accusing glare. The smile mocking as if she knew she'd ride his back for the rest of his life.

Why won't you leave me alone? You won't let me forget, will you? God, how many years have you been dead now? I DIDN'T DO ANYTHING!

Mrs. Brennen bustled out of the kitchen, lips rising cheerfully, but her lanky grey hair hung in strands around her head, and the bags under the eyes showed many a sleepless night. She waved Lynn and John forward. "See what I did with the birthday cake," Mrs. Brennen said brightly. "So beautiful if I do say so myself. Caitlyn would love it. She always likes pretty deserts and candles."

John moaned silently to himself and glanced sideways at Lynn who refused to return his look. "Sure, Mom." His wife rose, and groped for John's hand, dragging him off the couch like a reluctant child into the kitchen.

In the middle of the table rested a huge sheet cake covered in white frosting. Pink and red roses were massed in each corner while the middle was ablaze in orange and green swirling candles. Balloon-shaped circles, small tails twisting in curliques the colors of the rainbow, took up the empty spaces. Bracketing the candles and below a smiley face, in blue icing, were the words, HAPPY BIRTHDAY CAITLYN.

Mrs. Brennen stood to one side so Lynn and John had a good view of her masterpiece. "I took four smaller cakes and shoved the squares together, covered the seams using frosting so the edges didn't show," she beamed, nodding at a job well done. "Took me all day, but I'm pretty proud. What do you think?" She asked Lynn and John anxiously, "Would Caitlyn love this?"

"Uh, looks nice," stammered John as he watched the wicks flicker and the wax drip down the sides of the candles, puddling in blobs on the cake. "Cute."

Lynn inhaled in awe. "Oh, Caitlyn would have been so happy," she exclaimed, pressing her hands together and swiveling her head from side to side, trying to have a view from every angle. "I think, though, we'd better blow out those candles before we set the house on fire." Lynn looked from her mother to John. "Ready? One—two—three—*blow*." She took a deep breath and exhaled with all her might.

The candles flickered and died. "I'll get the plates," Lynn announced, opening the cupboard.

"I'll make us some coffee," agreed her mother moving toward the coffee pot.

The two women hurried around the kitchen, dodging John who stood helplessly by trying to decide what to do to hasten the process along. He realized his best course of action was retreat and said uneasily, "Uh, I guess I'll wait in the other room. I'm in the way here." He wandered back into the living room, refusing to acknowledge the picture, which followed him with a dark, haunting stare, and sat on the sofa, angling himself so he couldn't see the photo. He switched on the TV and concentrated at the screen, not caring what he watched.

How long does it take to make coffee and cut three slices of cake? John ripped his phone from his back pocket and scrolled through the messages, trying to listen to the muted conversation issuing from the kitchen over the drone of the television. He heard his name mentioned a couple of times, and then Mrs. Brennen emerged balancing a tray with cake and cups of coffee. Lynn trailing her holding a sugar bowl and small pitcher of milk.

"Rest yourself, Lynn," her mother urged, setting the tray on the coffee table. "Your feet must be killing you. I know mine were when I was pregnant carrying you and Caitlyn." She passed a plate of cake and fork to John.

Lynn picked up her coffee cup and took a sip. "My mother and I were discussing a name for the baby. We know she's a girl. What do you think of Caitlyn?" Both Mrs. Brennen and Lynn watched John expectantly.

John took a bite of the cake. The gooey frosting tasted overly sweet in his mouth making his stomach nauseous. He suppressed the urge to vomit and blanked his mind. Robot-like, voice empty of emotion, he replied, "Sure. Why not. Good a name as any, I suppose."

Relief flashed over Lynn's face as she exhaled and took a forkful of cake.

Mrs. Brennen clapped her hands together. "I have a surprise I want to show you two. You'll both be so delighted." She sprang up and hurried along the hallway.

John placed his plate carefully on the coffee table and followed Lynn and her mother to Caitlyn's room.

Unopened boxes were stacked in the corners, pushed aside to make space in the middle of the room. A new crib, complete with musical mobile, little owls and moons hanging down, rested in the middle of the floor taking up a majority of the space. "For when I babysit," Mrs. Brennen explained. She brushed off the plastic lining on the mattress. "I still need sheets, blankets, and a changing table, but isn't this cute?" She wound up the mobile, and the soft strains of "Hush-a-bye" played in the air.

"Oh, this is wonderful, Mom. Thank you." Lynn embraced her mother warmly and stepped back, studying the mobile. "You remembered?"

"How could I forget? Every night your father made you and Caitlyn read the silly poem. I couldn't find one with owls and pussycats, but owls and moons work as well." Mrs. Brennen smiled softly. "Your father always said to train you girls up right. You needed poetry in your souls, and so will my granddaughter as she grows up."

"This will be the perfect new home for Mr. Piggy," Lynn exclaimed.

"You mean you still have your old doll?" Mrs. Brennen said in surprise.

"Of course. How could I abandon Mr. Piggy," Lynn replied. "Soon I'll have a new doll to play with and this one," she patted her belly, "will need a faithful companion." Lynn whispered confidentially to John, "He needs a job anyway. Since I graduated from college, all he does is lay around on the bed. Lazy bum."

John refused to listen, but he knew he must say something, Lynn expected him to acknowledge the gift at least, and he wanted desperately to run out of the room. "Yeah, thanks," he replied as he turned away. "Uh, why don't we polish off our cake before the coffee is cold?"

After the three finished eating, Lynn and John strolled back to their own house. Lynn paused at the gate and said, "I want to thank you for agreeing so quickly with my mom about naming the baby Caitlyn." She studied him anxiously. "I know you weren't happy about the idea, but you made her day. I saw her eyes light up. You're not mad, are you?"

The numbness cloaking John was fading away, but he needed to be out, relax, toss off the tension still seething inside him. "Uh-huh. Well, Caitlyn is a name. What does it matter what we call the baby, right? Not angry exactly, but my parents were hoping we'd name her after my grandmother, but Gandma's dead, anyway. I'm sure she won't care and my mom will get over the change." John and Lynn reached the backdoor of their house. "I'm running down to Funzy's for a few minutes. You don't mind, do you? I won't be gone long."

"No, go ahead," Lynn replied. "Think I'll lay down and take a nap before supper. My mom was right, my feet are sore and so is my back. *Oh.*" Lynn placed her hand on her belly. "Little rascal kicked me in the ribs. Here, feel. I think she's going to be a cheerleader like her namesake. Want to feel? I think she's gonna hit me again."

You had to say that, didn't you? If I didn't know better... "Ah, okay." He placed his hand on her stomach. He felt nothing. "Must be naptime," he joked, "or the football game is over and everyone's gone home for the day." He patted her fanny. "See you later. Go inside and relax. Enjoy."

After Lynn disappeared into the house, John hurried to his car, thumbing the speed dial on his phone at the same time. "Herbie…? Yeah, it's me. Heading down to the bar, you busy…? No? Great, I'll meet you there. I'm leaving now….Thanks."

His friend hadn't yet arrived as John hurried to a seat and dropped down at the counter. He told the bartender, "Bottle of beer," and flipped a bill in front of him. As soon as his drink arrived, he took a long swallow, feeling the alcohol start to work its magic as the liquid rolled down his gullet.

My life is going to be worse than ever now. The old lady's trying to make me hate my daughter. Lynn said the baby would change things. Keep her mind occupied. Now I'll have twice as much Caitlyn shooting out of her mouth. Does the woman suspect something? Is this all a plot to make me confess? To punish me? Drive me insane? And Lynn saying the cheerleading crack. She knew all along what her mother was thinking about. It's been years now, drop the dead sister act, already, both of you, will yah.

John took another long draft of his beer, staring into the mirror behind the bar with his reflection gazing back. *Never let me forget—Never.*

He tipped the bottle to his mouth again. The contents were finished. He pushed the empty out in front of him and waved to the bartender. "Another."

His third bottle was half-gone when Herbie walked through the door and dropped onto the bar stool beside him. "What's the matter, buddy?" he asked as the bartender brought him a beer. "You didn't sound happy on the phone. Problems?"

"Mother-in-law troubles," John grumbled, making small circles using the bottom of his bottle on the counter as a crayon.

"Telling Lynn what a worthless so-and-so you are, huh," Herbie quipped, "and how she coulda done better if only she'd listen to her mother?"

John drained his bottle. "Nah, nothing as bad, thank goodness. At least not yet, anyway."

The bartender wandered back over and Herbie said, "Give my friend another beer, and a shot of rum, too. He's needs to unwind from a hard day."

"Hey, I've gotta drive and go to work tomorrow," John protested, but he shrugged and downed the clear liquid when the shot glass was placed before him. He washed the rum down with a swallow of beer. "Thanks, I need something strong."

His problems faded, body relaxed—the world appeared better around him. Herbie said, "So what happened? Talk to me, buddy. Don't keep your problems bottled up inside. BSing is what friends are for. To unload when you need to."

The alcohol was having the desired effect. All his worries shrank to small points in his mind. "Oh, she wants us to name the baby Caitlyn. I guess I'm making a big issue over nothing important, I was upset and needed to blow off some steam. Who cares anyway what the kid's name is. Doesn't matter, right?"

"Where'd she think up Caitlyn? Who...?" Herbie stopped, trying to place the name. "You mean Lynn's sister? The one who took off and never returned?"

"Yeah," John breathed, "one and the same. Every time, and I mean *every time*, we see Lynn's mother or go to her house, all she says is Caitlyn this, or Caitlyn that. The woman is driving me nuts. Now we have to name the baby after her. Caitlyn's dead. I...." John stopped abruptly, rubbed his forehead, and took another sip of beer. "I'm— I'm sure Lynn's sister will never return. Too many years. No word. God knows what happened to the girl, but if she hasn't returned by now it ain't happening. Why can't Lynn's mother leave the dead alone and get on living her life? Gosh, the woman made herself so sick, she wound up in the hospital once, remember. Mrs. Brennen's nuts and she's driving me crazy along with her."

Herbie hunched over his glass, twirling the bottle in front of him while he thought. "Maybe she can't stop," he said, not glancing at John. "People, sometimes people keep reliving events over in their minds. I know I do think about the past and how events coulda been different, you probably do the same, too, right?" he adjusted his glasses and tapped his bottle. "Best I can tell you is to ignore her, block your mother-in-law out of your mind when the conversation starts. Like you said, it doesn't really matter."

John chuckled. "I've tried doing the exact thing. The lady is insidious, like a cavity giving you twinges until your tooth begs to be ripped out." He realized he clutched his bottle so hard his hand shook. John placed the beer on the bar top, and then picked it back up and took a swallow.

"Sounds bad," Herbie agreed. He dug an elbow lightly into John's ribs. "The only advice I can give you to feel better, refer to the kid using a nickname. What did Lynn call her sister, Cat?"

"I think so. Yeah," John agreed.

"You see? After all, it's short for Caitlyn, right? Everybody shortens names. How many people do you know call me Herbert?" He beamed at his own wit and lifted his bottle. "From now on Caitlyn's dead and buried, baby Cat is about to be born." He raised his hand and held the bottle out to John. "The wise godfather has solved the dilemma again. Problem unraveled. Remind me to tell her when she's older who thought up her nickname."

John clicked his bottle against Herbie's. "Hear, hear. Caitlyn's body is a rotting in the grave. Long live the Cat."

Herbie finished off the rest of his beer. "Gotta leave now, buddy. You going to be alright?" He stood and stretched.

"Yeah. Thanks for stopping by and talking," John replied. "Think I've shook the bugs out of my system. See yah later."

John ordered another beer. The bartender looked at him dubiously but served him. John closed his eyes. Presently he drifted into a world of his own.

Herbie was right. No matter what Mrs. Brennen called his daughter, the baby would always be Cat to him. Caitlyn was dead. She never existed. A bad nightmare of a long ago past he vaguely remembered anymore. Whatever Mrs. Brennen said or did didn't matter.

John drove home and fell into bed beside Lynn. The next morning he awoke with a headache, and was late for work.

***

"John, not another stuffed animal?" Lynn's mouth flickered upward, pleased, but she tried to appear stern as her husband withdrew a stuffed tiger from behind his back and held the toy over the baby's head. "Her eyes are barely open and if you put any more playthings in the crib there won't be any room for her."

"Nonsense. Look, I think she's trying to reach for big Mr. Pussy." He squished the toy lightly into the baby's stomach with a wiggle. "Cat wants a pretty kitty?" he cooed.

The baby started crying.

"Uh, oh. Want did I do?" He pulled the tiger back out of her reach and stared helplessly from his daughter to Lynn. "What happened? I didn't break her, did I?"

Lynn bent over the crib and sniffed suspiciously. "I think Cat used the litter box," she replied ominously, picking up the baby and cuddling her while peeking into the back of the diaper. "Yep. Time for a pit stop."

"Uh, I'll go warm a bottle," John said quickly backing away from the crib. He disappeared out of the bedroom door.

"Coward," Lynn called after him. "Next time I'll warm the bottle and you change the messy diaper." She heard no reply. Lynn didn't expect any.

Lynn gazed down at the perfect features of her daughter as she gently cleaned the baby's bottom using a wet wipe. *You are so beautiful. Everyone says you resemble me, but you're too young to look like anyone yet, are you. Maybe you have my nose and eyes, but you have John's brown hair. We will see, won't we?*

Lynn thought taking care of a baby would be simple, and it was. Between her mother staying most of the day helping, and Trish stopping by at night after work, Lynn hardly did anything at all. Her mother even cooked and brought supper over so Lynn didn't have to, explaining, "You need to rest, Lynn, and cooking for three is really no problem. I always make too much anyway. Habit I suppose."

Even when no one else was around to help, baby Cat slept most of the time for the first few weeks, only waking when she was hungry, diaper changed, or bathed. After a short cuddling time, Cat fell asleep and the routine started all over again.

Being stuck at home all day except for brief periods when John watched the baby was no problem either. Between visits from her mother and Trish, who now insisted on the title Auntie Trish, she enjoyed plenty of company to keep her occupied. After the novelty of the first month wore off, though, Lynn felt herself trapped in the house unless she loaded herself down totting diaper bags, wipes, bottles, car carriers and stroller for a five minute run to the supermarket. Lynn thought back and marveled at the women she'd seen in the stores, baby in carrier, one holding onto a hand, and wondered how mothers managed to watch their children and still buy what their family needed. She'd tried grocery shopping once. Cat decided the time was right to cry. Lynn found herself feeding the baby with a bottle in one hand, while pushing the cart grimly onward using the other. She dumped canned vegetables and milk into the wagon and fled the store breathing a sigh of relief.

Lynn was always tired. Middle of the night feedings weren't bad, but she found the ability to go back to sleep impossible, lying in bed, hoping Cat wouldn't wake up again. In addition, Lynn still enjoyed waking in the morning and fixing John breakfast. A few peaceful minutes to herself and then talking quietly to her husband over a cup of coffee about what the day would bring, or events outside their home, she no longer felt a part of anymore.

John tiptoed into the bedroom, holding a warmed bottle and wearing a smile. "Safe to come in now?" he said in a loud whisper. He inhaled deeply. "Should I find a gas mask?"

"No, everything is all clear. I'm finished, but I need you to hide the evidence." Lynn added an extra squirt of powder to Cat's bottom, taped her up, and handed the dirty diaper to John. "Here, I'll trade you," she said accepting the bottle.

Lynn cradled the baby in one arm, holding the bottle to Cat's mouth. She reclined in her rocking chair and swayed gently back and forth watching the eyelids flutter shut. "She's going to sleep already," Lynn whispered. "Let me put her to bed, and then I have to start supper. Mom went out tonight and didn't being anything over." The baby's eyes closed. "I think I'll take a nap after we eat. I'm exhausted."

"You know, I could do one of the feedings. You never have a full night's sleep. All the waking up isn't fair to you, and I don't mind, really."

Lynn placed Cat back in her crib. "Let's go," she said softly. She patted John on the chest. "Getting up in the middle of the night is no big deal, and I have to keep *you* well rested for work. Diapers and formula aren't cheap." Lynn bent over and picked up the toy tiger John left on the floor and tucked it into the corner of Cat's crib. "Neither are stuffed animals."

"The rocking chair your mother bought for us is a blessing," Lynn remarked, closing the bedroom door. "I really enjoy holding Cat in it. She was right."

"I wasn't going to say anything," John remarked, "but Mom completely forgot about it between buying everything else and the move. I picked the chair out. I'm glad you like it."

"Really?" Lynn hugged John around his waist. "How sweet of you to remember. I'll treasure the rocker forever." They entered the kitchen and Lynn pulled out pots and pans from the cabinet. "For thinking of me you get a special dinner. What do you want?"

John wrapped his arms around her and kissed her neck. "You always."

Chapter Fifteen

"Lynn, you look terrible."

Lynn jumped and spun around as her mother entered the kitchen holding a casserole dish. "Oh, hi, Mom. You scared the wits out of me. I didn't hear you enter." She shifted Cat from one arm to the other. "Put the plate down on the counter and sit, and thank you, by the way. You know you don't have to cook every meal for us." Lynn bent over and sniffed the food. "Smells wonderful. I'll pour us some coffee." With the deftness acquired by constant practice, she hooked two coffee cups from the cabinet using her fingers and set both on the table. She filled each from the pot warming in the coffee maker and walked toward the refrigerator. "Milk or creamer?" Lynn asked her mother.

"Honey, I'll do this," her mother said, heading Lynn off at the fridge and taking out milk. "Sit and rest."

Lynn dropped into a chair, exhaling a groan of pleasure and cradled Cat against her chest. "Thanks, Mom. This little one is heavy after a while."

Mrs. Brennen found spoons and sugar, setting both before Lynn within easy reach and peered at her daughter and granddaughter.

"Why, you have circles under your eyes." Mrs. Brennen stirred her coffee and took a cautious sip. "You look like a raccoon. Haven't you been getting enough sleep?"

Lynn released a yawn. "Oh, yeah. Last couple of days, though, friends I haven't seen for a while from the school stopped by to see the little monster." She held Cat up, and then placed the baby on her knee, holding her under the arms and bouncing the girl. "The administration wanted to know when I'm returning to work." Lynn said to Cat, "Mommy can't make any money watching you, can I." The baby gurgled in glee. "She's gotten her morning naps, but I haven't found the time to have mine." Lynn cooed to the baby, "You're too popular for mommy to keep up." She said to her mother, "I don't know how you managed to do the books for dad having both Caitlyn and me in diapers."

"Practice and a husband who made his own hours," Mrs. Brennen replied. She peered toward the living room. "Speaking of husbands, where's John? Today is Saturday. Why isn't he here watching the baby so you can sleep?"

Lynn exhaled a sigh. "The company called him into the office this morning. Some client of his flew in last night from the Midwest and wanted a face-to-face talk. Couldn't put the meeting off until Monday. Client's leaving again tomorrow to go home." Lynn stifled another yawn and shifted Cat to the other leg. "Don't worry about me, I'll be fine."

"Of course you will, honey." Mrs. Brennen stood and lifted the baby off Lynn's knee. "Come here to Nana, Caitlyn, and let your mamma have a nice nap." Cat gurgled at her grandmother and smiled as Mrs. Brennen kissed her on the cheek, reaching out chubby baby hands.

"Gee, thanks, Mom, but you don't have to…"

"Nonsense. We'll play, sing songs and watch TV," Mrs. Brennen scoffed, cuddling Cat and tickling the baby's belly. "The weather is nice today. Maybe we'll take the stroller and go for a walk in the fresh air. I can be a proud grandmother strutting around the block showing off my cute granddaughter to all my friends." The woman rocked Cat in her arms as the baby kicked her feet. "See? My granddaughter wants play. Don't you, Caitlyn?"

"Well…." An overwhelming desire to take advantage of the opportunity for some me time washed over Lynn. She looked from her laughing daughter to her smiling mother. *Mom watching Cat for a couple hours won't hurt. I know John doesn't like to leave the baby alone with Mom, but he's being ridiculous.* She hadn't slept soundly for the past two months, always on the alert and ready to investigate for the slightest noise of Cat waking. *Why not. He won't be home until this afternoon. Sleep, glorious sleep.* "If taking care of the baby is really no problem. I'd love a couple of hours for a nap. Uh"—Lynn waved toward the living room "—stroller's in the front closet if you decide to go for a walk." She stood and disappeared into the living room, and returned carrying a large canvas bag. "Here's the diaper bag. Bottles are in the fridge if she gets hungry." Lynn felt like a kid going to the park. "Cat should be ready for her own nap in about an hour. Give a yell if you need me, okay? I'll be in the bedroom. Don't be afraid to wake me up."

Mrs. Brennen chuckled. "Don't worry. I'm an old pro at this. I took care of two. Remember? I can certainly watch one for a few hours and not lose her." She added hesitantly, "If you were planning to return to teaching, even as a substitute, or you're called full-time, don't hesitate to ask me to babysit."

"Oh, I couldn't impose on you, Mom," Lynn replied. "A couple of hours is fine, but all day? Maybe every day? It's way too much to ask."

"Watching my granddaughter is no problem, really. Now your father is gone, and Caitlyn not returning yet, and you out of the house, I don't have much to keep me busy, now do I? You would be doing me a favor."

"Well, I'm not ready to return to work yet, and I haven't been called to teach full time," Lynn replied, trying to think of a way to broach the subject to John when the time was right. "But I thank you for the offer. I'd have to talk it over with John anyway."

"Well, think about it." Mrs. Brennen stood and said to the baby, "Let's see what trouble you and Nana can get into, Caitlyn. Lynn, go lay down."

Feeling a sense of relief, Lynn entered her bedroom, closed the drapes to block the morning sun streaming through the window, and stretched out on the bed, pulling a light blanket over her. She stretched, twisted, luxuriating in the sensation of total relaxation of no responsibilities, and rolled on her side, drawing her knees up to her chest. Lynn fell asleep at once.

Images of Cat floated in her mind's eye and more pictures of people Lynn knew but couldn't place. She drifted above them all, staring earthward as she swooped and dove.

"Lynn, wake up." A hand shook her roughly.

"Huh?" Lynn uncurled and opened her eyes, rolling onto her back, unsure of where she was. John looked down at her, his eyes full of worry.

"Where's Cat? The baby isn't in her crib."

Lynn bolted upright, still disorientated. "Uh, my mother has her," she mumbled, sweeping the hair out of her face. "What time is it?" Lynn glanced at the window. The morning sun no longer shone through the blinds. "Why didn't Mom wake me up?"

"Two o'clock in the afternoon," John said. "Your mother has Cat?" Concern clouded his voice and he glanced at the draped window as if expecting to see his mother-in-law crawling over the sill carrying the baby in her arms. "I told you never to leave Cat alone with her. I got home fifteen minutes ago. How long has your mother had her?"

Lynn found a pair of sandals and slipped them on her feet, standing. "Since nine o'clock this morning, but Mom babysitting is really no problem." She tried to act upbeat, ignoring the worry in John's voice. "If Cat's not here, they're at Mom's house. If not, she said the two might take a walk around the neighborhood. C'mon, let's go rescue the poor woman. I bet the baby is driving my mother crazy by now."

"Why did you let your mother watch Cat?" John said as they filed out of the house. "Of all the stupid, idiotic things to do." John waved his hand, glaring at Lynn as they hurried across the back lawn. "You know I don't like her being alone taking care of the baby. Your mother's crazy. What happens if she decides to bake Cat in a cake for your dead sister's birthday? Or, take her to the police station and tell the cops she's located her missing daughter and they don't have to search for Caitlyn anymore? Do you want police swarming all over our home asking questions? We'd be the laughing stock of the whole town."

John is so upset over this, acting like a jerk. Why is he so mad? "Oh, stop complaining, will you? You're being ridiculous," Lynn replied, annoyed. She smelled the odor of alcohol on his breath. "Have you been drinking again?"

John snorted, giving her a disgusted look. "I was talking to a client, *working*. I took him out to lunch. Yeah, we had a few drinks, told a couple of jokes afterwards, but that doesn't mean I can't think straight, or don't know what I'm talking about when the subject comes to your mother."

I figured as much. Lynn's brows contracted as she bit back a nasty remark. They entered her mother's back door and she rolled her eyes. "Are you suggesting my mother is going to *eat* Cat?"

"Who knows? Wait, I hear someone." A voice echoed through the house, growing louder as Lynn and John walked into the living room, issuing from Caitlyn's bedroom. The sound changed to words.

"…now take your nap, Caitlyn. When you wake up, we can start unpacking your things. You should have put away your clothes years ago."

John shot Lynn a look of alarm and his jaw muscles bunched as he strode down the hallway. Lynn heard John talking to himself, as if chanting, "They never listen. They never listen."

Mrs. Brennen was standing over the crib. A vacant expression on her face, holding up a white sweater and skirt. "I never threw your uniform away," she said. "I knew you'd be back one day."

"Mom."

Mrs. Brennen glanced up. "Oh, Lynn. I was putting Caitlyn down for a nap. I didn't hear you enter."

John lunged forward. "If you've hurt her…" He grasped the railing on the crib, staring in.

As quick as he acted, Lynn was faster. She reached down and lifted Cat from the crib, clutching the baby to her chest. "There you are, precious. Mommy was looking for you." Lynn said to her mother, "Thanks for watching the baby. You shouldn't have let me sleep so long." She surveyed her mother closely. "Are you feeling alright?"

Mrs. Brennen drew back, startled. "Of course. Why would you ask me a question like that?"

John grimaced and snatched Cat from Lynn's arms. "C'mon. I'm taking the baby back to our house, before this crazy lady hurts somebody." He shouted to Lynn, "I think you'd better take this one," he flicked his head toward Mrs. Brennen, "to the hospital. She needs help. Maybe next time you'll listen to me."

Lynn's mouth opened wide, shocked. "John, what a horrible thing to say about my mother."

"You heard her. She's looney," he snapped back.

Mrs. Brennen glared at John. "Why, John Baker. How dare you say something so nasty about me? I was putting my daughter to bed. You act as if I were hurting…"

"See, I told you she was nuts," John snarled at Lynn as he took a step toward the bedroom door.

Cat started crying.

"See what you've done now?" Lynn yanked Cat from John's arms as he passed her. "Stop being a stupid jerk, will you?"

John's eyes closed, his fists balled up at his side. His whole body quivered in anger as he tried to control the emotions inside him. "She's not Caitlyn. Caitlyn's dead. Don't you two understand this?"

For the first time in her life, Lynn was afraid of John. *Is he going to hit me?*

***

John opened his eyes, his breath snorting in and out of his nose like a bellows as he struggled visibly to contain himself. He pointed a shaky finger at Mrs. Brennen. "Don't you dare leave Cat alone with your mother anymore," he said in a low voice to Lynn. He swung on his heel, stalking out of the room, back stiff. He shouted over his shoulder, "I'm warning you!"

All the way home, John kept repeating to himself, *Stupid. Stupid. The old lady's insane. Can't Lynn see? Why doesn't she do something" Say something?*

He paused at his back door, hand on latch, and changed his mind. He continued around the house to his car. *I gotta get out of here before I explode, say something, do something I'll regret. Damn Lynn, makes me so mad.* As he passed the window to the crawlspace, he slammed his fist into the wall, unable to contain his rage. *There's one for you, too, bitch.*

His constant companion, the pain in his head, returned. The name *Caitlyn* pounded in his brain, rhyming to the throb. John reached into his pocket, taking out the bottle of pills he carried on him, and popped a few into his mouth before he sat in his car. His hand shook so hard he fumbled for the keys in his pocket, and then he couldn't locate the one he wanted. Cursing, he managed to twist the correct key into the ignition and tore out of the driveway. He swung onto the main street and drove the few blocks to Funzy's. His phone yammered at him. *To hell with you, Lynn. I don't need your comments. I've had it up to here with you and your mother.* He switched the annoying instrument off, slammed into a parking space in front of the bar and stalked inside.

John dropped on a stool, and yanked out his phone, refusing to check the messages. He called Herbie. "Hey, buddy, sitting here at Funzy's waiting for you. Come on down, we'll, have a few…. What? Sounds like a lame excuse to me….No, I'm kidding….Well, if you change your mind, you know where I am." He shut the phone off again.

Don't need anyone else to help me get drunk. I can do the drinking all myself. Up yours, world.

Six beers and three shots later, the pain was no more than a whisper, the day brighter. He floated in a haze where he felt happy. John looked out the long plate glass windows of the bar. It was dark. "Think I'll start heading home," he told the bartender.

"I think you're right," she agreed whole-heartedly. "I was about to cut you off anyway. Do you want me to call you a cab?"

"Nope. I'm fine," John assured her. He gave the woman a sloppy salute and threw a ten dollar bill on the bar. "For you, beautiful. Don't worry, I'm only driving a couple of blocks."

"Well, don't let the hair of the dog bite you," she joked, returning his gesture with one of her own and scooped up the money.

Lynn was watching TV when John slipped in the door. She said bitterly, "You had my mother and Cat in hysterics. Took me an hour to calm them both down."

"Yeah, this is me. Always the bad person." He dropped beside her. "Hey, I'm sorry, but I worry, you know? And you have to admit, your mom wasn't acting right. She called Cat her daughter." He refused to argue. The last thing he wanted was to have another fight with Lynn so late in the evening.

"I'll take care of my mother, but you don't need to talk to her like you did. I called you four times. You couldn't call me back? Where were you anyway?"

John kicked his shoes off. "Funzy's. Shut my phone off. I wanted to think."

Lynn cocked her head, lips twisting down. "Thinking at the bar? Good place for rational thought, complaining alongside all your friends. Bet you handed the bunch an earful."

"Couldn't find any friends. They were all busy." John stood, walking toward the bedroom. "I guess you're right, Lynn, I don't think much," he agreed wearily. "I'm heading off to bed."

Lynn replied in a cold voice, refusing to look at him as she switched her attention back to the television, "Go ahead. Go lie down. You need to sleep the booze off."

John removed his clothes and crawled into bed. The room spun around him and no matter how hard he tried to concentrate, the ceiling would not hold still. The next morning when he awoke, the space above him still revolved slowly and his head pounded. He sat on the edge of the bed, took a pill, hoping the drug would ease the pain. He stood, and his stomach threatened to rebel.

What did the bartender said last night about the hair of the dog biting him? *Damn dog. Feels like he ate me up and puked me out on the floor before he died.*

He wandered through the living room searching for Lynn. When he didn't see her or the baby, he walked into the kitchen, still feeling as if he'd been dragged behind a car by a rope. *Oh, man, I need something. What the heck, hair of dog won't hurt, might help.*

He kept vodka in the cabinet and he thought Lynn stashed a bottle of tomato juice from her last shopping trip in the refrigerator. A short Bloody Mary should calm his stomach and place him in the right. He made a quick trip to the bathroom, dropped another pill into his hand and fixed himself a cocktail, washing down the pill in two quick gulps.

He drained the glass, made himself another drink, and sat at the kitchen table. A sheet of paper rested on the top. Scrawled across the front was, "John, gone shopping with Trish—took Cat along. Be back later," in blue ink.

The pills kicked in, spreading their soothing effect. His headache disappeared, and his stomach calmed as the vodka swept like a wave over him. John never realized how good tomato juice tasted in the morning. He fixed one more drink, promising himself it would be the last, relaxed on the couch in his underwear watching cartoons, and waited for Lynn to return home. *Wonder if I should shave?* The clock on the wall read nine o'clock. *Nah, Sunday morning. Don't have nothing to do or nowhere to go.* He noticed his glass was empty and made another Bloody Mary.

When Lynn did walk through the door he gave her a kiss on the cheek and told her how sorry he was for the way he acted the day before.

"I'm sorry, too," Lynn said quietly. "Let's not argue anymore," averting her sight from the cocktail resting on the table. She carried Cat to the playpen and placed the baby stomach down, the stuffed tiger in front of her within reaching distance. "I talked to my mom this morning and she admits she might have been confused last night. I'm making a doctor's appointment for her Monday. I don't know. This could be the first signs of Alzheimer's. We'll have to see what the doctor says."

Deep down, John realized Lynn was trying to apologize to him also. He tried to think of something else to say, but somehow the words wouldn't form in his brain.

The clock on the wall read three o'clock. He mumbled, "Sunday afternoon. Think I'll take a nap."

***

John was late reporting for work the following Monday. He snuck in the back door and hurried to his cubicle figuring no one would see him and he'd hide for the morning. As he sat, the officer manager walked over. "John, Mr. Cahn wants to see you." He hurried away before John asked what his boss wanted.

Mr. Cahn was busy at his desk reading a printout when John entered the office. The old man looked up and made a rumbling sound in the back of his throat for John to take a seat opposite him.

"So tell me, John, what happened this weekend," his boss asked.

The tone of Mr. Cahn's voice made it clear John messed up somehow.

"Huh?" He reviewed in his mind his Saturday morning conference with the client, trying to think of anything he'd said or done that might provoke a chewing out.

What happened? He'd met the man at the office, shook hands. They'd covered business, mostly depreciation of equipment from the client's factory. He was positive he'd encompassed all the information he would need, double-checking with the client each item and number. Afterward he'd taken the man out to lunch and shook hands again. The client appeared satisfied.

"Nothing, sir. We talked, went over figures, exchanged a few jokes afterwards. Told me he'd see us next time he was in town and glad I was on his account. Why? Something the matter?" John frowned, puzzled.

Mr. Cahn cleared his throat and crossed his arms, peering over his glasses at John. "He remembered he brought additional information he wanted to supply us— more papers he'd left in his hotel room and forgot to place in his briefcase to bring to the meeting. He tried calling you on your cell phone and left a message, two, in fact. One right after he returned to his hotel room and another later during the evening. You never answered." The old man shifted in his chair, plainly unhappy. "This is why we hand out our personal numbers to the clients, John, so the customers can reach us when they need to. My company prides itself on the individual attention each one of our people receive. Courtesy, care to detail, every step of the way. This is what sets us apart from the rest of the accounting firms out there. I thought you understood this."

A sinking sensation lodged in the pit of John's stomach. He'd messed up big time and he knew he had. *Damn Lynn's mother, she'll get me fired from this job, and then maybe she'll be happy.* Half rising from the chair, he said, "Oh, gosh, I'm sorry, sir. I turned my phone off and forgot to switch it back on. I'll give him a call right now and apologize. I apologize to you too, sir. I…"

Mr. Cahn cut him off with a wave of his hand. "Don't bother. When he couldn't reach you, he called *me.* I tried calling you and received no reply. I attempted again the next morning. I finally set up another conference for early Sunday afternoon without you before the client left, and took care of the meeting myself."

John ran his fingers through his hair, not knowing what to say. He stammered out. "I'm, I'm sorry, sir. Saturday and Sunday were hectic around the house. I never realized…. I should have, but I thought everything was finished. I…"

Mr. Cahn frowned, as if tasting a rotten piece of meat. "We leave our problems from the office at the office, John, and our home problems at home. Learn the difference. 'I *thought* everything was done' doesn't work around here. Remember the old army expression?"

"What saying, sir?"

"Almost only counts in horseshoes and hand grenades. Woulda, coulda, and shoulda aren't why I hired you to work in this office."

John winced, wondering if he could shrink to a small ball and disappear into the chair. "I promise, sir, I'll never..."

"I'm sure you won't." His boss picked up the paper he was studying. "No harm done in the long run, but the client wants you taken off his account. Don't blame him, myself. We need people here we can rely on twenty-four seven." He glanced up at John. "For God's sake, keep your phone on and answer your calls. I hired you in the first place because I thought you were reliable. Don't let me down."

John stood. Face burning red. "Yes, sir. This won't happen again. I promise. I'd better go back to my desk and start working." He hurried out of the office to his cubicle, popped a pain pill, and shuffled through folders of different accounts. For the rest of the day he bent over papers, typing numbers into his computer, but he barely realized what he did while he fumed.

He stayed late at the office, making sure Mr. Cahn saw he was still hard at work as the boss left. After work, he stopped off at Funzy's before going home to relieve the stress. He had a lot of anxiety to release.

Chapter Sixteen

Lynn ran the water in the tub, preparing to give Cat her daily bath. She tested the water, twisted the tap to off as hard as possible. A slow, but steady, stream continued to flow from the spout, and water trickled where the nozzle entered the wall. Lynn scowled at the drip, dividing her attention between baby and leak with increasing annoyance at the valve failing to work properly.

I've asked John a hundred times.... Always an excuse....If he didn't spend so much time at the bar talking to his friends....Should I ask him again...? What's the use, he'll yes me to death, get drunk, and I'll still have a leak.

Bath time over, Lynn was determined to take matters into her own hands. If John wasn't going to fix the dripping faucet, she'd call in someone who could. She grabbed the phonebook and commenced flipping pages until she found plumbers.

"Oh, my, gosh. There must be a thousand in here," Lynn mumbled, scanning names and advertisements. "Who do I use?" She slammed the book closed in disgust. John never employed a plumber, didn't really need one. She'd have to ask around and find one who knew what they were doing and wouldn't rob her blind. Lynn called her mother. "Hi. Have a question for you....Know any plumbers...? The tub....No, and I've asked him a million times....Well, thanks anyway, if you remember anyone give a yell, okay? Talk to you later."

Who else might know? Of course, Trish. She knows everything, or can give me a lead. Lynn hit her speed dial. "Hey Trish, what's happening...? Yeah, me too.... Hey, have a question for the girl who has all the answers. You wouldn't happen to know any plumbers, would you...? Your parents keep a list of service people. You must be kidding. Maybe I should start one. Yeah, I'll hold on. Let me grab a pad and paper." Lynn riffled through a drawer holding the phone to her ear. "Ready, shoot." She jotted down numbers. "Thanks Trish, you're a lifesaver....Oh, the tub, darn thing's been dripping for ages, but now the drip is a flow. I want to have the faucet fixed before we all float away."

Lynn called the plumber next. "Hello? I need someone to swing by here and replace a leaking faucet in my tub...." She supplied name and address. "How much will this be...? Estimate? Fine....How much? To change a faucet...? Can't we do this cheaper...? By the hour? How can we cut the time down a bit...? Well, the main shut-off is under the house, but I can twist a valve. Save some time crawling in and out.... When can I expect him....You have one now? Fantastic....Okay, I'll be here. Thank you."

"I should have gone to plumbing school instead of college and becoming a teacher," she said, glaring at the phone. "Glad I didn't have to wait two weeks for the man to show up. I wonder if this will get me into the union." Lynn took the stroller out of the closet, retrieved Cat from her playpen, and tucked a flashlight into her pocket. "C'mon, you," she said to the baby, strapping Cat in, "we have work to do."

Lynn pushed the stroller to the breezeway and parked it before the window leading under the house. She'd seen John go in this way and recalled him saying the valve was all the way back against the wall. "Let's see what we have here, Cat." Lynn dropped to her hands and knees, pulled the window up, and dusted cobwebs out of the way. Cautiously, she poked her head inside the dark space and shone the light around searching the interior.

The shut-off wasn't hard to locate. Besides the light from the flashlight, sunlight filtered in from the front windows. As John's bulk grew larger over the years, he'd scooped away dirt, creating a shallow trench from window to valve. Lynn said to Cat, "You wait here, shorty. Mommy will be right back, I hope." She lay on her stomach and wiggled in through the window.

The baby stared at her wide-eyed, reached out her hands, and smiled happily.

Spooky! No wonder John doesn't like crawling around in here. Let's make this quick and scoot back out. Lynn flashed the light around in a fast survey studying walls, earth, and the underside of the floorboards above her head. A spider clung from a web, directly in front of her face, watching with what she assumed was evil intent. Lynn squirmed forward faster, brushing the bug aside using the light and kept her head averted. *What do I do if one chases me? There's no place to run.*

Lynn made her way to the shut-off and twisted the valve closed. *Great. Let me scat out of here fast before something bites me.* She shone the light over her head and along the back trail, making sure no fuzzy little animals or wriggling things snuck up behind her. Her beam centered on one mound bigger than the rest in the far corner of the crawlspace. *I hope nothing lives inside. Looks as if giant ants built a nest, maybe some animal made a den under the house.* She crawled toward the light of the window, keeping the flash centered on the pile of dirt so nothing emerged without her knowledge. *Maybe snakes? Do they make burrows? What if one slithers into the house? Let me get out of here before I'm attacked.*

Cat squealed in delight as Lynn emerged from the window dusting dirt off her shirt and pants and sweeping her hair back off her face, breathing a sigh of relief.

"Yeah, your mother is a handyman now, kid. I can use a good helper," a voice from behind her said.

Lynn spun around, startled. The plumber stood in the breezeway, toolbox in hand, wearing a grin. She breathed a sigh of relief and said, "Just the man I was waiting for." She waved toward the window. "Water's off, all set for you to work your magic. I'll show you what needs to be done."

The plumber asked Lynn to crawl under the house three more times, once to switch the water back on, and then turn the valve off again, and flip the faucet open to check for leaks when he finished.

"Needed to put in a whole new pipe," The plumber informed Lynn as he wiped off his tools. "Old one was rotted at the threads. This ancient plumbing, you know. Copper corrodes after so many years. Should hold—lucky you didn't lose the whole wall."

After two hours and many dollars shorter, he'd completed the repairs, cleaned up his mess, and left. Still complaining about the outrageous price under her breath, Lynn turned the shiny new faucet on and off three times to guaranteed the plumbing worked properly. *At least the repair's done. Thank goodness. I hope John doesn't blow his top when he sees the bill.*

John was late arriving home from work. Lynn placed his supper in the oven to stay warm. As the hour grew later, she fidgeted, checking her phone to see if he'd left a text, and debated if she should call him at the office. When he finally walked through the door, listing slightly, Lynn knew where he'd been and what took him so long.

"Sorry I'm late," he mumbled, a silly grin on his face as he kissed her. "I, err, was delayed at the job. Last-minute details, you know. Wanted to stay and complete paperwork that's been piling up. Didn't want to go in tomorrow."

"Yeah, and at Funzy's to finish a couple of brews, I see," she retorted, turning away, disappointed. "Supper's in the oven."

"Well, maybe," John replied with a chuckle as he walked into the kitchen. "Stopping by and having a beer is not my fault. Hard day at work as always. Mr. Cahn is a slave driver, you know. Always on my back. They give me the hardest accounts. Expect me to act like a superstar using crummy numbers, when no one else wants to do the dirty work. I mess up one little column of figures and he's all over me like I'm an idiot. Needed to relax and work the kinks out."

Cat woke up while John ate dinner. Lynn retrieved the baby and sat with John at the kitchen table, bouncing the child on her knee. "I called a plumber today," she said, "for the faucet in the bathroom. The outlet wouldn't stop running and water was seeping from the wall. Repairman said if we'd allowed the leak to continue any longer we'd have to replace all the sheetrock. Lucky the tiles didn't fall off into the tub."

John dropped his folk on his plate with a groan. "I told you I was gonna fix the faucet," he complained, shaking his head. "How much?"

Lynn told him.

John grimaced. "Oh, man." He picked up his fork and savagely jabbed a potato.

"Woulda been more," Lynn commented. "They charge by the hour, you know. I saved some time and money by crawling under the house and switching off the water for the plumber. Wanted me to do go under four times, in fact." Her brows gathered in concentration. "Now I know why you don't like shimmying in there. Not a fun job wiggling around in the dirt. Maybe it's why repairmen are paid so much."

"You what?" John stopped eating, his fork halfway to his mouth. "Of all the stupid...," he sputtered. "You didn't go messing around with anything else under there, did you?"

Lynn drew back from the outburst. "Of course not. Why should I? There's nothing much in there anyway. All I did was switch the main on and off a few times. I don't know why you're getting so upset. It's not like I enjoyed crawling around in the dirt."

John glared at her, released a sigh, and picked up his napkin.

Lynn tried reading the expression on John's face, but couldn't tell if he was relieved or still angry. She held her tongue to see if he'd say anything else. When John started eating again, Lynn felt the time was safe to continue.

"Oh, by the way, I saw a big mound under there. Don't know if anything is living inside, spiders on the floorboards, and God knows what else crawling in the dirt. Think we should call an exterminator? I don't want creepy-crawlies running around up here." Lynn switched knees and continued bouncing Cat. "I have enough problems keeping track of this one and out of mischief. The last thing I want are bug bites on the baby or us."

John's face blanched white. "We don't need any more strangers poking around under there. I still can't figure out why you called a plumber and then went messing around underneath the house in the first place. What were you thinking?"

A hurt expression passed over Lynn's face. *Why won't he drop the subject? Isn't he listening to me?* "I was trying to save money. It's not as if I have nothing else to do. I could have let the plumber do the whole job and charge us for the time he spent." The indignation from how he was acting finally got the better of Lynn. Her eyes flashed and she blurted out, "If you'd fixed the faucet as I asked a hundred times and didn't discover something more important to do like running off to Funzy's...."

John placed his fork on his plate. "Okay. Okay. I meant underneath the house is dirty and dark. I didn't want you to be hurt, that's all," he said, trying to backpedal. "You're right. I should have done the job myself," he said in a low tone as he studied his food, "Next time tell me what you're doing before you start making home repairs or calling in workpeople. That's all I'm asking." His voice promised dire consequences.

***

*T*he mound Lynn's talking about. She saw the grave. "You didn't go messing around in the dirt, did you?"

Lynn's face was a mask of surprise. "Of course not. I crawled in. I crawled out. What do you think, I went digging for a rat who's going to run out of his nest and bite me? Why are you getting so bent out of shape for, anyway?"

"Did the plumber go in with you?" What if he'd seen something? Would he report his suspicions to the police? They might be on their way here right now to arrest him. *Stupid bitch.*

Lynn stared back at him, nose crinkling in disgust as she tried to figure out what John was complaining about. "Of course not. I told you. I knew you'd be upset when you leaned I'd called a plumber and how much those people charge, so I tried to keep the price as low as possible. If you listened to me weeks ago when I first told you about the leak we wouldn't be having this...."

John relaxed, breathing a sigh of relief. "You know what a worrier I am. If something happened to you while you were under the house, who would find you? And the last thing we need is to have a lawsuit because some plumber was scratched by a rabid squirrel, or you, too. Never know what could have sneaked in, raccoons, possums, maybe even a fox. We've never had an animal living under the house before, but...."

Relieved to see John's temper cooling, Lynn asked again, "Did you want me to call an exterminator? Now you have me worried. I was kidding about a rat. All I was thinking of were bugs and snakes, but remember last fall when the squirrel fell down the chimney? We had to chase him out using a broom. What if a mouse or raccoon really does hide under there and gnaws through the floor?"

"Well, I don't think a rodent would chew through the wood, but calling an exterminator isn't necessary," John replied quickly. "Tomorrow is Saturday. First thing in the morning when I wake up, I'll run to the hardware store and buy one of those humane traps and a package of bug bombs. Between the two, they'll take care of any creatures under the house. Don't worry about varmints. I'm on the job."

"Good. As long as you're so filled with ambition, maybe I can have you clean out the junk in the basement that I've asked you to do for ages," Lynn said. "I was down there the other day, and there's still stuff from your parents, for God's sake. I saw a gun down there too. With the baby now, I really don't think we should leave firearms laying around, do you?"

"Of course not. I completely forgot about Pop's shotgun. Should have sold the thing years ago." He kissed her wetly and lightly scratched her back. "I'll place the basement on my list right below bug killing. First thing tomorrow after the crawlspace. I'll start working on sorting and tossing, might even dig into the garage, too, and see what we can dump. I promise."

The next morning John drove to the store early and picked up his supplies. As Lynn and Caitlyn watched, he tossed the bug bombs beneath the house and set the traps inside the window opening. "There, all finished," he declared, dusting his hands off in satisfaction and straightening up. "Even baited the trap using a peanut butter sandwich as a lure. Doesn't get any better than a homemade lunch if you're a mouse, rat, or raccoon." He wagged a finger in Lynn's face and said sternly, "Better take the kid to the park for a couple of hours until the bug spray settles. Wouldn't want the poison to seep up through the floorboards and make anyone sick. Not after all the hassle we've been through this morning." He kissed Lynn on the cheek and patted her backside. "From now on, stay out of there, understand me? My job, my responsibility. Don't be a dummy when you don't have to be."

Lynn ignored his remark. Instead, she said, "Maybe we can all go to the park." She checked the sky. Blue showed overhead, a few white clouds blown by a warm gentle breeze indicating a perfect day for relaxing outside. "Beautiful morning for a family outing. Good suggestion," she said, hoping now the episode of the tub was behind the two, there'd be no more arguing. An idea popped into her mind. "Maybe we can stop at the diner afterwards and have lunch as we use to do. I miss our Saturday trips." Lynn watched John, hoping he'd agree.

"Uh, you and Cat go. I'll meet up with you later." John pretended to study his phone, scrolling through messages. "Almost twelve o'clock. I have a couple of things to do first and I still have to go into the basement to see what needs throwing away."

Lynn frowned at his excuse and knew exactly what those things were that he planned to do for the rest of the day. They didn't have anything to do with cleaning out the basement or the garage. Sitting and drinking at the bar, and afterward staggering home and passing out on the couch was more likely. At least he'd taken care of the bugs, though. She didn't know who he thought he was fooling, but the person certainly wasn't her. "Yeah, and I'm sure your appointments are important too." She paused and added sarcastically, "Have fun."

John struggled with his temper when he saw the expression on Lynn's face. *Stupid idiot. Wasting my time doing this nonsense. If she'd left things alone—her and her jerk mother always causing problems whenever they can. Sneak under the* house. *Stick up flyers on every damn telephone in town. No wonder the guys laugh at me at Funzy's. I'm the head of the idiot household. If I want a drink, I'll go have a drink. It's all their fault, anyway. Those two and the people at the office. Make me do all the grunt work. Use me, everyone uses me, and still haven't made me a junior partner after all I've done. I deserve to enjoy life, too.*

John brushed his hair off his forehead, infuriated, wishing he were anywhere away from the house. "I will. Thanks." Without another word, he walked to his car and left.

The bar was empty when he arrived. "Too early, I guess," he said to the bartender as she set a bottle before him. John took out his phone, started calling friends. For some reason everyone he knew was busy. Disgruntled, he slipped the instrument back in his pocket and worked on his drink.

The time was well past seven o'clock when he returned home. No lights shone in the windows. The door was locked. To make matter worse, when he pulled into the driveway, he clipped the garbage can sitting at the curb, spilling kitchen waste all over the road and lawn.

"Damn Lynn," he muttered scooping up broken baby food jars and coffee grounds using his fingers. "She knows better than to stick the can so close to the drive. What does she think I am, a marksman?" John threw two more bags of kitchen waste in the garbage and surveyed his cleanup job with distaste. He wiped his hands on his pants, finished parking his car, and managed to slice his hand on the railing of the stoop as he walked up the steps.

If I didn't have bad luck, I'd have no luck at all. He stuck the cut in his mouth and fumbled with his house key using his other hand, unlocking the entrance. He called in, "Hey Lynn, where is everyone?"

No answer.

John walked through the living room in the dark, smashing his shin against the coffee table and cursing loudly before he located the light switch. He looked around, walked into the kitchen flipping on the light as he went. A note rested on the table:

"Cat and I are hanging with Trish. Be back later," scrawled hastily in Lynn's messy handwriting.

"Typical," John grumbled, crumbling up the paper and tossing the note on the floor. He opened the oven door. Nothing. "Couldn't even leave me a plate of supper."

Tomato juice was in the refrigerator. He found the three-quarters full bottle of vodka he'd bought the night before. "Life is good for some people," he said aloud to the ceiling, as he mixed himself a cocktail. "Plenty of time for her friends, running around, shopping and spending my money. No time for me, though, right?" He picked up the bottle and his drink, walked into the living room and flipped on the television. "Bet she's talking about me behind my back, telling her precious friends what a bum I am." He raised his glass to the images talking on the TV. "Everyone's sucked their money's worth out of the drudge today, haven't they? Kick me to the corner when I'm not needed, too busy for me unless someone wants something. Here's to the supper of champions and God bless me." He gulped the drink down.

***

"I don't know what his problem is." Lynn pushed Cat in the baby swing. The park was crowded. Saturday visitors, children with mothers and fathers in tow, ran for the slides and monkey bars screaming in delight at the top of their lungs. Wiser adults with older children rested in the pavilions at picnic tables, occasionally glancing up to make sure their offspring hadn't vanished.

"What problem?" Trish asked, taking a turn pushing Cat.

"The first year of our marriage was wonderful. The time together was as if the honeymoon never ended." Lynn swung Cat. "In our own little world, no arguing, no troubles. All of a sudden when Cat's born, he's—" Lynn paused trying to find a word. "Reclusive? I don't know if his attitude is because my mother visits more, or what."

Trish peeked at Cat's face and stopped the swing. "I think you've had enough, little one." The self-appointed aunt lifted the baby from the seat. "Baby's starting to turn green," she informed Lynn. Trish hoisted Cat onto her hip and surveyed the park. "C'mon," she said to Lynn, "baby slide is open." They strolled across the sand to where a small plastic slide stood. "Well, you know," Trish said, placing Cat on the top of the slide. Lynn took a position at the bottom, "John never did like your mother. I think you've told me a thousand times. Ready? Here comes super girl." Trish released Cat and the baby slid to the bottom where Lynn caught her. Cat crowed in delight. "Again?" Trish ask as her mother carried the little girl back to the top of the slide. "How is your mother doing anyway?"

"Oh, fine. Hasn't gone through a memory loss for ages," Lynn exclaimed. "The doctors prescribed her pills, changed her diet. They say a lot fruit and vegetables, using olive oil for cooking helps Alzheimer's. Nothing can stop the disease, but I'm told it'll be years before confusion and the other symptoms become a real problem for her." Lynn released a snort of aggravation, still thinking about her husband. "Now if I could have John change his attitude as easily, there'd be no headaches." She put her hands out. "Ready to let her fly?"

"I hate to say this, but his drinking doesn't help either." Trish released the baby. "Here she goes again. Wheee!"

Lynn grabbed Cat as she glided to her. "He always drank, and I don't mind, but the drinking is becoming worse. Every time we have an argument, he heads straight for the bar or brings home a bottle, hangs out in front of the television and broods." She checked her phone. "Oh, gee, I didn't realize we'd been here so long. I have to hurry home and start supper."

"You said John's at the bar?" Trish asked as they walked toward their cars.

"Oh, yeah. He didn't say where he was going, but I could tell by the way he acted. Why?"

"Come on over to my house. My mom hasn't seen Cat in a while. What time do you think John will be home?"

Lynn released a snort of amusement. "Oh, probably not for hours." Lynn opened the door of her car and strapped Cat into the car seat. "You know," she said after a moment's thought, "maybe I will drop by for a while. I left John a note. He can make himself a sandwich when he wanders in, wait for me to arrive and cook, or join us. Maybe missing a hot meal will give him a hint not to stay out all night. Let's."

Trish's mother invited Lynn to stay or dinner. As the family was finishing their meal, Herbie stopped by, bringing his new girlfriend. Cat fell asleep in her carrier and Lynn decided to let the baby sleep instead of trying to move her to the car. The hour was late when Lynn arrived home.

When she entered the house, all the lights were on, the TV blaring. John lay on the sofa, asleep, the empty vodka bottle next to his hand on the rug.

Lynn didn't bother to wake him.

Chapter Seventeen

"John, Mr. Cahn wants to see you in his office." The office manager's face was impassive and he refused to look John in the eye.

"Oh, geez. What did I do now?"

The man shrugged, turning his back to John before he could question the man further. John tucked his shirttails into his pants. He'd been late getting into the office again, hadn't had time to shave and his head still pounded from a hangover. He ran his hand through his hair, hoping to smooth the brown strands back into a reasonable semblance of combing. *Stupid Lynn, shoulda woke me up. She knows what time I have to be at work. I love having my ass chewed out so early in the morning. Makes my whole day.*

Gonna be a good one, this time, John decided as he hesitated outside Mr. Cahn's office. He knew he'd messed up on the Miller account, even before the Internal Revenue Service called for an audit. He hoped the old man would understand. Screw-ups happened to everyone. Heck, baseball players batting five hundred missed the ball half the time, and he was doing better than that. Probably Mr. Cahn made a few strikeouts in his day.

As he knocked and pushed the door open, John pasted his best smile on his face, projecting self-assurance he didn't feel. He saw the look on his boss's face and the confidence faded away into a sinking sensation dropping to the pit of his stomach. Whatever he'd done this time was worse than the Miller account, for sure. The tongue-lashing he knew was about to occur wouldn't be a pleasant one. Knees weak, he sank into a chair opposite Mr. Cahn.

"I'll come straight to the point, John," Mr. Cahn said. He cleared his throat noisily. "Your services are no longer needed at this firm. We're letting you go."

John had difficulty understanding what the old man meant. A continuous buzzing in his ears was all he heard. He stared blankly at Mr. Cahn, the man who'd hired him and said, "What?" This couldn't be right. He wasn't the low man in the office hierarchy, and if the firm was cutting back accountants for some reason, others were hired after him. He possessed seniority in the firm.

Mr. Cahn frowned. "You heard me. I'm sorry, but you seemed to have forgotten the promises you made when we hired you. Lately you're making mistakes, not showing up on time, always calling in sick with a lame excuse." He raised his hands helplessly. "What would you have me do? This type of behavior is intolerable."

"I, but..." What could he say? There must be something to make this right again. The walls closed in on him, the ceiling lowering until he felt trapped in a box. "I promise I'll straighten up, sir," he said desperately. "Problems at home, my wife, mother-in-law." He touched his forehead. "I still have this stupid pain in my skull from the war." Fear and the humiliation of firing pressed inward threating to crush his chest. "I swear, sir. I'll turn over a new leaf. Please, have faith in me."

The old man drummed his fingers on his desk, staring at the green inkpad covering the surface. He switched his attention to John, studying him over the top of his glasses. "I like you, John, but I can't have unreliable people working for me. Look at yourself." He waved a hand in John's direction. "Unshaven, hair's a mess, clothes rumpled. I told you once not to bring your problems to the office." The finger thumping started again. "I think I know what your problem is, and the trouble is not the family." Mr. Cahn leaned back in his chair, slapping his palms on the desk as he made a decision. "Okay, here's the deal.

You're on an unpaid leave of absence as of today. I'll give you six months to fix whatever problems you have at home, and clean yourself up. You never took the second part of your CPA test over again. Take the exam and pass. Also," he nodded to himself, "I want you to go to Alcoholics Anonymous."

"Huh?" Was Mr. Cahn intentionally trying to be insulting? Drinking wasn't his problem. Wife, mother-in-law—those two were the ones causing all the trouble. He drank, sure, but only because he needed to relax from the crap they put him through.

"Sir, I don't think I have…"

Mr. Cahn raised his hand and stopped John before he could protest further. "You can't fool an old soldier. I know what's happening inside your head. I went through the same thing myself for a few years when I was your age after the army discharged me. Forty years sober now and I've never had any regrets."

Cahn's an alcoholic?

"You can attend the meetings or if you wish, I'll take you. If you want, I'll sponsor you also, but this is the only way you're returning to this firm. After six months, we'll see how you're doing and talk things over." The muscles in Mr. Cahn's jaw tightened as if he wanted to say something else. Instead, he shook his head and said, "Now clean out your desk and go."

John rose quickly. "Yes, sir. Thank you, sir. I'll do anything you say, even if it means going to AA meetings. I would be more than honored if you'd be my sponsor. I won't abuse your trust again." He rushed out of the office, a glimmer of hope clutched in his brain.

Face burning from the embarrassment, John refused to look at his fellow co-workers. Nor did anyone say a word to him as they passed his cubicle, casting curious glances in his direction. He stuffed his few belonging from his desk into his briefcase and scurried out of the building.

He drove aimlessly, making left and right turns without thinking where he was going. In his mind he kept repeating, *What do I do now? How will I support my family? Tell Lynn? I'm sinking, going down in defeat and I don't know why. What's happened to me?*

John found himself driving on the causeway heading toward the beach. In front of him, a brick monument constructed to honor the builder of the beach complex jutted to the sky with a traffic circle winding below, a red needle welcoming tourists and natives alike to the serenity of the ocean.

I could step on the gas and crash into the building, solve my problems fast, and end my life. Would anyone care? Remember me?

John's foot pressed down on the gas pedal. The car sped up, weaving around other vehicles slowing to enter the circle.

At the last moment, he slammed on the breaks skidding into the turn, avoiding hitting other motorists by mere inches. Horns beeped. John's body shook. *Coward. Afraid to take your own life.*

He drove along the beach road, passing the pavilion where he'd kissed Lynn so long ago, remembering her flushed face and the smell of coffee in the air. A line of customers stood there now, patiently waiting to place their orders.

I wonder if those people are happy? What a beautiful day to be out by the water. They wouldn't be here, enjoying themselves if they had problems.

The parking lot was crowded with cars. Pedestrians wandered back and forth, carrying towels, umbrellas, and coolers. John drove slowly, watching. He stopped for a mother holding a toddler in tow who carried a plastic bucket and shovel. The pair reminded him of Lynn and Cat.

Lynn and he should have the perfect life together. Where did their life all go wrong? If it weren't for the *thing* in the crawlspace....Why did he even worry about the corpse? Did Caitlyn's body matter now? The girl died ten long years ago. So much had happened in between. No one remembered, no one searched, not even Lynn. Her mother yes, but she was crazy anyway.

Was he a fool all this time? Worrying over nothing? Allowing his guilt, fear, to override his better judgement. Drowning his conscience in a bottle?

Mr. Cahn gave him six months. Pass the rest of his CPA test? Piece of cake if he weren't working. College was starting in another month. Lynn would be back at school, teaching; he could watch Cat while he was home.

The old man was an alcoholic? He never realized. So embarrassing to go to Alcoholics Anonymous, stand up and announce your name, say you had a problem. Could he go through the excruciating discomfort of admitting he was a drunk? Sure, why not, if humiliating himself meant having his job back. He didn't *need* the alcohol. John thought back. Sitting at the bar, talking about events that didn't matter, wasting his time and money, and then throwing up the next morning. This isn't what he'd planned to do all his life. He was twenty-eight years old, his whole life spreading out ahead of him and with higher mountains to climb. Did he want to wind up as one of those old bums, divorced, no family, getting drunk every night and staggering home to some old rundown apartment, because they couldn't work and no one wanted them around? No way.

He drove out of the parking lot and back to the causeway, starting home, more determined to turn his life around than ever. The sun was past its zenith. Without looking at the time, he knew the hour was late. He was sober, and determined to stay so. First things first. He would apologize to Lynn today for the way he acted these last few years, explain to her he'd lost his job. She'd understand, Lynn supported him. She'd do so now, John was sure of it. Lynn and he could work this out together as they always did.

Tomorrow AA, and start on the sober road. He'd call Mr. Cahn tonight and find out when the next meeting was. Afterwards, start school again. Maybe in the interim he would do taxes; he always made money doing people's taxes.

The sickish sensation he'd had all day vanished. His spirits rose, a controlled purpose of life flowing through him.

***

Lynn waited at the food court, banging her fingernails on the tabletop, impatiently waiting for Trish to arrive for lunch. She scanned the shoppers strolling by and finally saw her friend approaching with a wave. Lynn released a sigh, undecided if her feeling were from relief or sorrow.

"Hey, babe, what's up?" Trish dropped opposite her and put her purse on the floor. "Got your text." She peered into Lynn's face and then peeked around at her side of the table. "You acted hysterical. I could hardly read the spelling. Where's my little niece? Everything okay?"

"Cat's fine. I left the baby at Mom's." Lynn bent forward and blurted out in a hoarse whisper, "I'm thinking of divorcing John. I didn't know who else to talk to."

Trish pressed her lips together and nodded wisely, reaching out a hand to cover Lynn's. "I knew it was gonna happen." She shook her head. "These last few years. He's been..." Her voice trailed off as she saw the desperation in Lynn's face. "I don't know. All John's drinking and his arguing every time I saw you guys together. Separating was a time bomb waiting to happen." A hush fell over the table as Trish breathed, "You two were such a cute couple in the beginning. Everyone thought you'd be the perfect match."

Lynn sniffed back tears, grimaced, and pulled her hand away from Trish. "I don't know if I should, though." Her teeth worried her lower lip and she clutched her fingers together. "I keep hoping he'll change, go back to the way he was. Nowadays, all he does is drink, ignore Cat and me, and go to work. The two of us are like roommates living in the same house, but not married at all. He'd freak out if he knew my mother was watching the baby. He avoids her like the plague, doesn't want me to bring Cat over to her house, and if Mom visits ours when he's there, he turns around and leaves." Lynn smiled bitterly, "Of course he returns hours later drunk as a skunk and tries to start an argument, or covers my face with sloppy kisses before he passes out."

Trish nodded in understanding. "Herbie tells me the same thing. He's been avoiding John; so are all John's friends if they can help doing so. Everyone makes up excuses not to hang out every time he calls or stops by their houses. All he wants to do is drag them down to sit at the bar, or he brings a bottle with him so they can get drunk."

Lynn couldn't control her emotions any longer. Tears dripped down her cheeks. She whispered, "I don't know what to do."

Diners at the nearby tables looked in their direction, and the talk quieted as each strained to listen. Trish reached over the table and squeezed Lynn's hand again. "I know divorce is hard, hon. None of this is your fault. Don't blame yourself. Maybe sometime in the future John will come to his senses, but you don't have to take the abuse along the way. Your mom's here for you, I'm here for you, and so are all your friends. We all have eyes and see what's happening."

Lynn choked out, "Th-ank you. I know you are."

"Have you talked to John?" Trish asked. "Do you want Herbie or me to speak with him?"

"If I say anything, I'm afraid he'll get mad and start shouting. You or Herbie?" Lynn shook her head. "I don't know. You can try. I'll attempt anything at this point."

Trish stood. "C'mon. Let's take a walk outside." She glared at the occupants of the nearest table who made no pretense of not listening. "We don't need to air your private problems in public."

They walked outside and found a secluded bench on the side of one store. Trish sat close to Lynn and placed her arm around her shoulder. "If you want to cry now, go ahead. I'm here to listen."

Lynn sniffed and smiled wanly. "Not here, maybe later. I think I'm all done for now." Her tears started again. "I don't want—don't want to divorce him, but I don't know what else to do. I'm so unhappy. I thought John loved me." Her face was flushed. Trish hurriedly pulled out a fistful of tissue from her bag and handed them over. "Thanks." Lynn wiped her face and blew her nose. "He used to treat me like a precious jewel, that's what he called me. Now?" She stared at her knees. "Herbie stopped over one night when John wasn't home. I asked if this was the real John. He said ever since John entered the army, he's been different. Withdrawn." She paused. "Maybe the war did something to him? Herbie said he acts as if he has a great secret deep down inside bugging him. I wish I knew what to say to him, what to do." Lynn whispered, *"I don't know."* Her heart felt squeezed, a sinking sensation traveling through her chest into her stomach.

Lynn's phone buzzed. "Text from John," she muttered, her voice dead. "Says we have important things to talk about. I'd better be heading home." She stood.

Trish rose also. "Give me a call tonight, and tell me what happened," her friend urged. "Do you want me to take the rest of the day off and stay with you for moral support? I can, you know. It's no problem."

Lynn stared thoughtfully at Trish. *I wish I could say yes. I feel so alone. This is better between John and me, no matter what happens.* "No, you're right. I should talk to John alone first. I'll call." Lynn glanced at her phone again. "You'd better be returning to the store. I don't need you getting fired on my account. I'll be fine."

Trish appeared dubious. "Okay, but make sure you let me know what happens, or I'll be calling you." She walked back to the mall, casting worried glances over her shoulder at Lynn.

Lynn drove home, wondering what to say to John, thinking up reasons why she should not divorce him, and dismissing the arguments as quickly, knowing in her heart their marriage was finished. *Maybe he'll tell me he still loves me. He said he has something important to talk about when he returns home. Wonder what he wants? What can we say to each other at this point we haven't said before? Poor Cat, growing up without her father. She'll have the Brownies, Girl Scouts, school and summer camps to go to. How do I tell Cat her mommy and daddy don't love each other anymore? She adores him.*

Flashing lights from police cars, firetrucks, and ambulances surrounded her house as she drove up the street. Lynn pulled against the curb and stumbled out of the car.

What in the world? Oh, God, I hope nothing's happened to Cat or my mother.

Lynn ran up the driveway and saw her mother standing in the front yard, surrounded by a group of strange men in uniforms. More walked in and out of her home, and into the breezeway. Mrs. Brennen clutched Cat close to her chest and looked up, saw Lynn running into the yard, and waved her over frantically.

"Everything is alright," Mrs. Brennen assured her daughter before Lynn could say a word. "I'm a stupid old woman, that's all, who doesn't think first and panics at the slightest thing."

Lynn released a sigh of relief. "As long as you and Cat are all right."

Cat, who stared wide-eyed at the flashing lights and stranger in trepidation, began whimpering, and stretched her arms out to Lynn. "Mommy!"

"Come here, baby." Lynn reached out and Cat grabbed for her. Mrs. Brennen handed the baby over. "Now for heaven's sake, Mom, what's going on around here? Why are all these people walking around in the yard?"

"The day was so pretty," Mrs. Brennen exclaimed. "I took Caitlyn out into the backyard to play. I—I must have fallen asleep in my chair," the woman admitted sheepishly. "I woke up and the baby was missing. I searched the property, every bush, ran into the house and checked all the rooms. I couldn't find her anywhere. I panicked and called the police." Mrs. Brennen continued, abashed. "The officers know me by name I've called so many times asking about your sister. The station sent"— she looked around at all the uniformed men, still amazed at the response she'd received— "everybody. I never thought to check the crawlspace under the house."

"Who would?" Lynn said. "Why in the world would Cat have crept in there?"

"I don't know, but the baby did." Mrs. Brennen waved vaguely toward the breezeway and gaping window just visible from the front yard. "The police brought dogs. The dogs found her." She added, "They're underneath the house now. I don't know why the officers are still searching. Caitlyn's safe."

Lynn looked over where her mother pointed. A fireman poked his head out of the window opening and waved frantically to a man dressed in a suit, who huddled close. The two talked in whispers.

"If the fire department and police found Cat, what are the people doing under there now?" Lynn asked.

"I told you, I don't know," her mother replied, exasperated. "The dogs ran in barking, Caitlyn was brought out. The dogs stayed in, still yapping away. Oh," Mrs. Brennen pointed to the man in the suit who squatted by the window. "I forgot in all this uproar, he needs to talk to you."

"Oh, okay. Probably wants information about Cat. Let me talk to him and get these people on their way." Lynn looked at all the men standing around. "I expect John home any minute. He'll blow his top if he sees this." She shifted Cat to her hip and walked over to the window. "I'm Mrs. Baker," she said to the man who rose at her approach. "You wanted to see me?"

"Detective Roberts," he announced. He smiled at Cat. "I take it you're her mother. This is your house? We spoke to your mother, but she insisted we hold our questions for you or your husband."

"Yes, my husband and mine. We live here. I'm so glad you found Cat. I'm so grateful." Lynn held the baby up, enabling Cat to see the window, and waved a finger at her. "No. You know you're not allowed under there. Your father will have a fit."

Detective Roberts asked, "You own this house? I mean, you're not renting the place from someone else, are you?"

What an odd question. "No, we own our home, or rather, we're paying a mortgage. We're buying the house from my husband's parents. They lived here before."

He nodded toward Mrs. Brennen, who watched apprehensively. "Your mother tells me your husband's name is John? This is correct?"

The way the detective said John's name made Lynn study his face carefully. "Yes."

"And I believe you had a sister named Caitlyn who vanished ten years ago in this neighborhood? Is this also correct?"

Prickles of uneasiness ran along Lynn's neck. Why was this man asking questions he plainly knew the answers too? "Yes, my sister vanished the day we moved in next door. No one has seen her since. My mother insisted we name the baby after her. Cat is short for Caitlyn. Why are you asking? The police know all this. My mother calls the station every day."

"Making sure." He withdrew a small plastic pouch from his coat pocket and held the bag up. Inside was a gold chain and corroded tarnished medal. The front was unreadable but he flipped the award over. A name and date were barely visible, etched on the surface. "Can you identify this?"

***

John decided to stop in at the bar one last time. One drink wouldn't hurt, he reasoned. He wasn't going inside to drink, rather to say goodbye. He watched the neon lights flash on and off advertising the name Funzy's and mentally kicked himself for all the money spent and time wasted in the place. He pushed the door open and walked in.

One of the regulars sitting at the bar looked over at his entrance and recognizing him. "Hey, bartender," he shouted, waving at John, "my buddy's here. Buy him a drink on me."

The temptation to sit and talk surged over John. A beer would taste so good about now, before going home. He took a step forward toward a barstool, hesitated, and stopped. *This is how the drinking starts. One, and two, and then I'm back in the same situation I was before. Should never have walked in here.* Summoning willpower he didn't realize he possessed, he raised a hand and said, "Thanks, but no thanks. I stopped by to say I'm going on the wagon and say goodbye to everyone. Next time you see me, I'll be a new John."

A murmur of assent rose from the other patrons of the bar. One man called out, "Anything to do with all those cops parked on your street? Didn't run anyone over did you? I passed by on my way here. You'd think the whole block burned down seeing all the firetrucks and flashing lights clogging the road."

A prick of apprehension stabbed John. "Hope nothing's happened at my place." John scanned his phone for messages from Lynn. He saw nothing. Everything must be okay at the house. He texted her he'd be home soon and they must talk. "Nothing here," he said, shrugging. "Maybe the firemen are practicing? Sometimes the department does that when they're bored, or, I think, isn't the Fireman's Fair happening soon? The guys like to drive up and down the streets, the sirens and lights blaring away to let you know it's time." He shoved his phone back into his pocket. "Anyway, goodbye and good luck to you people." He waved and left.

"Hope they still don't have the street all clogged up," John muttered to himself as he drove home. "Hate to walk all the way down the block and back up later to retrieve my car."

The street was clear enough for him to pull into his driveway, but an ambulance and two police sedans were parked at the curb along with a black car he didn't recognize. John slammed his car into park and rushed into his house, wondering what was taking place inside.

Had something happened to Lynn or Cat? An accident? Why hadn't someone called him to let him know what was going on? Maybe Lynn's mom had hurt herself or wandered off. She'd been acting alright lately, but you never could tell.

Four uniformed police officers waited inside, standing next to Lynn and her mother. Another man, whom

John assumed was a detective, sat on the couch with the women. The three stopped talking and stared at him as he entered.

John froze in the doorway and threw a puzzled glance at Lynn and her mother. The baby was nestled in her mother's arms, sleeping. Everyone seemed fine.

The women said nothing. John stepped deeper into the room and asked Lynn, "What goes on here? Did someone hurt themselves?"

Lynn shook her head, refusing to answer.

He switched his attention to the man in the suit. "What is this? Why are the police here, the ambulance? Will someone tell me what's going on?"

Two of the policemen moved in behind him, closing the door. The detective stepped in front of John, flanked by the other officers. "You are John Baker?" the man said.

"Yes, of course I am. This is my house. What in blazes is going on here?" John searched the faces of the officers, expecting an answer. He received none. "Did someone try to break into the house, a robbery? What? Anybody, tell me what happening."

"I'd like to ask you some questions." Detective Roberts held up a bag, watching John's face. Inside was an old school ring. "Is this yours? The band has your initials engraved inside."

John took the bag from Roberts and studied the ring closely. The "J.B." was still visible, etched into the metal.

He owned no school ring. What did this have to do with him? Dumbly he glanced at his fingers, vaguely wondering if his wedding ring somehow fell off his hand and transformed into the object in the bag. "This is some dumb kid's school ring," he said, still searching his fingers. "I haven't owned one since..." he stopped, afraid to say anything more.

The detective wouldn't stop asking questions or watching for a reaction. He said, "Did you ever meet Caitlyn Brennen?"

Who was Caitlyn Brennen? She never existed, never was. A bad memory best forgotten. This man was talking nonsense, probably a friend of Lynn's crazy mother.

"You mean Caitlyn Baker," he mumbled. John waved vaguely toward Lynn and the baby. "She's my daughter. There is no Caitlyn Brennen." He noticed how worn his wedding ring was around the rim. At one time, glittery scalloping decorated the edges of the white gold. It was now badly banged up and dull.

"You're under arrest for suspicion of murdering Caitlyn Brennen."

Rough hands grasped his arms from behind. Handcuffs snapped around his wrists.

This isn't happening. Impossible. IMPOSSIBLE.

John looked up, seeking Lynn's eyes.

She stared back in horror.

"Lynn, you gotta believe me," John pleaded, "They're not looking for me, I wasn't even there. I was in the army." He begged her to understand. "Mrs. Brennen, Mom, you know, tell the police."

The officers switched their attention to Mrs. Brennen.

Lynn's mother looked confused. "I don't know," she answered slowly. "The police canvassed the neighborhood. I remember your mother saying an officer stopped at your house, but you'd already enlisted." She shook her head. "I'm an old woman. My memory isn't as good as it used to be." Mrs. Brennen closed her eyes, resting her forehead in her palm. "After all these years," she murmured, "my daughter, dead under a house, buried next door to me." Mrs. Brennen took a shuddering breath as tears poured down her cheeks.

John nodded his head frantically, staring at the detective. "Did you hear her? Your people stopped and asked. I remember my mother telling me so." He shoved his face toward the bag the detective held and thought desperately. "The corpse was buried under our home? She had the ring you showed me? The piece of metal was so corroded it could be any school." He drew back and stood upright. "J.B.? There must be a thousand J.B.'s in the area. Anyone of them could have sneaked under my house and buried a body. Anything else for that matter, for all I know. Maybe she was going out with a guy from the city named J.B. *I was in the army when she disappeared.*"

The strain of tension disappeared from John. The police had no case, no proof he was anywhere involved in this mess. Lynn showed indecision. His wife stared into space, the set of her jaw indicating she didn't know what to think anymore.

The detective said gruffly, "You're still our prime suspect. We're taking you to the station for questioning." He said to Mrs. Brennen. "One way or the other, we'll get to the bottom of this."

The police took John to the police car, pushed him in the back seat and drove to the police station. The questioning began.

"Did you kill Caitlyn Brennen?"

"Of course not. I've told you I wasn't there."

The questioning continued. John kept to his story.

A different officer talked to him. "Hey, listen. We know you're a vet, went through a lot of bad experiences in the army. Tell us the truth and we'll go easy on you, maybe cut a deal. What do you say? Be honest and explain what really happened between you and the girl."

John glared at the officer and snorted. "Haven't you people been listening to me? *I was in the army.*" The room was hot, and John was sweating profusely. "Even if I did know Caitlyn, what possible motive would I have for killing her, huh? Answer me, *but I was never there."* When the officer didn't reply, John said, "How long are you going to hold me? Am I charged with something? Do I have to call a lawyer?"

The police detectives conferred. "We're releasing you," one said finally, "but don't leave town, we'll be watching. We still have questions for you and this investigation isn't over yet."

Yellow tape and curious neighbors surrounded his house when John arrived home. He ducked inside. Lynn wasn't there. He fell on the couch, brain numb and rubbed his hands together over and again.

The cops will learn eventually. The detective is bound to. The police will check my army records. See my date of induction was the day after Caitlyn disappeared. This is the end. Discovery is only a matter of time.

John stood and peeked through the drapes of the front window. Most of the neighbors were vanished. A black car parked across the street, two men inside.

The police are watching me like vultures. Hoping to storm inside and rip this place apart, haul me way again. I wonder what the cops would do if I ran downstairs and grabbed my dad's shotgun and started firing? John laughed hysterically at the thought of a standoff. What a way to go out.

John recalled Herbie telling Lynn and him about the kid Ron Billings. *He's still rotting in jail. Me and old Ron. Lynn will divorce me for sure. My parents after thirty years? Mom and Dad will be dead. My friends all moved away. And Cat? Maybe visit me in prison once a year. A Christmas card, perhaps, for her jailbird dad, if she even remembers what I look like. What do I do when I'm released? Live in a crummy room, a single lightbulb hanging from the ceiling? No one will hire me. I'll be a bum sitting on the curb watching the cars go by.*

John felt a glow of peace flow through him. Better to go out blazing. At least the end would be over quick without the shame and humiliation he'd face for the rest of his life. Much better than twenty years? Thirty years? In jail for murder.

His dad's shotgun.

He walked down the stairs into the basement. The gun leaned in the corner. John retrieved the weapon and a box of cartridges resting on a shelf above, examining each closely. Both appeared in working order. He loaded the gun, fondling the wooden stock and trigger, and carefully walked upstairs and dropped on the couch.

Everyone, I'm sorry. I never meant for any of this to happen. Baby Cat, I love you. Lynn, I love you too.

He placed the barrel of the shotgun in his mouth. The trigger was too far away for him to pull. *Of course, silly me.* As if this was an everyday occurrence, he kicked off his shoe and slipped his sock from his foot. His big toe fit nicely into the trigger guard. He put the barrel back in his mouth.

The rear door of the house opened. "John? John? I know you're here," Lynn called as she walked through the kitchen into the living room. "John, we have to talk. John? *John. NO!*"

John glanced sideways at Lynn and mumbled around the barrel of the shotgun. "I never meant for this to happen."

He pushed the trigger.

Epilogue

Detective Roberts waited patiently for Lynn on the steps of the police station as she walked up. "Mrs. Baker, I'm glad you drove down as soon as I called." He glanced past her. "Your mother isn't with you? I called you both. We couldn't reach you, your phone number was changed, and when we sent a car to your home, we saw a For Sale sign on the lawn."

"My mother and friend are watching my daughter, and I'm staying at my mom's for the time being," Lynn explained. "I couldn't stand living in the house any longer. I took a few personal items. The rest I'm leaving. Whoever buys the house can keep everything else in there or dump what they don't want."

Roberts nodded. "I can understand you wanting to move after all you've been through."

"And the people driving by, staring," Lynn shook her head in disbelief. "Even knocking on the door. Why, three people walked up to the door holding a camera. I think they were from a movie company, wanted to stop by and take pictures of my living room. The man in charge said their network was thinking of making a television show and needed photos for realism."

The detective conveyed his understanding of the ignorance some people showed with a nod. "The movie industry can be like that. No respect. All those bloodsuckers are looking for is a buck in their pocket." Roberts waved toward the police station. "If you're ready, we can wrap this up quickly. You'll pass all the necessary information to your mother? She's the one who's been asking."

Lynn bobbed her head up and down in the affirmative. "I can take whatever papers you want to give us. She still doesn't understand what went on." Lynn sighed. "Neither do I."

The detective nodded. "Fine. Let's go inside and we can wrap this up. I know you've been through a lot of stress for the last few months and I don't want to add to your pain."

Roberts guided Lynn to a small office. He dropped the blinds on the window and took out a manila folder from a desk, withdrawing a sheet of paper. "This is a summary of your sister's autopsy." He pushed the paper over to Lynn. "Basically we found no sign of physical violence. The body was quite degraded, but as far as the medical examiners can determine, your sister died of a heart attack."

"My father died of a heart attack," murmured Lynn, staring at the paper. She looked up and said sharply, "Caitlyn was only seventeen years old, though. Seventeen-year olds don't have heart attacks."

Roberts sat on the edge of the desk. "I didn't think so either at first, and I've never heard of a case, but I'm told it can happen under the right circumstances. Tell me, was your sister big in sports?"

"Caitlyn was a cheerleader. I guess you'd call cheering a sport."

"Lots of exercising?"

"Well, yeah," Lynn agreed. "You have to be in shape, of course. You're running, jumping, clapping. You've seen cheerleaders at football games, right? The girls are doing handsprings, cartwheels. Sometimes flips."

The detective nodded. "Dieting too, I suppose?"

Lynn released a small laugh. "Constantly." She smiled to herself remembering her sister. "'Top of the pyramid', Cat always called herself. My sister kept the weight down, because she stood on top of the other girls, but I don't see…."

Roberts ticked off points on his fingers. "Constant heavy exercise, dieting, possibly borderline anorexic—all indications of stress on the heart. You told me she was upset about the move out here from the city, too?"

"Yes, but…"

"Might have been internalizing her feelings, causing more strain. Tell me, the day she disappeared, was she acting sick, complaining about pains? Can you recall?"

Lynn thought back, trying to remember. "I think Cat mentioned she was coming down with something. A cold, maybe the flu? I can't…we talked such a long time ago."

"All the signs and causes of a heart attack. Your sister was having one and never realized what was happening. As you said, seventeen year olds don't have heart attacks."

Oh, Cat. If we'd known. Mom is devastated. I knew you'd never return, but … "Are you trying to tell me John had nothing to do with Caitlyn's death? Then why…?"

Roberts spread his hands wide. "Why he did what he did is something we'll probably never know. The two people who could tell us are dead."

Lynn returned to her mother's house. Mrs. Brennen and Trish waited anxiously inside. She walked blindly past both into Caitlyn's room, picked up her baby, Mr. Piggy, and sat in her rocking chair. She cuddled both close.

John.

Lynn cried.

Lynn cried for a long time.

The End

About Arthur Butt

Army Veteran, graduate of Florida State University, former police officer and plant manager. Native Long Islander now living in Florida was wife, two puppies and SnoopyCat. (and yes, a coffee drinker!)

Social Media Links:

Amazon:
http://www.amazon.com/s/ref=nb_sb_noss?url=search-alias%3Ddigital-text&field-keywords=Books+by+arthur+butt

Facebook Fan Page:
https://www.facebook.com/Arthur-Butt-The-Fantasy-SyFi-Author-1528729850734703/

Twitter: https://twitter.com/artyny59 @artny59

Goodreads link:
https://www.goodreads.com/search?utf8=%E2%9C%93&query=Arthur+Butt

Instagram Link:
https://www.instagram.com/artyny59/

Acknowledgment:

To the United States Army, Editor in Chief, K.C. Sprayberry, and all the people at Solstice Publishing.

If you enjoyed this story, check out the other books by Arthur Butt:

Dragonkiller

Hope is a monster killer, First Family of her town, and condemned to death if people knew she is the mother of a half-human, half-dragon child. When summoned to another dimension, she discovers love, and a man who accepts her son. In order to stay, however, she must vanquish a demon army that threatens to destroy this new land, and the old world she is leaving behind.

http://bookgoodies.com/a/B00USNA7TI

Gail is Gaea

To the people who enslaved her she is a priestess trained in the art of prophecy. To the new land she escapes to, she is an outlaw. To the natives she leads in revolt, she is a goddess.

http://bookgoodies.com/a/B0193QH2SE

The Girl Who Rode Dragons

All Jackie wanted was equal treatment and to ride a dragon. When her cruel brother-in-law takes over as head of household, and makes her quite school, she is forced to do all the chores, and collect wood in the forest. Jackie finds a dragon's egg, and although law forbids girls to ride dragons, she secretly hatches the egg, and dons boy's clothes. After she brings the gift of fire to the dragonriders, she becomes an accepted member of their band.

Civil wars breaks out, dragonrider against dragonrider. Jackie leads the loyalist faction against the rebels. The stakes – the fate of the kingdom and the life of her and the man she has grown to love.

http://bookgoodies.com/a/B0117QI24Q

Troubleshooter for Earth

Sometimes smuggler and full-time Space pilot Don Weiss teams up with Puddlefoot, a mischievous fairy, to defend Earth. Their greatest challenge, locate and subdue the Vas, an evil race of spider aliens bent on destroying our solar system, and turn them into peaceful non-belligerents.

The problem: The Vas do not exist.

The solution: Annihilation.

http://bookgoodies.com/a/B01434A8SM

30

When the Gaea manifests herself on Earth, she seeks one man who feels the planet's pain. She finds none, and the human race pays the price.

http://bookgoodies.com/a/B01C37Z8WC

2050

The end of civilization as we know it.

http://bookgoodies.com/a/B01HSOSY26

www.ingramcontent.com/pod-product-compliance
Lightning Source LLC
Chambersburg PA
CBHW051147030726
47504CB00004B/1082